COURT
APPOINTED

COURT
APPOINTED

A Novel

PRISCILLA
AUDETTE

SUNSTONE
PRESS

SANTA FE

Sunstone books may be purchased for educational, business, or sales promotional use.
For information please write: Special Markets Department, Sunstone Press,
P.O. Box 2321, Santa Fe, New Mexico 87504-2321.

Book and cover design › Vicki Ahl
Body typeface › Book Antiqua
Printed on acid-free paper
∞
eBook 978-1-61139-379-8

Library of Congress Cataloging-in-Publication Data

Audette, Priscilla, 1953-
  Court appointed ; a novel / by Priscilla Audette.
    pages cm
  Includes bibliographical references.
  Summary: "A series of vignettes of elderly people as they helplessly and ultimately
ineffectively struggle against the intrusion of a court appointed guardian who has
taken over their lives" -- Provided by publisher.
  ISBN 978-1-63293-067-5 (softcover : alk. paper)
  1. Guardian and ward--Fiction. 2. Older people--Abuse of--Fiction. 3. Abused
elderly--Fiction. 4. Psychological fiction. I. Title.
  PS3601.U34C68 2015
  813'.6--dc23
                        2015014115

WWW.SUNSTONEPRESS.COM
SUNSTONE PRESS / POST OFFICE BOX 2321 / SANTA FE, NM 87504-2321 /USA
(505) 988-4418 / ORDERS ONLY (800) 243-5644 / FAX (505) 988-1025

To the nightingale

Some say the nightingale's song is a lament.
Others say it is simply a night song that inspires love.
Perhaps this novel is both.

Contents

Preface _ 9
Acknowledgements _ 10

Part I
A Sign of the Times

1. Lila _ 13
2. Bonnie _ 22
3. Darling _ 32
4. Lucille _ 40
5. Dr. Lee _ 50
6. Mr. G _ 58
7. Annabelle _ 71
8. Wren _ 79
9. Faith _ 88
10. Sarah _ 94

Part II
The Sands of Time

11. Shirley _ 111
12. Beatrice _ 122
13. Ellen _ 130
14. Wendy _ 143
15. Eugene _ 156
16. Edna _ 169
17. Hector _ 185
18. Cliff _ 193
19. Morgan _ 205
20. Hope _ 220

Suggested Readings _ 227
Readers Guide _ 228

Preface

Conservators perform a necessary function in a society top heavy with elderly who need care and attention. As is the case with a lot of clichéd professions, a few bad apples do often seem to spoil the whole crop. However, just as all lawyers aren't shysters and all contractors aren't cheats, all conservators aren't people full of greed with God-complexes. Unlike Morgan in this story, the conservators I have known have always put the interests of their clients first and foremost.

Acknowledgments

To the caregivers I have known who mother our infantile parents who are journeying through the last chapter of their lives: Bless you, Luce, Mari Lou, Maria, Vickie, Wendy, Bernice, and countless others whose names may have been forgotten but whose kindness and dedication will always be remembered.

Part I

A Sign of the Times

"A test of a people is how it behaves toward the old. It is easy to love children. Even tyrants and dictators make a point of being fond of children. But the affection and care for the old, the incurable, the helpless are the true gold mines of a culture."

—Abraham J. Heschel

"Strive to preserve your health; and in this you will the better succeed in the proportion as you keep clear of the physicians."

—Leonardo DaVinci

1

Lila

> "Such is the audacity of man, that he hath learned to counterfeit
> Nature, yea, and is so bold as to challenge her in her work."
> — Pliny the Elder

Hope Nightingale strode down the hallway, pausing briefly at the front desk to sign in then continued on her way toward room one hundred. As Hope traversed the labyrinth of hallways to her destination, she skirted around patients in wheelchairs. Most ignored her, but others reached out to her as she passed. "Help me, help me," one always croaked in an aged whisper to anyone who would listen. Today there was a plea coming from an open doorway. "Let me die. I just want to die." Hope shuddered and wished for the person who was pleading a timely and gentle passing into that Good Night, although knowing that instead of a release the great god, medical science, would, in all likelihood, keep the person going for years to come. From another doorway came audible breathing interspersed with a gasping sound of despair that wasn't a word in any language — the universal cry of the soul whose suffering simply went on and on. The nurse, at her cart filling little paper cups with pills, glanced up and smiled. "I always know it's you, Miss Hope, by the clicking of your heels on the floor."

Hope smiled in return. "How is she today?"

"Same as always. She's had her shower and is back in bed now."

"And the port site?" Hope tapped her fingers on her abdomen.

"Just fine now, no more redness."

Hope continued on her way, passing the nurses' station. An aide stood behind the counter writing something in a patient's chart. A nearby man in a wheelchair kept repeating with some urgency, "I need help getting to the toilet."

The aide's response was, "Just do it in your diaper, Mr. Sims; they will clean you up later."

Hope brushed a sympathetic hand over the patient's shoulder as she passed him by. He recoiled from her giving her a murderous look. Not only wasn't she one to help him, she was also a witness to his humiliation. She hated that these people were stripped of dignity at every turn. For cripes sake she thought to herself, help the poor man to the toilet! How hard would that be! A year ago she would have said that out loud to the aide, but over time she realized she needed to pick and choose her battles. She had learned the hard way that there were snitches everywhere and more often than not the things she said when in the facilities got back to her boss, usually with embellishments. So she swallowed her criticism of the aide, choking back the words that now sat like a brick in her stomach.

Stepping into room one hundred, Hope observed her client. Lila was a big-boned woman who weighed close to 160 pounds. Hope could never figure out how she maintained that weight considering she hadn't had a meal in over two years. Well, a conventional meal that is where she used a fork or a spoon to shovel food into her mouth. Lila was fed with the aid of a PET tube, which stood for percutaneous endoscopic gastrostomy tube, or simply speaking, a stomach tube.

Lila was a woman in her eighties who had never married and never had children. When the Alzheimer's progressed to the point where she could no longer care for herself, and there was no family to step up to the plate and help out, the state of California did the stepping in and a court-appointed guardian was assigned to her. The guardian is technically called a conservator and, at least in the early years, a conservator had complete legal control over the incapacitated individual's person and estate. In more recent years the court belatedly rediscovered that not only does power corrupt, but that absolute power corrupts absolutely, so these days it is sometimes likely that the court will appoint two conservators for one individual: one over the person and one over the estate. That way there is at least a semblance of checks and balances in this less-than-perfect way of handling the life and assets of someone who no longer has the mental capacity to deal with day-to-day living.

Lila, one of the early victims of the system, had only one conservator who had control over both her person and her considerable estate. And this one person, Morgan Smyth, was Hope's boss. Hope, the case manager for Morgan's clients, visited Lila twice a month in the facility where she had been placed. Hope's job was to act as liaison between the client and the conservator. She was the middle man or woman, as the case may be, who did all the work and had none of the decision-making power. If a client was still in his or her home with a caregiver, Hope visited the home and made sure that the caregiver was doing the job correctly. If the client was in a facility, Hope made sure that the client was cared for according to acceptable standards. In other words, as case manager, Hope was the conservator's eyes and ears out there in the field earning twenty dollars an hour plus mileage while the conservator sat behind a big desk, made the big life-altering decisions, and collected the big bucks.

Before Hope started working for Morgan, Lila had been in her home with a caregiver in attendance. But, according to Morgan, it was just easier for the clients to be placed in facilities than to try and keep them in their homes; and if there weren't family members to kick at the decision, the conservator moved them into a facility as soon as possible after receiving the court papers of guardianship. As is the case with the majority of seniors placed in facilities, Lila had gone downhill rapidly after being moved to California Palm. During the early days of her institutionalization she had felt bludgeoned by the system. Soon after her incarceration she began refusing meals. Her plan, if she had one, was probably to let herself starve to death — death being the lesser of two evils. But fortunately, or unfortunately as the case may be, Morgan ordered the insertion of a PET tube and the rest, as they say, is history. Not only couldn't Lila starve herself into a release of her personal hell, but her conservator, who controlled her estate, could charge the estate enormous amounts of money every month for taking care of her. The longer Lila lived the more money lined the conservator's pockets. While the morality of the situation was certainly questionable, the math was easy.

"Are you going to talk to me today, Lila?"

"No!" Lila's voice boomed out loud and angry. *No* was probably the first word she had learned, and evidently it was going to be the last word she remembered.

"You doing okay?" Hope knew the answer she was going to get before she got it.

"No!" Lila turned her head away from the annoying questions and closed her eyes.

"Aren't you happy to have a visitor, Lila?" There was no response to that. Unlike most of Hope's other clients who loved company, Lila was the exception. Lila was very good at ignoring outside disturbances. Hope glanced around the sterile room. Not surprisingly, the second bed was still empty. Lila had not had a roommate for quite some time. That was mostly due to her yelling at all hours and disturbing whoever was unlucky enough to be assigned the bed next to her. Hope rested her hand on the cold, metal guard rail that was raised to keep the patient from rolling out of bed and looked down at her client. She was wearing her limb splints and thera boots. The staff put those on her for several hours every morning. The purpose was to keep her unused muscles from atrophying. It was then that Hope noticed the unsightly bruise on Lila's upper arm. She did a speedy survey of all other exposed body parts. There were no additional bruises visible; just the one on Lila's arm.

"Do you need anything, Lila? Can I get something for you?"

Lila turned her head back toward the sound and bellowed, "No!"

The tone of Lila's voice and the volume didn't surprise Hope. She had been visiting Lila for over a year and nothing had changed. Once upon a time a college professor, today the woman was no longer capable of carrying on a conversation, and in fact had been unable to do so for as long as Hope had known her. Once upon a time she had also been a semi-professional golfer, and now she couldn't even walk, let alone sit up in a wheelchair. If the staff wanted to get Lila out of the room for whatever reason, she was placed in what is called a geri-chair: geri for geriatric. It was more of a wheel-bed than a wheelchair. The patient could remain supine and be moved from place to place.

Hope continued to observe her client, but she did so from a safe remove. As Lila was prone to violent outbursts, often of a physical nature, Hope knew to stand well back from the edge of the bed. Early on, Lila had struck out with her arm and bashed Hope alongside the head. Only momentarily stunned, the blow had hurt her pride more than anything else, but it was also a keen lesson in keeping one's distance from Lila. She could hardly blame the woman for her anger and striking out. Hope's attitude was, "If I was in her place, I'd be pissed off too."

Regarding the bruise on Lila's arm, Hope peeked out the doorway and caught the nurse's eye just before she popped into another room to dispense her ubiquitous pills. "Yes, Miss Hope?"

"Hi, Ruth, I haven't checked Lila's chart yet, so I expect an explanation is in there, but I noticed the bruise on her arm. Any idea how that happened?"

"We discovered it this morning and, yes, we did record it in the chart. We think she just bumped it against the railing last night. You know what that Coumadin does to patients—one bump and they bruise so easily."

Hope made a notation in her book and thanked the nurse. "By the way, how's she doing for shampoo or body lotion? Do I need to bring anything next time I come to visit?"

Ruth checked the bedside drawer and shook her head. "No lotion or shampoo needed; all that is fine for at least another couple of visits, but she does need more blouses for when we get her up and take her to the activity room. The ones she has are literally falling apart." Ruth had gone to the closet and was extracting the threadbare blouses and showing them to Hope.

"New blouses; got it." Hope made another notation in her book. "I'll order them today." Ruth smiled her thanks then left the room.

Hope turned her attention back to the client. She looked at the IV stand where a bottle of *food* hung. A long, snake-like tube ran from the bottle to Lila's abdomen. The last time Hope had come to visit Lila she hadn't been in her bed. Hope had gone to the activity room to see if she had been taken there. Not that Lila could participate in any of the activities.

Often the patients in the activity room were simply sitting slumped over in their wheelchairs or geri-chairs listening to loud, and to Hope's mind, inappropriate music. She believed that these people, in their eighties and nineties, should be listening to music from their heyday, not this modern hip hop noise that passed for music. When Hope suggested that to the administrator his comment was, "But the people who work here like hip hop."

Hope tried reasoning with him. "If I was a patient here I'd consider that music cruel and unusual punishment, and then I'd wonder what my crime was other than outliving all my peers." She had wanted to add, "You should have a little respect for these people." But she didn't dare take her outrage that far as she knew it would get back to her boss, and then she'd have to endure another pious lecture about all Morgan's good and unselfish deeds for these clients.

"Well, most of them can't hear that well anymore anyway," was the administrator's parting comment.

Other times, when Hope visited the activity room, a therapist would be there gently tossing a huge beach ball to each patient and would then wait for the patient to toss it back. Sometimes it was a long wait that entailed a lot of coxing, if the patient had even bothered to catch the tossed ball in the first place. When taken to the activity room, Lila just lay back in her geri-chair with her eyes closed and her head turned away from all the noise and activity. But Lila hadn't been there that one time, and so Hope went in search of the nurse to find out where she was.

"Oh, we just called the conservator this morning. She had to be taken to the hospital to get the port for the feeding tube fixed. It was starting to ooze and her abdomen where it had been inserted was reddish and inflamed; we were concerned about possible infection."

Ah yes, the feeding tube, Hope thought, as she observed the thick sludge moving from the bottle, through the long tube, and disappearing under the client's hospital gown. That tube was nothing more than a man-made umbilical cord without which this woman and countless others like her would not be alive.

In some instances the PET tube was indeed a life-saving device. In others, it was akin to a medieval torture prolonging the inevitable. It was in cases like Lila's that the quantity-vs.-quality-of-life debate raged. Of course, said debate regarding devices like the PET tube had as much to do with dollars and cents as it did with ethics and morality. In Lila's case the tube was mostly a convenience. None of the aides wanted to be bothered to hand-feed each and every elderly patient as they would an infant. It was simply easier to put in a plug and provide life-sustaining nourishment via the PET tube. Not only had these patients lost everything, they had also been robbed of oral gratification. No wonder so many of them begged to die.

Every person Hope knew in this business who worked with people like Lila had their own DNRs in place. A DNR is a legal "Do Not Resuscitate" order. Not that a PET tube could be compared to, say, a respirator. There was a gray area about what exactly a DNR should entail—or if it would even be honored. If a person had one, it was best to spell out in no uncertain terms just what was covered and then cross one's fingers that the doctor would comply. Many doctors just didn't want a death on their watch which would end up in their statistical record; so they would go all out to save a patient even if it was the patient's wish not to be saved. Talk about a slippery slope. And yet, talk to any person on the street and you'd discover one universal truth: nobody wanted to end up like these disenfranchised members of society, although more and more did. After all, the warehousing of the elderly and keeping them in a limbo between life and death was the bread and butter of people like Morgan Smyth. Indeed, a whole industry had grown up around caring for the people that medical science kept tethered to life—if you could even call it life. "This poor woman," Hope whispered to herself. Then a little louder she said, "I'll see you next time, Lila." She waved toward the unresponsive woman as she left the room.

Lila, and so many others like her, was caught up in some kind of time warp—timelessness really—the sameness of every day with no variation must be some kind of hell here on Earth. Hope couldn't help the little sigh that escaped her as she sat down at the nurses' station with the patient's chart. She read the notes on Lila from the past couple of weeks and jotted down pertinent information in her own notebook.

"What the heck?" she whispered to herself. They'd started giving Lila massive doses of Vitamin D. Hope just shook her head. Vitamin D had recently become the vitamin de jour. When she'd been a kid in school studying the different vitamins she recalled that D was not water soluble like most of the other vitamins and so everyone was cautioned not to overdo it. But, evidently things had changed. She guessed someone had published a study (probably the people who manufactured D) indicating that lots of D was necessary now and, voila, the doctors were prescribing it left and right for her elderly clients. Hope recorded the Vitamin D increase in her notebook. Then she took her leave.

Hope always tried not to sigh with audible relief when she left Lila's facility. The bimonthly visits were all the same...and it was the sameness that was so disheartening. Lila would never get better. Nor would she get worse, at least not for a long, long time. This suspended animation was a living death and was so fiendishly wrong. The minute Hope stepped outside into the fresh air, or what passed for fresh air in southern California, she inhaled deeply, not even minding the exhaust fumes. She didn't exactly hold her breath when in facilities like this one. But often the smell of bodily discharges did permeate the air inside, and it wasn't the most pleasant aroma.

Getting into her Honda, Hope automatically flicked the lock button and simultaneously slipped off her shoes. Checking her iPhone for voice and emails, she got caught up, then tipped her head back on the headrest, closed her eyes, and took several deep, cleansing breaths. When she opened her eyes, they were focused on her reflection in the rearview mirror. "Well, my dear," she said to her reflection, "there but for the grace of God go you."

Hope was not a religious person, but she realized that since she'd become a case manager for Morgan she had started evoking the deity more and more. She'd find herself praying for the peaceful passage of these unhappy souls to that better place all religions claim exists beyond this earthly plane. And when that didn't happen, when these people lingered and lingered and lingered, she truly did wonder if there was a God. Could He be that cruel? What ever happened to that bit about caring for every sparrow and every blade of grass? Of course, she had to admit, if nature had taken its course in most of these cases these people would not be lingering on in nursing homes begging to die. And yet, where does aiding and helping the ill and sick stop and overstepping bounds of what nature intended start?

And truth be told, not all of her clients were in Lila's state of limbo. Many of them were simply unable to fend for themselves any longer in the most basic ways, and because of the state's imposed conservatorship, they were getting the care they needed. However, conservatorship in general was one thing; working for a conservator with a God-complex was quite another. Morgan was a conservator who enjoyed having power, who enjoyed wielding control over others, and who wouldn't brook any contradiction once an order had been issued. Whether Morgan was the exception to the rule when it came to conservators, Hope didn't know. What she did know was that she sure wouldn't want Morgan making decisions regarding her end-of-life existence. So, baby boomers beware, she sent that mental warning out into the universe; your number is coming up sooner than you think. And you'd better hope you don't end up in Morgan's sites.

Hope adjusted the mirror and applied a fresh coat of lipstick. When she looked into her own eyes she had to acknowledge the irony, for reflected back to her was nothing more than hopelessness.

If Hope had been asked to describe herself to someone, she would say that she was a woman *of a certain age*. She loved the diplomacy of that European phrase that softened the harsh reality of being classified as middle aged. No longer young, not yet old, that was Hope. People, well, one sister, told her she was pretty. Some men even described her as hot; personally, most of the time she felt she was neither pretty nor hot, at least not anymore. She just felt tired. She was of slim to average build with light brown hair, now-a-days highlighted with blond to help camouflage the ever-encroaching silver strands that kept appearing. She was a cerebral person often lost in thought, abstracting, dissecting this and that. Her demeanor to those who did not know her was quiet, polite, interested, and the slightest bit aloof. Hope had two sisters. One who was spiteful, odious, and smug. The other was courageous, talented and as generous as the other sister was stingy. Talk about extremes. And here was Hope, the middle sister caught between the two extremes. She often identified herself as *the responsible middle child*. As far as appearance, Hope's most arresting features were her deep blue eyes, now framed with fine lines that she felt added character to her face, and her disarming smile. She also had a nice laugh. "Laugh and the world laughs with you," she often quipped, "cry and you mess up your makeup."

And now that her makeup was freshened, Hope glanced down at her watch. She was scheduled to supervise Bonnie's weekly visit with her husband before meeting Darling for lunch.

2

Bonnie

"Love is lovelier the second time around."
— Arthur L. Porter

Hope zipped into the parking lot at the Sunrise for Seniors facility and saw that Dan's truck was already in the lot. No matter how early she tried to arrive for the weekly visit, Paul and Dan always arrived first. Paul missed his wife so much that being apart from her was torture. And yet, the short hour they were allowed to see one another had to be another kind of torture. It just didn't make sense that the court system would permit a jealous sibling so much power.

The automatic door opened outward and Hope entered the lobby where Paul sat regally in his wheelchair with Dan, his driver, comfortably slumped in a gaily cloth-covered wing-back chair. "Here comes Doris Day," Dan sang out as Hope approached them. Paul actually smiled at her, which was a first. Dan really must have worked his magic on this angry husband.

"Hello, Hope," Paul greeted her. "Dan tells me you used to live in Maine."

"True." Hope couldn't believe that Paul was engaging her in small talk. This really was a miracle.

"I did summer theater there once, in Ogunquit. It was a memorable time."

"Yes, it's a wonderful theater," Hope recalled. "Shall I go get Bonnie?"

"Please," Paul nodded. When Hope turned her back to Paul and focused on Dan she raised her eyebrows and silently mouthed the word, "Wow!" He just smiled and winked at her as she headed down the hallway to Bonnie's room.

The room was empty so the next stop was the activity room. There Bonnie sat in a wheelchair, head hung despondently. When Hope first started visiting Bonnie, she was as spry as spry could be. But the months of incarceration here had taken its toll. In addition, she'd been in and out of the hospital with pneumonia and each time she lost more ground. Hope had asked her physician/acupuncturist once why so many of her clients ended up with that horrible viral pneumonia that they just couldn't shake. Dr. Lee explained, "Those facilities are like Petri dishes full of all kinds of stuff that just grows and grows, explodes really; there is no containing it or eliminating it. When seniors go into places like that, it's just expected they will end up with the virus sooner or later. But there is another explanation." Dr. Lee continued, "We acupuncturists believe each organ of the body is a vessel containing certain emotions. For example, the liver contains anger, the kidneys fear, the heart joy etc. The lungs contain a person's sorrow and grief. I believe so many of these people contract pneumonia because they are grieving." And Hope could certainly believe that seeing Bonnie in her wheelchair, staring down at her feet with the most dejected expression on her weathered face. It was the saddest picture in the world. At least the beauty shop in the facility had rinsed Bonnie's hair since last week. Paul had been so upset to see the gray roots in his wife's hair. "She never let herself go like this. It's criminal!" he had expounded.

Approaching Bonnie, Hope slipped an arm about the woman's shoulders and leaned down to speak as her hearing wasn't as good as it once was. "Bonnie, guess what? I have good news. Paul has come to visit you."

Bonnie's eyes lit up and she sat up straighter in her wheelchair. "Paul? My Paul? Oh!" And she started to cry. "Oh, I want to see my Paul!"

"Come along then." Hope took the brake off the wheelchair and began pushing her down the warren of hallways to the lobby of the facility. "Let's not keep him waiting."

"Oh, Paul. My Paul's come to see me." The woman's joy was so great she could barely contain it. When Hope rolled Bonnie up to her husband they reached for each other and clasped hands and, for the first moments, were simply wrapped up in gazing into each other's eyes. They took such a deep and profound delight in each other's company it was almost a sacrilege to witness it.

Bonnie was in her nineties and a victim of Alzheimer's. She was one of those gracious older women who always did her best to make people around her feel comfortable. She didn't like discord and she would do anything in her power to keep things around her smooth and on an even keel. The sad fact of the matter is, however, that discord usually seeks these very people out and thrusts them into the role of peacemaker. And such was the case with Bonnie.

Bonnie had married for a second time later in life to a younger man. Back then, Bonnie, a youthful and very pretty seventy-three year old, had been widowed for nearly twelve years and was attending a potluck dinner at her church in Bel Air when she met her second mate. There was Paul, sixty-five years old, tall, sexy and about as handsome as she could imagine. They had a nice conversation and the next day she baked him a cake and delivered it to his apartment herself. They were married in less than a year and for the next twenty years they were as happy as any couple could be.

But there was someone who had not been happy for those past twenty years and that was Bonnie's baby brother. He was many years her junior and that made him about a decade younger than Paul. When Bonnie's parents had died in a train accident while her brother was still very young, she took over raising him and she promised him that he would never want for anything. Bonnie had gone on to marry a very wealthy man, and while they tried to have children, they were never so blessed. When her husband died she was left a rich widow. Because she was suddenly so alone, and her brother had never married, she relied on his companionship, while, of course, footing the bill. He had his own apartment, and dabbled in real estate, unsuccessfully, so it was Bonnie who supplied him with a new car every couple of years, nice clothing and jewelry, watches, rings, and even the gold necklace he was fond of wearing, as well as all the sun and fun vacations to the Caribbean that he wanted.

After Bonnie married Paul, her new husband pointed out to her that her brother was a big boy and he needed to start taking care of himself. Bonnie agreed. Baby Brother, of course, took considerable exception to that; he had felt entitled to his sister's wealth and didn't appreciate the interloper cutting him off. But Paul was a force with which to contend and Bonnie loved him with a deep and abiding passion. Baby Brother didn't have a snowball's chance in hell of convincing her that Paul was, in his decided opinion, an interfering bastard. But time and failing health seemed to be on Baby Brother's side.

Bonnie was now in her early nineties and Alzheimer's had her in its grip. In addition, over the past couple of years, Paul had undergone several abdominal surgeries and needed a wheelchair to get around. Because of their health issues, Paul hired a live-in caregiver to help them. The caregiver was a strapping young man who was able to help Paul into and out of his wheelchair. He got them to doctors' appointments and kept all their medications straightened out. He was a fabulous cook and did light house cleaning as well. All in all, he was a godsend; he was also gay. Things fell apart because Paul wanted to thank the caregiver and give him a special Christmas present. He sent him on a two-week-all-expense-paid vacation to Hawaii.

Baby Brother and Paul had been engaged in a pissing contest for the past two decades, but Baby Brother was younger, healthier and had nurtured twenty years of rage that had festered in his gut. Somehow Baby Brother got wind of this caregiver's sexual orientation and the recent vacation to Hawaii; using his imagination he concocted a very persuasive tale. It was revenge time and he was not to be denied. He convinced the court that Paul was a homosexual man who had hoodwinked his sister and was absconding with her wealth by giving it to his young gay lover. Baby Brother had documented evidence that this young gay lover lived in his sister's house and that Paul kept his paramour happy by sending him on expensive vacations.

Twenty years of devotion between husband and wife stood for naught. Baby Brother had successfully painted Paul with a black brush and the court, hearsay notwithstanding, without even investigating to see if what Baby Brother claimed was true, appointed Morgan Smyth conservator over Bonnie. Paul, unfortunately, had never seen it necessary to talk his wife into putting his name on her bank accounts or other assets, so everything was in Bonnie's name. So when the court froze all Bonnie's assets and then handed said assets over to Morgan, Paul was left with merely his social security check to his name. The only lucky thing was that when they were first married, Bonnie had refinanced her house for tax purposes and at that time had put Paul's name on the deed. The fifteen-year loan had been paid off and the house was free and clear. Other than that, the couple was screwed. Neither Paul nor Bonnie was in any shape to fight the system:

Bonnie because of her diminished mental capacity, and Paul because of his ill health.

Baby Brother, manipulator extraordinaire, had Morgan's ear and filled it full of invective. Hope got the story second-hand from Morgan who had been convinced by Baby Brother's story that Paul was indeed gay. "So what if he is gay?" Hope was always one to defend the underdog. "Who's to say he and Bonnie didn't have some 'understanding' when they married. They say the best friend a woman can have is a gay man. What right does her little brother have to interfere in a marriage, let alone the court system? *What God hath joined together, let no man put asunder.* Ever hear that?" Hope asked Morgan.

"Whose side are you on, Hope?" Morgan's voice was dismissive. "Cases like this are our bread and butter."

Morgan's first action was to get rid of the caregiver that Paul had hired and put a different one in the home. Paul balked at Morgan's handpicked choice, sensing that they now had a spy in their midst. So Morgan, in retribution, let the new caregiver go, yanked Bonnie out of the house, and had her placed in a nursing home. When Paul strenuously objected to that, Morgan's *nobody-fucks-with-me* attitude kicked into high gear, and Morgan went one step further getting the court to agree that as Paul was a negative influence on Bonnie that he could only visit his wife one hour a week.

Paul was completely outraged that the system could just step in to his life and rip his wife away from him. And Hope, what Morgan had asked her to do, well it just made her sick. Her job was to monitor the weekly one-hour visit between husband and wife. And when the hour was up, it was Hope's responsibility to see that Paul left the facility in a timely fashion. Good Lord! Now she had to play the role of warden. Hope was to arrive at the facility at the appointed hour, go get Bonnie from her room, escort her to the lobby area of the facility, where she could see Paul for that one slim hour then Hope had to escort her back to her room. Bonnie always cried as she was being escorted away. She would turn around and reach for Paul and cry out, "I love you!" And he, sitting in his wheelchair, would reach for her and answer, "I love you too, baby. I love you too." Hope always felt so ill afterwards. She would get Bonnie settled in her room. The woman would lie on her bed, roll over on her side, and just weep. Conversely, the next week, when Hope would show up in the room to get her and bring her to Paul for the visit, Bonnie's eyes would light up and she'd say, "Paul, oh my Paul has come to see me." And she would almost skip down the hallway to the lobby. But as the weeks wore on, Bonnie wore down. And that she was depressed was clear. She spent more and more time in bed, refused some meals, and was starting to waste away. She was now relegated to a wheelchair.

Needless to say Paul hated Hope with a passion as she represented everything that had gone wrong since the court had gotten involved in his life. And because the court now controlled all the money except for his monthly social security check, he could no longer afford to have a caregiver in the home for himself. So each week he had some friends pick him up and drive him to the facility and after the visit the friends would drive him home, and Hope could leave too, breathing a sigh of relief that that obligation was over until the next week.

Hope viewed the system as a behemoth that took no prisoners. In her mind it required dismantling: to be torn down and rebuilt. Some of the existing rules needed to be revised or maybe simply thrown out. Morgan's insistence that Hope monitor the visits between husband and wife struck her as shameful. The couple deserved their privacy, but to disobey Morgan was to court unemployment. And while Hope was at a place in her life where unemployment wouldn't have ruined her, she still needed something to fill her days.

So the monitored visits went on week after week—husband and wife seeing each other only for that one allotted hour. At least that's what Hope thought.

Morgan, as it turned out, had a snitch in the facility and, certain things soon came to light. It turned out that often Paul's drivers would wait until Hope had driven away from the facility, and then they would bring Paul back for a longer visit with his wife. In time, they started showing up nearly every day. But Paul, who proved to be quite cunning, had been sold out. Not because of what he was doing, but because of his haughty countenance. People don't like the arrogant. They love knocking them down a peg or two and that was what happened to Paul.

When Morgan discovered that Paul was ignoring the court order the doo doo hit the fan. Morgan at first tried to revoke the weekly visits between husband and wife altogether, but the court would not go that far. So instead, Morgan got a restraining order against the neighbors who drove Paul to and from the facility and made sure everyone in the facility knew to call the authorities if the restraining order was not obeyed to the letter of the law. So now Paul had to find a new driver. A veteran of World War II, he knew all veterans were brothers under the skin. So he went to the VA and hung out chatting up some of the guys there. He found his salvation in Dan, a big, strong, strapping Viet Nam veteran who could help him get to his visits to see his wife. And so far so good.

Bonnie was reaching for her husband before Hope had pushed the wheelchair halfway across the lobby. Their reunions were so touching. Not wanting to behave like a voyeur, Hope always sat in a wing-backed chair not far from the two lovers, but far enough away to grant them a semblance of privacy. Dan, also sitting at a comfortable remove, leaned toward Hope and whispered sotto voice, "You know I've fallen very much in like with you."

Oh, oh, was Hope's first thought as her mind went on red alert. But out loud she just chuckled and said, "Have you now?" Then she quickly changed the subject. "I took a quick look at Bonnie's chart when I was back there. No change in her medications except for one thing. They've started giving her a cranberry capsule a couple of times a day."

"Cranberry? What for?"

"A lot of my female clients end up with bladder infections. It's wearing those diapers all the time, I guess. At any rate, rather than having them succumb to that ailment, doctors prescribe cranberry as a preventative measure. And, truth be told, it's better than taking drugs when an infection flares up."

"So in other words she's become incontinent?"

"Not necessarily. It's just with age body parts don't work as efficiently as they used to."

"Tell me about it." Dan rubbed a knee.

"Arthritis?"

"Something." He looked over at Paul and Bonnie, heads together, hands clasped. "That there is a love story."

"That it is."

"How did it go so wrong?"

"Oh, Dan, who knows? It's mostly greed. That Bonnie's brother was so greedy he couldn't stand it. And now Morgan. Bonnie's estate is substantial which only makes the conservator less likely to let things go back to the way they were."

"I always knew I should have died in the war. Getting old is going to be a lot worse than that. It's like old age is hanging over all our heads like that ole' sword of Damocles. It can't be hid from or outrun."

Hope nodded in agreement. "I couldn't have put it better."

Partway through the visit, Dan had to help Paul to the bathroom as it was a two-man job with the wheelchair and doors etc. Unfortunately, when they got back, Bonnie decided she, too, had to go to the bathroom. Hope looked around for assistance but, of course, there were no aides available. "It figures," she thought to herself.

"Guess you're elected." Dan was grinning.

"Yeah, well, you get to be doorman." So Dan graciously held the door to the bathroom while Hope maneuvered the wheelchair through the opening. When the door was closed, she helped get Bonnie out of the chair and on to the toilet. The woman did her thing and was at least self-sufficient enough to be able to pat her self dry with a bit of toilet paper. Hope helped her hoist the bulky Depend diaper back up and then got her back into the wheelchair. She nudged the door open and there was Dan, ready and willing to hold the door for them.

When she got Bonnie parked next to Paul again and had taken her seat, Dan asked, "So how did it go?"

"I think I'm going to ask for combat pay," she told him. That got a laugh.

"You are a very kind woman." Dan's words surprised her.

Refusing to blush at the complement, Hope said, "Are you flirting with me?"

"Always, but I'm sincere. I read something somewhere, I don't remember where, it went like this: *Be kind, for everyone you meet is fighting a hard battle.*"

"Wow. You sound like a philosopher."

"Maybe I'm a student of philosophy, in my own way." They locked eyes for a beat of time until Paul's throat-clearing broke though.

Holding his wife's hand Paul got Hope's attention and began in his sonorous voice, "What the court has done to us is so incredibly wrong. My wife and I have lost so much time. And at our age, it's time we don't have to lose. What's happened to us is monstrous — it's a monstrous rape of all the ethics, morals, and values that keep society whole — leaving an irreparable tear in its fabric."

"Paul's not wrong." Dan added his two-cents worth. "You really have to color me astonished that things like this can happen. As a veteran I can steadfastly say, that's not why I fought for my country. I fought for freedom, the American way. This conservatorship business is not the hallmark of a country built on the blood of patriots who shed that blood for freedom."

Hope felt both embarrassed and humbled. "I'm not the person who needs to be hearing this. I can't do anything."

"If not you, who?" Dan asked.

"I may not be a well man." Paul nodded his head regally sitting in his throne on wheels. "But I am still a fighter. What the court has decreed here for us is unimaginable. I've sent a letter to my senator. It's a scathing indictment of a system that allows something as heinous as this to happen. I want my wife back in my home and I want our caregiver back. I want our lives back."

Hope hadn't taken her eyes from Paul during his pronouncement. She admired his spunk, but had her doubts about the outcome. "You have better faith in politicians than I do."

That made him smile. "Actually, I don't. But I have to start somewhere." He noticed his wife give a little shiver. "Are you cold, sweetheart? Here." And he removed his yellow cashmere sweater and placed it around his wife's shoulders.

"So tell me," Dan asked Hope, "you got a boyfriend?"

"I did, but not any more."

"What happened?"

She looked Dan dead in the eye assessing then said, "He didn't value my worth."

"Guy was a fool."

"Can't argue with you there." She appraised him some more. "Are you interested, Dan?"

"Big time!" His grin spread over his wide, handsome face. "But I'd better fess up. It's just flirting. I'm a married man."

"How many years?"

"Twenty-eight years. They were the best fifteen years of my life."

That made Hope laugh. "A man with a sense of humor; I hope your wife appreciates that."

"Maybe I should remind her."

"Maybe you should," Hope agreed.

The hour passed quickly and before anyone was ready it was time for Hope to push Bonnie back to her room.

●●●

Heading across the parking lot Hope spied Dan helping Paul into the passenger seat of his truck. Paul waved her over and said, "You know, I always did like you."

Hope put her finger to her lips and leaned in as if to tell a secret. "Your nose is getting longer, Paul."

He chuckled. "Well, maybe it was your butt I liked as you walked away across the parking lot. I may be old, but I'm not dead."

"Well, then, I guess it's time for the show," she said as she turned and headed across the lot toward her car. "Take care," she hollered over her shoulder. "And good luck with that letter to your senator. See you guys next week." Hope got in the car, flipped the lock button, started the engine, switched on the air, and pulled out her phone to let Darling know she was on her way to the restaurant.

3

Darling

> "If it's the Psychic Network why do they need a phone number?"
> — Robin Williams

"Hey there, girlfriend!" Darling rushed toward the booth, not the least bit apologetic for her tardiness. "As I always say, I'll be late for my own funeral." She slipped in opposite Hope. "Been here long?"

Hope shook her head. "Just long enough to order my margarita."

Darling waved to the waiter and pointed at Hope's glass. "So, how's that man of yours?"

"That man is making me wonder what I've gotten myself in to. I've had enough."

"Oh, oh, man trouble already? It's only been...what? A month or two?"

Hope had been divorced for five years after a thirty-year marriage and in all that time hadn't dated anyone because she didn't want anyone in her life. She loved her independence and the fact that she could do what she wanted, when she wanted, with whom she wanted, without checking in with someone else first; that was the ultimate freedom in her opinion. But then, a few months ago, she'd met first one man and then another and before she knew how it had happened, she and the second man were, to use a quaint old-fashioned term, keeping company.

Fred had taken one look at her and his eyes had ignited with a glow that Hope hadn't seen in a man's eyes in, well, a very long time. Fred had an intensity about him that had just swept her along, or sucked her in. She wasn't sure which. He was high energy and so arrogantly sure of himself. And, as it turned out, he also had an ex-girlfriend who had started causing trouble with a capital T.

"Come on, tell Darling all about it."

Hope sighed. "When we first started seeing each other, I told him that at this stage in my life I just wanted one of those nice, comfortable relationships with no bullshit."

"Yeah, yeah." Darling had heard a ding and eyed her purse beside her in the booth.

"Well, looks like I'm hip deep in bullshit and it's not good."

"Did you guys quarrel? Have a falling out?" Darling was all sympathy.

"If you want to call it that."

"It's that ex-girlfriend of his, isn't it?" Darling dug through her purse looking for something. "I told you that woman wasn't history. Didn't I tell you that? I saw that coming. That she was going to cause more and more trouble."

"That you did."

"Let me guess." Darling emptied half the contents of her purse on the table and finally found her cell phone. The contents of Darling's purse reminded Hope of life: disorganized and chaotic. Darling clicked a couple of buttons and stared at the screen, simultaneously reading a text while she talked to Hope. "Oh it's Amy. Always something with my kids. All that drama mama stuff. Anyway, back to you and that bimbo; I bet she's started calling him up at all hours and now she's stalking him. Well, here's what you do." She looked up from the phone screen and leveled a gaze at Hope. "You've got to freeze her ass out of his life...and yours. Now, you write her full name down on a piece of paper, three times, that's important, three times, and then sprinkle it with sea salt and say, 'I freeze you out of Fred Tailor's life.' Say it three times, got that, three times. Then fold that paper up into a teeny tiny little square and put it way back deep in your freezer. That'll freeze her the hell out of his life. And yours!"

Hope blew out a breath. She loved Darling and her mumbo jumbo; at the same time she did take it with a grain of salt, make that sea salt. "It's not worth it, Darling, it's just not. I don't have enough invested in this relationship to fight for it. He's the one who went after me; it wasn't my idea to get involved. It just happened."

"Ah, come on, you can't let that bitch get away with that. Dig in and give her what for." She slid the contents of her purse that were on the table top out of the way as the waiter put down her margarita.

"You senoritas ready to order?"

"In a minute." Darling looked over at her friend. "So? You going to give it the good fight?"

"No." Hope was shaking her head. "I don't care enough to fight for the relationship, if that's what it even was. Life was easier without Fred in it. And it's not just Diana. There's more than just that, and no, I don't want to go into it now."

"Ummm, Ummm, girl." Darling's fingers were flying over the buttons on her phone. "It's too soon to give up *hope.*"

"Don't start on those word games with me. You know how I feel about my name."

"Yeah. Yeah. Well, sounds like you made up your mind." Darling was focused on her reply text message then hit send before looking back at her friend. "Are you really through with him?'

"Yes, I am. Seriously, he was just nothing more than a...a geographical convenience."

"Humph," Darling snorted, "What a way to put it. Hey, you said he was rich. Why don't you toss him my way?"

"I might have considered that, except for the fact that he's a bigot."

"What? He's prejudice. Hasn't he heard that once you go black you don't go back?" Darling batted her eyelashes.

"Guess he missed that memo."

Darling put her phone down and focused on her friend. "Okay, I can tell you don't want to talk about ole' Fred so change of subject. Tell me, who did you see today?"

"I had to supervise Paul's weekly visit with Bonnie."

"Isn't Paul the guy who hates your guts?"

"Not anymore. He has a new driver now, Dan, and I think Dan is starting to get Paul to understand that I'm just doing my job."

"What happened to the old driver?"

"Morgan got a restraining order against him because he wasn't following the court order that allows Paul only one hour a week to see his wife. They were sneaking in to the facility to visit Bonnie at other times and Morgan got wind of it. The you-know-what hit the fan. So...now a new driver. This guy thinks I look like Doris Day."

"Say what?" Darling started laughing.

"That's what he said to me the first week he took over as driver. Whenever Paul and Bonnie have their visit, I just sit a ways away and unobtrusively read my book and let them hold hands and cry and tell each other how much they love each other and miss each other etc. It's really none of my business to intrude on their hour together. So, a couple of weeks ago, this guy, Dan, shows up, but I'm not feeling like making a new acquaintance. It's the end of the day and I'm tired and bitchy and just want to find out what Jack Reacher is up to, so I sit in a chair and dive into my book. Then pretty soon I hear a 'Hey.' Not a sharp 'Hey' but just a low, smooth, sensual kind of 'Hey.' I look up and Dan is looking at me and he says, 'You look like Doris Day.' I say, 'I do not!' and he turns to Paul and says, 'Paul, don't you think she looks like Doris Day?' So Paul looks over at me and those eyes are narrowed as he really hates me, and he stares at me for a moment then the turns to Dan and says, 'No, she doesn't!' But Dan won't let up and he says, 'Well, you're wrong cause she sure does look like Doris Day.' My comment to him was, 'I hope you're talking the fifties or sixties Doris because Doris today isn't quit as gorgeous as she used to be.'"

Darling gives Hope a serious appraisal. "You know, he's right, you do look a little like her. It's the blond highlights in your hair and the way it's cut with the bangs and all. And that cute little nose with just the hint of faded freckles. Yep, I can definitely see where ole' Danny boy was coming from."

"Whatever. Anyway, today when I arrived to supervise the visit, Dan and Paul were already there waiting for me to go get Bonnie and bring her to the lobby and Paul seemed more relaxed around me. So I think Dan is working some magic and driving home the point that I'm not the bad guy."

"So, what about this Dan guy, if you're through with Fred?"

Hope shook her head. "He's wearing a ring."

"Of course he is." Darling shook her head too. "Doesn't it just figure? Come on, let's order. I'm hungry."

●●●

"Earth to Hope," Darling reached across the table patted her friend's arm. "Where were you just now?"

"Oh, just...daydreaming."

"Daydreaming, hell, you were all but thinking out loud about that Fred moron."

"Okay, okay, you twisted my arm; I'll tell you what happened? The other night after we'd gone out to dinner..."

●●●

After a supper out on the town, Fred pulled in to Diana's driveway. "What are we doing here?" Hope wanted to know.

"I'm just going to invite her over to the house so the three of us can have sex."

It was rare to find Hope speechless, but, the longer she associated with Fred it was becoming more and more common. She found her voice just as Fred reached for his door handle. "Fred, clearly, in all this time, you have not gotten to know me very well. I am not going to participate in a threesome."

She had more to say, but before she could get it out his eyes flared and he said, "When we get married, I am going to expect you to say the word *obey* as in Love, Honor, and Obey."

Laughter bubbled up from her throat. "Of all the...not only will we never get married..."

"Of course we are," Fred interrupted.

"No we're not, Fred. Because I wouldn't say *obey* anymore than you would be willing to say, *forsaking all others*." She jerked her thumb toward Diana's house. "So, just so you are perfectly clear, not only aren't we getting married, not only am I not going to be participating in a threesome with you and your ex girlfriend, but you and I have just reached the end of the line." She opened her own door, "Don't bother seeing me home. I can find my own way." It felt so good to walk away from him, down the driveway, across the street, and back into her life.

She heard Fred's car door slam at the same time that an upstairs window was opening.

Diana poked her head out the window and hollered, "What's going on?"

From across the street Hope waved at her then pointed at Fred who stood in the driveway staring at her with his hand on his hips. "He's all yours, Diana. I won't be in your way anymore." She continued on in the direction she was heading, not in any hurry, just enjoying the heady rush of freedom. The air was sultry, the sky was cloudless, the stars and the nearly full moon were the perfect touch to what was turning out to be a perfect night. As Hope wasn't used to walking in heels, she slipped her shoes off and let them dangle from her fingers as she strolled along the avenue with the yellow moonlight lighting her way home.

●●●

Darling gave a rude snort and said, "He did not! He did not really expect you to participate in a threesome."

"Evidently he did."

"You?"

Hope crossed her arms over her chest. "Excuse me?"

Pausing before popping the last bite of enchilada into her mouth, Darling roared with laughter. "God, that's so funny. I would have loved to have seen the expression on your prissy face."

"Yeah, well," Hope glanced at her watch. "You're going to be late getting back to work."

"Naw, I'm in no rush to get back. You done for the day?"

"Yes, well, almost. I'll pop in on Dennis on my way home. Then I'm done."

"Damn! Nice short work days. Wish I could get by on a half-day job like you have."

"It's not always half days; I am on call twenty-four seven. You know that." Darling was staring at Hope, giving her a considering look. "What? Do I have something on my face?"

"No. I was just thinking, maybe you shouldn't be too hasty about tossing Fred back. Women our age we don't have a lot of options."

"We have plenty of options," Hope disagreed. "The problem is nobody our age comes without baggage. And right now, I'm not interested in anyone else's baggage."

"Humph, depends on the baggage," was Darling's rejoinder. "Say, not to change the subject, but what do you think?" She patted under her chin with the back of her fingers and then tapped the corners of her eyes. "Time for Botox?"

"Oh good grief, Darling, what's wrong with growing old gracefully?"

"Nuh Nuh, girl. I got to get me a *new* boyfriend. That Mr. Derek keeps saying he's going to stop seeing me and go back to his wife. So..."

"That's good news."

"Say what?"

"You're too good for him. You know that. Let the wife have him."

"Well, I guess she's got him, but now it's time for me to find me another man. Know anyone?"

"Sorry."

"Not only do I need another man, I need another job. Hey, think Morgan would hire me?"

"You don't want to work for Morgan, believe me."

"Sure I would. I could drive around all day like you not stuck in some stuffy office."

"No, just stuck in traffic on the freeways breathing in all the exhaust fumes. But, I repeat, you don't want to work for Morgan."

"Why not?" Hope just leveled a look at her friend. "Okay. Okay. I hear you. What was it you called Morgan the last time we had lunch: a pile of shit?"

"Actually I think my exact turn of phrase was 'a mound of doggy doo doo.' But it amounts to the same thing, doesn't it? To call Morgan insensitive wouldn't even begin to explain Morgan. Morgan is a person who can't even appreciate the drastic changes in our clients' lives, the cataclysmic changes. The poor babies are just so old and basically helpless. They've all grown older than they ever expected to be."

"Yes, then they up and die on you. I've seen how you get when one of them dies."

"It's not their passing that's hard. It's what they have to endure to get there that grabs at me. It's a profound thing, being blessed to share the final months and years with them. Most people don't get that. What I do isn't just a job, it's almost like I'm some kind of emissary. Oh," she threw up her hands. "I can't explain it."

Darling, applying some lipstick, said, "Tell me something."

"What?"

"Why is it that most of your clients with Alzheimer's are women? Why don't the husbands get it?" Darling put her lipstick and compact back in her purse.

"It's not just women."

"No, but mostly, why is that?"

Hope thought for a moment then sighed. "Who knows? Maybe the men are such control freaks that the woman, after years of putting up with that shit, turn to the only escape they have, in their heads."

"Ha!" Darling threw her head back and guffawed. "Escaping into dementia in self-defense, I like it!"

"I figured you would." After a thoughtful pause Hope added, "Extreme old age is like..." She was grasping for a way to describe it.

"Is..." Darling prompted.

"It's like life is a loan shark who's come to collect. It's not pretty; it's not nice; it's basically cruel. Without being aware of it, time has slipped through their fingers."

"All the more reason to make as much as we can of what time we have left." Darling, ever the optimist then reiterated, "So, I gotta get me a *new* boyfriend. Say how's your cute little Mr. G doing?"

Hope laughed. "You going to go after him?"

"Think he'd have me?"

"I'll find out tomorrow when I go and visit him."

Darling suddenly leveled her ebony eyes at her friend, pointed a sharply manicured finger at her, and spoke in a resonate voice. "Somebody's coming. Somebody else. Mark my words there'll be a new man in your life before too long. He's going to be a tall one. And handsome too. You go ahead and tell that Fred Fucker to get lost. Make room for this new one that's coming toward you." With that Darling jumped up and headed for the rest room.

The woman sitting in the booth behind her turned and spoke to Hope. "What she was just saying to you, it sounded like she was making a prediction. Is she psychic?"

Hope nodded, "So I've been told."

"Is she usually right on?"

"Ooooh, about half the time."

Laughing the woman said, "Well, hell honey, *I'm* usually right...about half the time."

"Me too, but don't tell Darling that." The two of them shared a chuckle.

Hope was pulling her car keys out of her purse when her phone rang. "Hi, Tanya, what's up?" Hope listened, then murmured, "Oh, dear." After a moment she said, "Okay, I'm on my way."

4

Lucille

"Old age is like a plane flying through a storm.
Once you're aboard, there's nothing you can do."

—Golda Meir

Lucille Simpson was a dear old soul. Her dementia had progressed to the point where she was confused most of the time, but a lifetime of breeding and good manners still showed through. She was a classic lady in every sense of the word and always greeted Hope with a smile as she reached out her hand for a polite shake—or gentle squeeze, to be exact. In her younger and middle years Lucille would probably have been described as *elegant*. Now the word *sweet* fit her better. She had become coy, little girlish, and loved to reminisce about her twin brother—Beauregard who, as a young man, was always in a dalliance with this girl or that girl.

Each time Hope visited her she had to reintroduce herself. In fact, she often had to reintroduce herself several times during each visit. Hope had discovered early on in this career that each client was a complete individual. Some didn't want to see Hope and ignored her as Lila did. Others loved to reminisce over old times as Dennis or Mr. G did. Hope found that what Lucille enjoyed most was going through magazines with brightly colored photographs. So Hope would always show up with a magazine and the two of them would sit side-by-side on the couch and page through it. Lucille would make comments about each photograph. If a dog was pictured dancing on his hind legs, Lucille would clap and laugh as if she were a small child at a circus. If a model was wearing a beautiful evening gown, Lucille would oohhh and ahhhh and stroke the picture as if trying to feel the texture of the material. If a scrumptious meal had been photographed, Lucille would tell Hope of the different things she used to like to cook. It was always a pleasant occasion for both of them, and when it was time for Hope to leave, Lucille, lady of the manor, would graciously ask her to come by and visit again.

Today, as usual, Lucille smiled when Hope entered the hospital room, but the smile competed with the lines of pain etched on her face. Hope put the magazine she'd brought with her on the bedside table realizing that today they probably would not be indulging in their favorite pastime.

"How are you feeling?" Hope took Lucille's hand and held it.

"It hurts." The sound of her voice was as pitiful as the mew of a kitten.

"Do you know where you are, Lucille?"

The elderly woman looked around and then shook her head. "Where am I?"

"You're in the hospital. You fell and hurt your hip. The doctor fixed it, but now you have to stay here for a while to mend."

"Oh."

Hope was pretty sure Lucille hadn't understood all that. "Would you like me to sit with you for a little bit?"

Lucille nodded. "Yes, please." In a few moments she looked at Hope and asked, "Where is this place?"

"You're in the hospital."

"Oh? What happened?" Hope ended up repeating herself again. Lucille listened to her intently following every word. Suddenly her eyes sharpened for just a moment. "You're the lady who tells me stories. Will you tell me a story?" She smiled coyly at her visitor.

Hope knew Lucille liked the ones that began "Once upon a time." And she particularly liked the ones about a damsel locked in a tower by a wicked witch. The damsel waits for her prince to come and rescue her and they both live "happily ever after." Lucille probably liked those stories because she, like the damsel, was locked away in a facility. But in her case no hero would come to the rescue — unless death himself took on that role. When Hope had finished the story, Lucille looked at her and asked, "Where is this place?"

"You're in the hospital."

"Oh? What happened?"

Hope ended up telling Lucille where she was several times until the woman finally drifted off into a fitful sleep.

Lucille had fallen and broken her hip. This type of accident was not uncommon amongst the elderly, but in this particular instance it was an accident that could have been avoided. And while nothing would come of it, Hope pointed the finger of blame directly at the caregivers of the facility where Lucille lived.

Before Morgan took over Lucille's conservatorship she had lived with her niece who had been granted the role of conservator of her estate and person. The niece, not realizing that conservative spending and accurate bookkeeping would have been a real good idea, thought being granted conservatorship gave her carte blanche and she basically blasted though the bulk of her aunt's savings in record time. When the court became aware of the mismanagement of the estate, it belatedly rescinded the niece's conservatorship and passed it on to Morgan. The niece erroneously had thought that Morgan taking over would simply mean someone else would pay her aunt's bills in addition to paying her thousands of dollars every month to continue caring for her aunt as she had been for the past several years. Morgan saw things differently and immediately arranged to remove the client from the family member's home and establish her in a small facility.

The day Morgan had informed Hope that Lucille was to be removed from her niece's dwelling and transported to Rest Haven Hope had gone to bat for the niece. Knowing Morgan didn't like anyone challenging a fait accompli decision didn't stymie Hope in this instance. Her visits to Lucille in the niece's home had convinced her that this was the best place for the client. So she decided to try and argue Lucille's case with Morgan telling Morgan that Lucille truly was cared for and just because the niece hadn't handled the money properly wasn't any reason to uproot the client from her familiar comfort zone. Hope argued, "Taking her away from her family member and all that is familiar to her just isn't right."

"Sometimes it's hard to know what the right thing is, Hope. You don't know all the angles. I'm the one who has to make the ultimate decisions."

"And just how do you decide, Morgan, rock, paper, scissors?"

"There's no need to get testy."

"You're right," Hope conceded. "You're the boss."

"You got that right. And right now your boss wants you to head on over to the niece's house and transport Lucille to her new home—Rest Haven."

"So soon?"

"The sooner the better."

"But why isn't Chester going to get her. He is really more qualified than I am to transport a client to a facility."

"He doesn't want to be going all the way into the heart of Orange County."

Hope shook her head. "Of course he'd be willing to go. Have you even called him and asked?"

"Do I have to spell it out for you, Hope? I don't think sending a big, burly black guy down into that lily white community to pick up a little old lady would go over with that prissy niece. She'd probably refuse to give up the custody of her aunt to the man and end up calling nine-one-one to boot. We don't need that mess. You've visited Lucille down there and it will just go smoother with the niece if you do the transporting."

Hope had only one more arrow in her quiver. "Can you at least place her closer to her niece? Rest Haven is so far away it will be almost impossible for her niece to visit very often."

"You know as well as I do that our clients are better off in places where family members can't interfere with things."

Hope didn't know that at all; nor did she agree with keeping the elderly isolated. The facts were that without visits and attention when moved into facilities, the elderly failed quickly. But Hope knew in Morgan's mind, the sooner they became vegetable-like so PET tubes could be inserted the better for the business. In that condition all they had to do was vegetate, remaining barely alive, but at least alive enough so that Morgan could continue to charge their estates on a monthly basis and not be bothered with other demands. Morgan, such a piece of work in Hope's mind, went to church every Sunday. When the other parishioners would ask Morgan how business was, Morgan would always reply, "I'm doing God's work." Yeah, right, Hope thought to herself, Devil's work is more like it. Today's particular *God's work* was to rip a demented old woman from the arms of her loving albeit spendthrift niece and drive her eighty-some-odd miles away to a facility in the valley where she wouldn't know a soul. "Some God!" Hope spat the words as she headed for her car to make the long drive south to pick up Lucille and transport her to her new home in the valley.

The drive to Orange County gave Hope plenty of time to think. She had visited Lucille three times at her niece's house. It was a modest house considering the location, but the bedroom for Lucille was roomy and the bathroom had been remodeled for an elderly person. Lucille had been happy, smiling and content during those visits. She would often babble on and on about her twin, Beauregard, and the flatlander he'd run off with.

"What's a flatlander?" Hope had wanted to know.

Lucille just pointed toward the distance. "Someone out...there," she finally answered. Visiting Lucille had always been enjoyable, but today would be different because today wasn't a visit. It was a legal kidnapping.

Getting Lucille out of the niece's home and into her car proved to be an adventure. The niece kept telling her aunt that she was going to go to court and get her back. That it would just be a few days and things would be back to normal. Lucille didn't really understand what her niece was talking about, but in her mind she equated court with jail. So she asked in a tremulous voice, "Am I being taken to jail?" Both the niece and Hope assured her she was not.

During the bumper-to-bumper drive on the freeway, Lucille kept asking, "Why are you taking me to jail?" Again and again, Hope gently explained that she wasn't going to jail, that she was going to be living in a nice new home with lots of nice people. The drive was interminable and Lucille started getting more and more agitated. In desperation Hope put in a Nat King Cole CD and, blessings of blessings, Lucille loved it and sang along with the songs all the way to the valley. And while Lucille sang, Hope mourned the fact that this poor woman's life had been so brutally sideswiped — completely knocked off track — never to be the same again.

Lucille ended up being placed in what is commonly known in the profession as a six-pack. A six-pack is a family dwelling that has been turned into a nursing home. Each one is run by a caregiver and the caregiver was allowed to have six clients to care for — hence six-pack. Sometimes it was a family run operation and sometimes it was run by a corporation that owned several six-packs. Most of these types of facilities were well-run and clean and very acceptable. Others, well, ended up on the other end of the spectrum. The facility where Lucille had been placed fell in between those two extremes. She had been assigned a nice bedroom with a private bathroom, but beyond that her life had taken a sharp left turn. No longer would she and her niece be jumping in the car to head to McDonalds for chicken nuggets, no longer would she take little day trips to the beach to watch the waves roll in which was a favorite pastime. No longer would she be allowed to walk up and down the sidewalk with her walker for her morning and afternoon exercise. She would now need to conform to her new environment.

This particular six-pack which bore the misnomer of Rest Haven—Haven being the questionable part of that name—was run by Sammy. Sammy was a registered nurse who had been hired by a corporation that owned several of these facilities. He had two helpers, also males, and while Hope never got the vibe that anything inappropriate was going on in this house of all elderly female patients run by men, it did smack of a peculiar set-up to her. Sexual abuse of elderly patients in nursing homes was not unheard of. And while the accusations were often unfounded, there were times when the abuse had indeed happened. It was true that muscle came in handy when getting patients into and out of beds or wheelchairs. And it was also true that modesty and dignity were luxuries that couldn't always be maintained in elder-care facilities. But it just seemed to Hope that a female presence would have added a legitimacy that seemed to be lacking in this particular six-pack.

When Hope had expressed those concerns to Morgan she had been told that there actually had been one incident about a year ago where a female patient had accused one of the caregivers at Rest Haven of inappropriate touching. It turned out the woman had needed a diaper change after a bout of diarrhea, and the necessary cleansing of the folds and crevices of her genital area that had become soiled was what had brought about the accusation. The explanation sounded plausible and was probably exactly what had happened. Still Sammy himself was a strange one and Hope never felt comfortable around him.

The other thing Hope didn't like about Rest Haven was the two yappy dogs that ran wild down the hallways and from room to room. They were small, but that only made it worse in Hope's mind. It wasn't that she didn't like dogs, but these ill-trained mutts were always jumping up at her when she entered the premise. Telling them, "Down!" was futile and the people who lived or visited there soon learned not to bother. One of them in particular always turned its head and gave her a cockeyed stare, looking as if it were pondering the advisability of nipping her ankles; then, reconsidering, it blinked, turned around, and skittered off down a hallway.

Getting Lucille settled into Rest Haven rendered Hope heartsick. Sammy immediately took Lucille's purse away from her — the symbolism of which was not lost on Hope. The woman had been removed from all that she knew and now was being stripped of any identity. It was more than wrong; it was evil. In this instance it was as if Sammy had taken a page out of Morgan's book. Morgan preferred it when there was nothing left linking the client to the past. When that attachment was broken, it often broke the client, making the client easier to handle. Taking Lucille's purse away was step one in this process.

Over time, Hope's visits to Lucille fell into a pattern. Lucille was always on the couch in the living room watching television; Sammy always hovered nearby hanging on every word. Hope would greet Sammy professionally and smile at him but never once had she received a smile in return. While Hope was only doing her job, Sammy made her feel as if she were an unwelcome intruder. It was not a comfortable feeling. The only time she ever saw him smile was when one of the patients in the facility had a guest or family member visiting. Sammy then put on a whole different face for the guest. He was all smiles and polite and solicitous of the patient who had the visitor — plumping pillows, soothing and, in Hope's opinion, putting on a pretense. But he did his job, kept his patients fed and clean and so there was no reason to complain.

And yet while Lucille was fed and clean it wasn't the same as when Hope had first met her. Lucille's hair, while not in complete disarray, wasn't combed and arranged with the pretty ribbon that had always before adorned it when at her niece's house. And while her clothing wasn't unkempt, she was no longer dressed with the accessories that make a woman feel pretty and well-put-together. If Lucille happened to look in a mirror she would pause, puzzled. She couldn't remember the word slovenly, but she knew that's how she looked now and it confused her considerably.

In her new environment at Rest Haven, Lucille had to follow a strict regimen and, as a polite and easy-going woman, she did her best to follow the rules, but she was mystified as to why she couldn't indulge in some of her usual habits. In particular, she was no longer allowed to exercise as she had been accustomed to doing. She had walked with the aid of a walker for a couple of years now, but before moving to this place had been in the habit of walking around the block every day and sometimes twice a day where she lived with her niece. She also had an exercycle at her niece's house that she used daily—with her niece's assistance, of course. Here in the facility, the caregivers didn't allow an exercycle saying it was too risky, an accident waiting to happen, nor did they want Lucille, or any of their charges for that matter, wandering around the block perhaps getting lost in the unfamiliar neighborhood. No one had the time to walk with them so it seemed. So every morning after breakfast, instead of getting her morning exercise, Lucille was placed on the sofa in the living room in front of a big-screen television that blared all day long. The sofa was a huge very soft piece of furniture that almost swallowed up anyone who sat on it—making it impossible to get up without help. The more the patient struggled to get off this sofa, the more stuck she became: think Br'er Rabbit and the Tar Baby. This was by design, not accident. The staff didn't want any of their patients to be able to move about the house. Once they were placed on the couch, they were expected to sit there all day until it was time for a meal, a diaper change, or bed.

Hope had complained to Morgan about that after her first couple of visits to Rest Haven to see Lucille. "These people need to be given exercise. They should at least be able to go outside on nice days. There's something wrong, even criminal, about just plunking them down and leaving them in front of the television all day long."

Morgan, far from sympathetic, said, "Hell, if they were living on their own, they would be sitting in front of their televisions all day long. What's the difference?"

Lucille, her dementia notwithstanding, was a wily old broad and in pretty good shape to boot thanks to her years of exercise. The unaccustomedly imposed sedentary lifestyle didn't thrill her at all. Somehow she managed to get up off the sofa a couple of times and, with the aid of her walker, make it out the door. The door happened to have a long, loud buzzer attached so whenever it was opened the staff was alerted. Both times Lucille had made it that far she was intercepted and taken back to her spot on the couch.

To control matters even more after those two incidences, the staff put

Lucille's walker clear on the other side of the room so she could not get a hold of it and take off for the walks she was so accustomed to enjoying and was so desperately missing. Once again Lucille managed to get up off the sofa, how she did so remains a mystery, and was crossing the room to get her walker when, Hope speculated, one of the dogs must have jumped up on Lucille, tripping her. One way or the other, Lucille fell, and broke her hip. If the walker had been beside her instead of clear across the room this accident never would have happened. If Lucille had been left to her own devices with her walker at the ready whenever she wanted to get up off the couch even if it was just to go back into her room for some privacy, all would have been well. But autonomy was no part of living in this particular six-pack. Hope just wished she had some pixie dust she could scatter over Lucille's broken hip to help it heal quickly.

●●●

Well past suppertime when Hope left the hospital, she postponed her visit to Dennis for another day and headed home. Hope drove the surface streets as the freeway was the opposite of free this time of day, arriving home in a little over an hour. Pouring herself a glass of wine, she wandered out on her balcony to drink in the night along with the light, crisp white.

Hope's condo was part of a triplex, an older home that had been broken into three separate apartments; hers was the only one that boasted a balcony that looked out toward the nearby hills. The balcony is what had sold Hope on the condo and it had become her place of respite. Often during the afternoons she would sit out there to relax or read. Other times she'd come outside side to stargaze as she was doing now.

God, she loved to look out at the heavens. Talk about mystery. Talk about immensity. Talk about giving a person perspective. There were times she received a jolt of pure joy just standing here beneath the stars. It was still as hot as Hades out, with no breeze, but she didn't mind the heat. She stretched her arms up, almost in supplication, drawing down the night into herself. This was the time of day Hope let her mind wander and often it turned toward her clients. For them time had become the enemy. There was no escaping its relentless march across the years and decades. It had reduced Lucille from a vibrant active woman to a broken old lady in a hospital bed grimacing in pain and confused as to how she had gotten there.

It was evenings like this that Hope would ponder God, fate, karma, destiny. Traditional religions didn't do it for her. And a lot of the new age stuff was too far afield for her to swallow as well. She was no philosopher, but she liked to ponder things, wonder why, and ask unanswerable questions of the universe. Her quest wasn't for knowledge per se — but for understanding the un-understandable. No one had ever given Hope a guide book — The Book of Life. She had to learn the hard way, by doing, by experiencing, by making a multitude of mistakes. She stood on her balcony looking out at the hills, pondering the whys and wherefores, knowing there was no definitive answer forthcoming. No, there didn't seem to be any answers, but she had her clients.

Each client provided her with a larger vision of — not the end of life so much — but of life itself. They gave Hope's life meaning — an irony because individually their lives were woefully rift of meaning. They'd had everything taken from them and for most even their minds and memories had turned against them too. It was such a bittersweet thrill when one of them remembered a tidbit from the past and shared it with Hope. That they didn't always remember things accurately was no big deal. Their own personal reconstructions of the past were perhaps even better than memories. After a moment of communion, Hope sighed, looked away from the heavens, passed back through the French doors into her condo, and booted up her computer. She still had client notes to record before she could call it a day.

5

Dr. Lee

"It is more important to know what sort of person has a disease than to know what sort of disease has a person."

—Hippocrates

Each morning Hope rolled out of bed, pulled on her jeans and a T-shirt, some socks and her tennis shoes, and headed out the door. A brisk morning walk was a part of her routine that kept her healthy and sane. She walked for an hour before breakfast, came home and cooked up some oatmeal, then hit the shower and got ready to face her clients. The walk and the oatmeal were her health insurance policies—literally. Her job was part-time which translated to no benefits, and the cost of living in California was such that keeping the wolf from the door didn't include enough left over for health insurance. Add to that the fact that Hope had philosophical differences with those who drove the health care machine.

Hope loved it that while she lived in the heart of the city she often ran into wildlife on her walks. It was her proximity to the Verdugo Hills that lent the area a more rural feel. During one early morning walk not long ago, Hope rounded a corner and up ahead saw a coyote that had wandered down from the foothills. It was trotting down the middle of the residential street like it owned the place. When he saw Hope he stopped, blinked his tawny eyes at her, turned around and trotted back in the direction from which he'd just come. Another time she startled a fawn that was apparently lost and looking for its mother. It had bawled when it saw Hope, then jumped someone's fence and disappeared into the person's backyard. She'd also seen a tortoise, numerous rabbits, squirrels, and even possum. Thank goodness she'd never come across a skunk. Yes, Hope never knew what to expect on her walks.

This morning, however, there was no walk on the agenda—thank God for it was the hottest day of the year so far. In the summer months, when temperatures soared upward toward one hundred degrees, Hope often got up before six a.m. to get her walk in. There was no point in courting heat stroke. Today, however, Hope had an appointment with Dr. Lee so she would forego the walk. Dr. Lee was an acupuncturist who also, happily, happened to be a medical doctor. Hope rarely needed a medical doctor, but one never knew; so going to an acupuncturist who was both was the best of all possible worlds. She saw Dr. Lee every six weeks for a tune-up, as she liked to call it, and today was the day.

Dr. Lee, a working mom, was a petit Chinese woman who, if she stood on tiptoe would still be shorter than Hope's five feet seven inches. She practiced a Japanese brand of acupuncture along with western medicine and maintained a small patient base so she could be what she called a full-service doctor to them. They could call her anytime and it was guaranteed that she would answer the phone — not her service, not a receptionist, but she herself. Dr. Lee's patients could also get in to see her on very short notice, usually the same day they called with an issue, and she never did the ten-minute-visit-looking-at-the-chart-in-lieu-of-the-patient thing while scribbling out a prescription that most modern doctors did. After an intensive conversation with a lot of hands-on and a lot of eye contact, it was more likely that she would prescribe vitamin supplements than pharmaceuticals. And the fact that Dr. Lee treated her patients like the human beings they were rather than as a means to make an expensive house payment meant the world to all of them.

The last time Hope saw Dr. Lee was shortly after Congress has passed the Obama-care bill. The doctor lit right in to Hope the minute she was in the office. "So, you will finally be able to get insurance. How do you feel about that?"

Hope tried not to roll her eyes then gave in to the gesture. "Dr. Lee, Congress is not going to make me change my mind about getting insurance."

"You are so stubborn."

"So I've been told."

"But it looks like you aren't going to have a choice. So what are you going to do when time runs out?"

"I'm not worried. There's a lot that can and will happen before the deadline to get insurance rolls around. Mark my words."

"I thought for sure the legislation would make you change your mind."

"Dr. Lee, the state of the health care system in this country is deplorable. I'm not going to jump on that sinking ship."

"I sense a diatribe coming on..."

"If the government would be honest with us and call it what it really is — not insurance but a tax — then maybe I'd fall in to line. But if they want to keep whitewashing it and playing semantic games..."

"Horsepucky, insurance isn't a tax."

"Of course it is. Just because they call it insurance and make it 'voluntary' doesn't mean it isn't a tax. And if they called it a tax and just automatically took a percentage out of everyone's paycheck, it would all be a moot issue."

"People in this country don't want socialized medicine. You know that."

"What I know is that they *have* socialized medicine. It's just being called something else. That's what I mean by the government not being honest with us. It's like those people who have no children but who kick because their property taxes go down that toilet called the public school system. They don't want to pay for kids' education, such as it is, but they have no choice. It should be the same way with health care. For example, those handful of people who are billionaires should each have to be taxed yeah number of billions each year. Those who make less then...say...twenty-five thousand a year should not be taxed at all. And everyone in between those two extremes should pay a gradation-scale tax. Then when people needed health care, they'd get it, nobody would be billed for anything, and it would be so easy to do."

With her tongue firmly in her cheek Dr. Lee said, "I wonder why nobody has thought of that before?"

"Ha ha."

"Seriously, Hope, I love your indignation. But you are still foolish if you don't get insured."

Hope looked pointedly at the picture of Thomas Edison on the doctor's wall that hung side by side with several diplomas. It was a photograph of the inventor with a pithy quote beneath it: *The doctor of the future will give no medicine, but will interest his patients in the care of the human frame, in diet, and in the cause and prevention of disease.* "It appears to me that you're sending mixed messages, Dr. Lee."

"Yes, I am a complex blend of Eastern and Western, of homeopathic and medical, of ancient and modern medical practices. Regardless, common sense still dictates that you need insurance."

As usual they ended on a stalemate. Hope knew her beloved doctor only wanted what was best for her. But Hope, a rebel at heart, had made the decision long ago to buck the system on this issue. She would not be dictated to by the insurance companies, the pharmaceutical companies, or the American Medical Association. She didn't want to sound like a conspiracy theorist, but she did think that the aforementioned mighty trinity had brainwashed the populace of the country. It had turned the citizens in to a pill-popping mass of hysterics who thought with enough insurance they would be able to beat death. Hope was fond of pointing out, to those who insisted that she needed to be insured, that no matter how rich or how well insured a person was, that that person was still going to die. "No one gets out of this space ship alive," she quoted when faced with someone who wanted to debate her stance.

"Blood pressure's fine." The doctor put the cuff away. "Anything going on that we need to look into today?" She patted the table.

Hope stretched out in preparation for the acupuncture treatment. "Nope, I'm fine, good as always."

"I sense a 'but'...how are things on the job? You might feel a small prick," she added as the first needle slid in.

"Oh, some days crawl by, some days fly. Mostly I'm just frustrated, as usual, with the way the system abuses my clients."

"Is it really the system that abuses them, or is it your boss and people like Morgan?"

"Conservators! It's just a job to them. They make decisions that alter lives then go home and have a cocktail. If they had to live with these people and suffer the consequences of their decisions along with the clients, they might make better choices."

"And your clients? Are they just lambs to the slaughter?"

"How can they help but be when most of them suffer from dementia of one form or another? When my clients exert their own wills, the doctors, with the conservator's full sanction, put them on enough drugs to force them into compliance, turning them into drooling automatons, and call it a job well done."

"Yes, it's troubling," Dr. Lee agreed. "Does that happen to a lot of your clients?"

"Enough of them. But not all. Some of them are lucky, like Dennis. Would you believe he's eighty-eight and not on one prescription drug? He's my hero." Hope smiled up at her doctor.

"I don't think you've mentioned Dennis before. Tell me about him."

●●●

Dennis, in his late eighties, was forever young. When asked his age he would always quip, "Seventy-five." He wasn't equivocating. He really thought he was still seventy-five. And honestly, if someone didn't know better, it was a comment that would be taken at face value. He was a vigorous man who still had a youthful air about him. At five and a half feet he was short for a man, but he was in great physical shape and still had a head of hair that others not so lucky would envy. True, he did keep it cut short with a military precision; he was one of those not-a-hair-out-of-place guys. He reminded Hope of Mr. Rogers, that beloved television personality that her children watched on TV when they were young. Dennis, like Mr. Rogers, dressed in clothes that could only be described as square — to use the parlance of Hope's youth. He even had the cozy sweater that buttoned up the front that he wore on chilly winter days.

A former World War Two veteran who had worked for the postal system all his life, Dennis had never married nor had children. After his retirement he resided in a little house and lived what most would call a pretty boring life. He never travelled, didn't date, never went to the movies, and rarely ate meals out at restaurants. He did have one pastime that he loved — he playing the ponies. He'd head on over to Santa Anita or Hollywood Park a few times a year to indulge himself, but that was the extent of his extravagances. He never overdid the gambling. Moderation in all things was a motto he'd always lived by.

As a mail carrier he had been accustomed to walking miles a day delivering mail, so continuing on with that habit in his retirement, he walked every day, sometimes several times a day. He was in good shape thanks to all that exercise and one day flowed into the next. And all was well with his world until one day he sauntered into his neighbor's house instead of his own, turned on the TV, and settled in to watch the news. It was at that point that the dementia was discovered. As he had no one to step up and care for him, Morgan was appointed. Dennis was placed in a six-pack in the valley where his life fell into a routine.

This particular six-pack was one of the nicer ones. The couple who owned it was from the Philippines. The woman was a nurse in her fifties. Her husband was considerably older and retired, so he was home to help with the day-to-day chores involved in taking care of the six elderly people that they housed. Their house was in a pretty little cul de sac away from the maddening crowd. The property was surrounded with a neat brick wall and the gardens were lovely. Flowers bloomed, shrubs thrived and the trees offered plenty of shade. There were little stone benches here and there to sit on if the clients wanted to spend time outside, and a fountain splashed merrily in the backyard. Dennis, who had always been a loner, was pretty much left to his own devices which suited him perfectly. He had a private room with a little TV for entertainment, a private bathroom with a roomy shower, a walk-in closet to hold not only clothes but shelves for other things, and the piece de résistance was a bay window that looked out on the beautiful yard if he just wanted to sit and contemplate the out-of-doors. He was fed three meals a day and, as was his habit of a lifetime, he enjoyed walking around and around the cul de sac for exercise in the late mornings or early afternoons. He never ventured further afield than the comfortable circle. The husband of the woman who ran the facility would go outside and do yard work, raking, watering or pruning rose bushes that stood outside the brick wall surrounding the property, when Dennis was on his walks. That way they kept an eye on him and made sure he got back to where he belonged safely, without impinging on his desire to walk alone.

Hope visited him every two weeks and the visits were always the same. They talked about his service days on a hospital ship in the South Pacific. His memories of that time of his life were so vivid. All that he described could have happened yesterday. Beyond that he didn't have much to say. He'd talk about the weather and the fact that he enjoyed his walks. If it was a hot or a cold day, he told her, he would wear a straw hat when he was outdoors. One time he stood, slid open the door of his closet, and took the hat off the upper shelf to show Hope.

One day, quite by accident, she learned that Dennis knew a lot about cars. She mentioned that she had to take her car in to the shop for service because it was acting up. In his humble way he started asking her specific questions about this and that regarding the car and pretty soon she was equipped with a wealth of information about what the problem might be. When she took the car in she'd be able to suggest to the mechanic where to start looking. Compared with her other clients visiting Dennis was like visiting an oasis. It was such a peaceful interval. She could sit and visit and not worry about his medications (because he didn't take any), not worry about his treatment by the staff (because they were top of the line), and not worry if he was getting what he needed (because it was evident that he had everything he needed). She could see he was clean and well fed and perfectly content with his daily existence.

●●●

"If all my clients could be as happy as Dennis, I'd be so pleased," she told Dr. Lee.

"What accounts for his happiness?"

"It's probably just his personality. But if someone had to end up with dementia, I'd wish for him—or her—an existence like Dennis's. He isn't expected to do anything other than what he wants to do. He's left alone and he does just fine. This is an example of conservatorship at its finest—the laissez fair approach. And I do my best to help Dennis keep a low profile. I simply refuse to bring him to Morgan's attention any more than is absolutely necessary. Luckily he isn't sickly. If he was, of course the caregiver would step in and be sure he saw a doctor. But, other than the dementia, he's in such good health. I don't know how he managed to fly under the radar as far as not being pumped full of drugs. But he's doing fine without the established medical community's interference. That's for sure."

Dr. Lee chuckled and looked at her fondly. "He sounds like a lucky man, considering."

"Yes, he is, considering."

"You know, Hope, not to change the subject, but speaking as a member of the established medical community, I really think you need to have that physical we talked about."

"And I told you I can't afford to do something like that out-of-pocket."

"It's important, Hope. Tell you what, I'll comp you the whole thing; that's how important I think the physical is. All you'll have to pay for is the tests."

"But how many tests? That's the thing. They're what cost the most; not the office visit. That basic blood test you gave me last year to see if I had iron-poor blood cost over three hundred dollars! When I got that bill from the lab I almost fainted. I used to be able to go to my doctor's office, get my finger pricked. The nurse would smear my drop of blood on a slide and check it right away, and then give me my hemoglobin results for two dollars! So that three hundred dollar bill was essentially economic rape. That's the system's way of getting even with people who refuse insurance. So, forget it. Sorry, Dr. Lee, not interested."

"Hope..."

"Look, first of all, I'm fine. Second, you take some tests, and voila, you know what happens? You invariably find...something. That's what doctors do. And once you find something, then you are going to expect me to deal with it. Plus," she rushed on when it looked like the doctor had something to say, "then it gets in my record and then I have a pre-diagnosed condition that wouldn't be insurable if I ever did get insured."

"Hope..."

"No. I take care of myself. I feel fine. My blood pressure is fine. If I were feeling ill, I'd know it. Let me just take my chances, my way."

"What if you had a life-threatening illness?"

Hope gave Dr. Lee a long, solemn gaze. "I'm not afraid to die, Dr. Lee. I look death in the eye every day when I'm with my clients and you know what? Death isn't all that scary. In fact, Death isn't even the enemy. There are a lot of fates out there far, far worse than Death."

Dr. Lee crossed her arms over her chest and leveled Hope with a penetrating look of her own. "You sure know how to get on a soapbox; I bet if I took your blood pressure now it wouldn't be fine."

"Ha ha."

"Yeah. Ha ha. That was the last needle." The doctor dimmed the lights in the room. "Now just lie back and relax and let the needles do their thing."

6

Mr. G

> "A man over ninety is a great comfort to all his elderly
> neighbors: he is a picket-guard at the extreme outpost; and the
> young folks of sixty and seventy feel that the enemy must get by
> him before he can come near their camp."
>
> —Oliver Wendell Holmes

When Hope stepped out of the air conditioned acupuncturist's office she was hit with a wall of heat that took her breath away. It was so hot that the heat waves shimmering on the sidewalk made her think, for a split second, that she was in the throes of an aural migraine. She slid into her car and started it up turning the air to high before grabbing her phone. Hope punched in Mr. G's number and waited. She frowned when the voice mail picked up. "Hello? Wendy, are you there? I was supposed..."

"Ma'am, yes, it's me." The caregiver sounded rushed. "I was just getting Mr. G into the car."

"Why?"

"The VA called a little while ago. He has an appointment in half an hour."

Hope looked at her watch. She was a good forty minutes away from the Veteran's Administration facility where Mr. G doctored. "Did they say what's up? He was just there last week."

"No. I've got to go or we'll be late."

"Okay, Wendy, I'll meet you there as usual, but I am going to be a few minutes late."

"Yes, ma'am, I'll see you there."

Mr. G, a feisty ninety-nine-year-old, was outspoken, and, up until about six months before, still able to walk without the aid of a walker or a cane. Several years ago his daughter had gotten a conservator involved in his affairs because she was sick and tired of putting up with his demanding and authoritarian personality. Mr. G, a World War Two veteran who had been shot six times in the line of duty, had a strong will that had served him in good stead all his life. And he saw no reason to allow his snip of a daughter, as he called the seventy year old, to start dictating to him. He'd been living alone since his wife died twenty years before, and getting along fine as far as he was concerned. He made it to temple every week, and he still drove to the market every day to buy his kosher food. He'd eaten kosher all his life and was proud of the fact that no other type of food had ever passed through his lips. But dementia does not discriminate and Mr. G's memory was beginning to fail more and more. His house was filthy, he had stopped taking baths, and who knew if he even remembered to take his medications, let alone get the prescriptions refilled when they ran out. Something needed to be done.

Mr. G, however, was having none of his daughter's interference in his life; and she certainly had no intention of battling the stubborn old man day in and day out. So his daughter, at her wit's end, did the only thing she could do to see that her father was cared for properly: enter the California court system. The court, agreeing with his daughter that he needed someone to oversee his affairs and to see that he was kept clean and cared for, appointed Morgan Smyth as Mr. G's conservator of both his person and his estate. And the battle of wills began. Mr. G did fight the good fight, but was shot down at every turn. And Morgan, God complex intact, had no problem stepping in and issuing dictates regarding what, who, when and how things would be done from now on.

Mr. G despised Morgan with a passion and never failed to state that fact. When Hope would visit him, the first thing out of his mouth was how much he hated Morgan and how he wanted vengeance for all the wrongs done to him. Hope would sit next to him on the couch, pat his gnarled hand, and tell him he'd have to "get in line" because a lot of people felt the same way about Morgan—that always made Mr. G laugh. He came to view Hope as someone who truly understood how angry he was that the court had taken away his right to make his own decisions. And she did understand, but, at the same time, she also understood that if help hadn't been forced on him, he wouldn't have a caregiver in his home to cook his meals, clean his house, and keep him clean as well, and then where would he be?

At least his daughter had cared enough to insist to Morgan that her father be kept in his home until the end; that neither he, nor she, would ever tolerate his being moved out of the home he had lived in for decades and placed in a facility.

Hope recalled the first time she had met him. She had pulled into Mr. G's driveway, scooped up her notebook and blood pressure cuff, and before she'd even gotten to the front door, Wendy, the caregiver, was holding the screen door open in welcome. "Good morning, Ma'am. How are you, Ma'am?"

"Fine, Wendy? I'm Hope. How's Mr. Goldstein doing today?"

"He's fine, Ma'am, come in."

Hope skirted around the caregiver and entered the living room. Mr. Goldstein was seated on the couch in the tastefully furnished room. She formally shook his hand and smiled into a face that could only be described as wizened. Talk about Mel Brook's *2000 Year Old Man* personified. He eyed the blood pressure cuff in her hand.

She held it up. "Do you mind?" He didn't, so she took his blood pressure and wrote it down in her notebook. "Tell me about yourself Mr. Goldstein."

"Just call me Mr. G. Everyone else does."

She acquiesced. "Mr. G. Tell me about you." The visit went well and over the months they both looked forward to seeing each other.

Mr. G's dementia was such that his memory was spotty, but he remembered a lot of things past, and often regaled Hope with anecdotes about his childhood. And of course, there was the war. That was always a lively topic of conversation. He would show her his scars and tell her how he had cheated death again and again. In time, he developed a little crush on Hope. He often broke into song, singing a cappella. Once he held her hand and looked into her eyes singing: *You made me love you (I didn't want to do it)*.

"And you've made my life complete," she had told him as she patted his liver-spotted hand. "Now, I will never be able to say that no man ever serenaded me." Hope always wished she could remember to smuggle in one of those voice-activated tape recorders so she could get his songs on tape. But she never did.

He would tell her his hopes and dreams, most particularly that he wanted to visit Israel once again before he died. He would ask her so sweetly, "Would you take me?"

Over the months, Hope saw the decline; imperceptible at first, but picking up momentum in recent weeks. Mr. G now needed a wheelchair whenever he went out. At home he could still walk from the bed to the couch to the dining table and back to the couch. But he was weaker and couldn't stand for long periods of time. They had gotten him a shower chair and soon after that the wheelchair.

Their last visit to Dr. Rubinstein hadn't gone as planned at all. Dr. Rubinstein had been Mr. G's doctor for literally decades. He knew the patient well and visits always went smoothly. Maintain the status quo was the doctor's motto. Don't rock the boat was a cliché he lived by when it came to his geriatric patients. But last time when they had waited in the examining room for the doctor, someone else walked through the door. A young woman, who introduced herself as Peggy, handed Hope her business card, and said she'd be taking over Mr. G as a patient. It turned out that Dr. Rubinstein had retired. This had been the fate of so many of Hope's clients. They were so old that the doctors they had been doctoring with for more than half their lives were now of retirement age. The tried and true doctors were clearing the playing field, leaving it to the now untried doctors. These new doctors had fire in their bellies and a gleam of determination in their eyes. They wanted to make a difference, but often their elderly patients only became upset and bewildered having no idea who these young upstarts were.

Peggy, not knowing the patient or his history, only having the chart to guide her, made her first big blunder—she took everything Mr. G said as gospel not realizing that with dementia a patient often says things that never happened expect in his mind.

Peggy had gestured to Hope and said, "Is this your daughter?"

"I hate my daughter," Mr. G bellowed. "I was swimming in her pool and she held my head under the water."

Peggy looked at Hope with a mixture of horror and loathing on her face. "What!"

"I'm not his daughter," Hope said softly. "I'm his case manager."

"Oh." Peggy paused then said, "But, did you call the authorities when his daughter did that to him?"

Hope responded, "His daughter lives in a lovely home, but it doesn't have a swimming pool."

Peggy's eyes narrowed. It wasn't that she didn't believe Hope, but apparently the tone of Hope's voice had been off-putting. Those in authority, Hope had learned long ago, didn't like others to question or challenge them on any level. By the end of the visit Peggy had ordered numerous tests, and then told Mr. G that his diet sounded abysmal and that he'd probably have to see a nutritionist to make sure his meals were balanced.

"I'm concerned that he's lost some weight since his last visit here." Peggy had turned her shoulder to Hope and spoke to Wendy. "Make sure he eats more at each meal. You need to start fattening him up."

As Wendy and Hope walked back to the parking lot pushing Mr. G in the wheelchair, Wendy said, "She was a nice doctor."

Wendy was a sweetheart, but not the sharpest crayon in the box. Glancing down at the business card she still held in her hand, Hope retorted, "She'd not a doctor. She's a physician's assistant."

Today, Hope zoomed into the VA parking lot about ten minutes past the hour wondering what the *physician's assistant* wanted with this unexpected appointment. When she got to the waiting room she spied Wendy and Mr. G in his wheelchair and hurried over to them. "Ah, good, I made it before you were called in. Did they tell you what this was about?"

"No ma'am. But at the desk they said we weren't seeing Ma'am Peggy but a dietitian."

"Excuse me?"

"That's what they said."

"What?" Hope had taken Mr. G's hand and was holding it while she talked to Wendy. She now focused on the elderly man and noticed he had tears running down his cheeks. "Mr. G? What's wrong?"

Sounding like a petulant child he said, "I want to go home."

"I know you do." She gently smoothed the back of his hand. "You'll get to go home soon."

"I want to take a nap; I'm tired; I want to go home."

Wendy dried his eyes. "It's okay, hon; it's okay." She turned to Hope. "He cries a lot now. More and more each day."

"I want to go to heaven." Mr. G looked at Hope with pleading eyes. "Why won't God take me to heaven?"

"You can be sure he will when it's time for you to go to heaven," Hope reassured the old man.

"But I want to go now. I want to see my mother."

When Mr. G started coughing a raspy cough, Wendy took a child's sippy cup out of her pack and gave him a few sips of water. "I'm glad you're keeping him hydrated in this weather." Hope nodded her approval.

"Sometimes I almost have to force him to drink more, or even eat. He just doesn't want to."

Yes, Hope thought to herself, like dogs, cats, horses, or other animals, humans also knew when their time was nearing the end, and not wanting to eat anymore was a big billboard advertising previews of coming attractions.

Hope continued to hold his hand while they waited, and waited, and waited to be called. Mr. G broke the silence. "Do you think there is music in heaven?"

"Of course there is." Hope gently squeezed his hand.

"Good," his response was feeble. "Good."

When his eyes closed and his head nodded on his chest, Wendy said, "He's tired, Ma'am. But he doesn't sleep at night. He just cries, or prays out loud in Hebrew. He prays a lot."

"He's certainly talking a lot more about heaven these days."

"And some days he doesn't even want to get out of bed. Even to go to the bathroom. I change his diaper just like he was a baby."

"Is it becoming too much work for you? Do we need to call in another caregiver?"

"No, ma'am. We are fine."

A miserable forty-five minutes later they were called into the dietitian's office. After introducing herself, the young woman picked up a clip board and started asking Mr. G questions about his meals.

"What did you have for breakfast this morning, Mr. Goldstein?"

"I don't know." He sighed as if the weight of the world were on his shoulders and looked over toward Wendy. "Do you know what I had for breakfast?"

"He had cereal, Ma'am."

The woman wrote something on the clip board and addressed her next question to Mr. G. "How often do you eat fruit?"

He just looked at her beseechingly as tears spilled out of his eyes. "I want to go home now."

"I need to get this information Mr. Goldstein, it's important."

"Important?" Hope's voice was soft and, for those who knew her, deadly.

"His last blood test showed that he was slightly anemic and so we need to alter his diet."

"He's ninety-nine years old. What's important is keeping him comfortable and happy. Right now, he's is not comfortable or happy."

The woman turned a cold shoulder toward Hope and addressing the patient said, "Mr. Goldstein, do you eat fresh fruits and vegetables?"

When Mr. G started sobbing out loud, Hope snapped, jumped up and hovered over the now cowering woman. "Okay, that's it."

"What...?"

"It's the hottest day of the year!"

"So?"

"Do you realize how many elderly people are going to die today because of the heat? You have us bring a ninety-nine year old man out today, of all days, for this?"

"But Peggy said..."

"Peggy!" Hope spat the name. "Peggy sees him once and suddenly she's an expert?" She raised her hand with the intention of slapping the clipboard out of the woman's hands then thought better of that impulsive desire.

"I...I didn't know he was ninety-nine," was the only thing the dietitian could think to stammer.

Hope pointed to the clipboard the woman was now clutching to her breasts as if it was a shield to protect her. "You have his chart. Doesn't it have his birth date there at the top? "

"I have a job to do..."

"So do I!" Hope started to turn to go, but stopped and turned back to the woman. "What are you doing here that you couldn't have done over the phone speaking with his caregiver? You get a ninety-nine year old man out on the hottest day of the year, make him wait nearly an hour in the waiting room and then ask him what he had for breakfast? He has dementia! How is he supposed to remember what he had for breakfast? You need to be directing your stupid questions to the caregiver. But not now. You...you should feel horrible for making this old man cry."

"Peggy will be very upset..."

"Peggy doesn't have a corner on *that* market! Tell Peggy to reschedule. And it had better be a teleconference with Mr. G's caregiver. Come on Wendy, let's get Mr. G home." She grabbed the handles of the wheelchair and headed for the elevator with Wendy doing her best to keep up. "Of all the idiotic, stupid...that woman, for Christ sake..." Feeling a prickling between her shoulder blades Hope glanced back. Both the dietitian and Peggy leveled her with twin malevolent glares.

In the parking lot Hope helped Wendy get Mr. G settled in the car. "Should I be fixing him something different to eat?" Wendy wanted to know.

"If he wants to eat bon bons three times a day, let him!"

"Ma'am?"

Hope started laughing, "Sorry, Wendy, it's just that it doesn't make sense to even care what a person eats when he's made it to ninety-nine. Hell, if I make it to ninety-nine, I'm going to start smoking cigars! And just watch somebody try to stop me!"

"Yes, Ma'am." Wendy did her best not to look confused. Settled in the car Mr. G started singing *Ghost Riders in the Sky*. Hope could still hear his mournful interpretation of that song as she turned and headed for her own vehicle.

Settled in her Honda with the air conditioning going full tilt, Hope called the office.

"Hello. Morgan Smyth's Professional Services. This is Tanya speaking, how may I help you?"

"Don't you ever get tired answering the phone like that?" Hope asked her.

Tanya laughed. "Hi, Hope. Morgan expects me to answer that way. Says it's more professional."

"Whatever. Morgan in?"

"Nope. Can I take a message?"

"No, thanks." Hope watched as Wendy's car pulled out of the parking lot and disappeared around a bend. "I just wanted to fill Morgan in on Mr. G."

"Oh wait, Hope, Morgan just arrived."

Hope could hear Tanya handing the phone to her boss. "What's up, Hope?"

Hope told Morgan about the visit to the VA ending with her diatribe against the dietician as well as the physician's assistant who were suddenly disrupting Mr. G's life. "I just thought you should hear it from the horse's mouth, so to speak."

"Well, I don't expect anything will come of it. But thanks for keeping me in the loop. If I get a call from the people at the VA, I'll deal with it. But just remember, Hope, these people are only doing what's best for the client."

"No, they are really not. I know what my people need and what they don't need. And they don't need to be taken out of their air conditioned houses on the hottest day of the year to talk about what they had for breakfast."

"You might think you know what the clients need, Hope, but you don't know more than the doctors do." Morgan was firm.

"The dietitian and that Peggy woman are not doctors."

"Well, neither are you! It's our due diligence to follow all orders and if the orders are for him to talk to a dietician then so be it. I have to account to the court..."

Due diligence! Hoping Morgan choked on those words some fine day, Hope interrupted with, "Well, maybe I'm accounting to a higher court."

"Look, I know you're peeved..."

"Peeved? You call what I am now peeved?"

"I think you need to calm down, Hope. I know you always try to fight the good fight for the little people. But you know as well as anyone else, you can't fight city hall."

"Fuck you, Morgan," but Hope had already clicked off so she knew that curse wouldn't reach its intended source. Hope sagged for a moment. She felt Mr. G had been ambushed by what passed as the *new normal* in today's medical field, not to mention the fact that she'd made a couple of enemies back there. That hadn't been her plan, of course, but it certainly had happened. And her boss—when had Morgan become her opponent? On a sigh, Hope put the car in reverse and backed out of the parking slot. The day was young yet and she had miles to go and people to see.

●●●

On her balcony, Hope stretched out on a chase lounge staring off at the hills that she could almost reach out and touch. The awning provided shade against a blazing white sun that wasn't quite ready to set, but she didn't mind the heat; it just made her feel languid and drowsy. The hills were so clear today she could see the individual shrubs and plants, and even noted a coyote trotting up the winding fire break. He'd probably head on down into the neighborhood after dark looking for something to eat. The view was so beautiful: the cerulean sky, the green-brown hills accented with the scattering of yucca plants, past their youthful bloom, but still a sight to see, rising up the hillside like sentinels, and the hawk soaring overhead was the perfect touch. If only she could paint, she'd capture that view so it would remain forever hers.

Hope loved her condo cradled in this little valley with the San Gabriel Mountains behind her and the Verdugo Hills in front of her. Originally an unusually large one-family dwelling, the house had been divided into three separate condos. Hope was not well acquainted with the other two inhabitants of the building. It wasn't that she was anti-social, it was just that she liked her alone time after dealing with clients. Usually the hour or so after work was the best time of day for her. She'd sit out on the balcony not minding the dry desert heat of summer, reading a book, with an ice-cold glass filled with Dr. Pepper on the table at her elbow. It was tranquil and the perfect way to wind down after dealing with clients and caregivers and doctors all day long. In fact, the balcony was what had sold her on the condo in the first place. If anyone took her balcony away from her, she'd be more than pissed. She'd be in fighting mode. It was her special place of peace and relaxation, where she could take her ease and simply...be.

But today, Hope was far from relaxed. Even her beloved hills weren't cheering her up. Her book was opened, but face down in her lap, and her thoughts were melancholy. For all the good that acupuncture did her this morning, she thought, so much for staying in balance, for remaining calm, cool, and collected. Well, maybe it had at least prevented her from committing a murder. Feeling a tear trickle down her cheek, Hope dashed it away with the back of her hand. "You will not cry!" She scolded herself. "Stop being such a baby!" But, the fact was, she was creeping closer and closer to burnout and she knew it. She was starting to lose a little more control each day and that was due to the helplessness she felt when dealing with her clients.

Atypical as today's rant was, it served as a wake-up call. It was forcing her to evaluate her situation. Hope was as good at denial as anyone else, but today's eruption had given her pause. The time was going to come when she wasn't going to be able to take any more. It wasn't a matter of if; it was a matter of when. Sipping her drink, she stared off into the middle distance and pondered her future. Nothing. She couldn't see a thing. Time swam past and still nothing. It was like there was a layer of fog between her and there. She simply couldn't see the future clearly and that perplexed her. One day she would have to give up this job for her own mental health. At the same time she knew that she was doing some good in her job — all the while feeling stress building and building each day she stayed on the job. Talk about being conflicted.

The individuals who peopled her life, clients, caregivers, staff of facilities, and her boss all spun her personal moral compass in different directions: first left then right, up then down, sometimes pulling it toward true north, but more often pointing it in some ambiguous nether direction where she was left alone to choose her destination. Ah, destination... destiny...if she could only see which way to go.

Hope's condo was on the far side of the building that stood next to some small homes that ran the length of the rest of the block. From a couple doors down she could hear some children playing outside. It made her smile reminding her of her childhood when she and her sisters would play *Mother May I* or *Red Light, Green Light* on the little patch of grass in the front yard of their childhood home. Kudos to the parents of those kids, she thought, as she heard them squealing in delight. So many kids now-a-days stayed inside playing video games instead of enjoying the great outdoors. A bloodcurdling scream pierced the air, then a little girl's laughter saying, "Now you scare me." They were so carefree with all the time in the world at their disposal. Every so often Hope could hear water splashing too. They might have a little wading pool, she thought, or maybe they were running through the sprinklers on such a hot afternoon. She glanced over at the neighbor's palm trees, not a bit of movement from even an errant breeze. Picking up her beverage, she took another sip.

Her thoughts turned inward away from the carefree children and focused on her clients, as a totality, all of whom were on the downhill slide. Not only didn't they have all the time in the world, for most of them time had become the enemy. Some just had too much time on their hands; others hoped every sunrise would be their last. She really loved them and wanted to help them in every way she possibly could. But in the long run all she could do was offer them...what? Hope? Ha! Hope for what? A better tomorrow? Tomorrow wasn't going to get any better, and they knew that. There was no hope.

She had always known her parents were nuts. Naming their three daughters Charity, Hope, and Faith proved it. Sheesh! At nine years old Hope had come face to face with the philosophical implications of her name. Her dad had given her a book on mythology for her birthday, where she found the story of Pandora's Box. Pandora, out of innate curiosity, opened the box she had been told not to open. When she did all the evils, such as pain, sorrow, etc., flew out of the box and, scattering to the four winds, were released into the world. The last part of the story differs depending on the version one reads. One version says the last thing in the box was hope, but Pandora slammed the box shut before it got out. So, does a reader construe that to mean that there is no hope in the world? Yet, another version of the story says, the last thing out of the box was hope, and goes on to claim that it was a boon to counteract and balance out the evils that had been given free reign. So in that interpretation, hope was a gift from the gods to the people on Earth. Hope, however, interpreted the myth differently. Oh, she believed that hope had definitely been released into the world, but she didn't see it as a good thing. Because, logically, if hope was in the box with all the evils, wasn't hope an evil too? After all, what is hope but hopelessness in disguise? Hope came to see *hope* as the gods' best joke on human beings; hope was a gift that was as hollow and as worthless and as empty as Pandora's Box now was.

Inside the condo, her phone began to ring. If it had been her iPhone, she would have had no choice but to answer it, being on twenty-four seven call as she was with her clients. But the land line was another matter—she decided to let it ring. It was probably Fred, but he was the last person she wanted to see especially when down in the dumps. Picking up her Dr. Pepper and wishing it were a glass of wine, Hope quaffed down half of it. She could almost feel the jolt of caffeine pass through her stomach lining and into her bloodstream. She took another sip and brushed another tear off her cheek.

7

Annabelle

"Old age is no place for sissies."
— Bette Davis

Annabelle was a piece of work in addition to being one of the most amazing women Hope had ever met. She was loud, obstinate, and obnoxious and Hope loved her with all her heart. In her mid-eighties, Ann had been under conservatorship for nearly a decade now. When Hope first came on board as the case manager, Ann had two caregivers, Lucy and Gwen who had been with her all that time. Lucy took days and lucky Gwen had nights when Ann slept. In Hope's estimation, Lucy was a sure-fire candidate for sainthood; she sure had her hands full with Ann.

Picture a big, burly Mack truck driver, remove the male genitalia and replace it with female genitalia and you would have Ann. She was as butch as they come, and as she was a dyke that was a good thing. An outdoorsman (woman) most of her life who wasn't afraid of anyone or anything, she had devolved into an agoraphobic who jumped at her own shadow. The only time she left her apartment was to go to doctors' appointments. And only because she was forced to go to those appointments. If it had been up to her, she never would see another doctor as long as she lived. She just wanted to be left alone behind closed doors to watch television. And, truth be told, it wasn't that Ann was afraid to live in the world, it was that she no longer *wanted* to live in the world. She was being forced to go through the motions of living and she resented it with all the passion she had left in her body, mind, and heart.

As a young woman Ann had single-handedly started a male-dominated business in the heart of Los Angeles and became a success, albeit not an overnight success. Shoulder to shoulder with the competitors, she'd had to fight the good fight for customers; and the hard-as-nails and wily businesswoman did just that. She worked like a stevedore, swore like a sailor, and earned the respect of all the men she worked with be they employees or customers. She would roll up her shirt sleeves and work side-by-side in the sun with the men hauling bags of concrete or other materials. She wasn't afraid of work; in fact she thrived on it. And her business was not only a success it became a multi-million dollar success. And behind every successful woman is, well, in this case, another woman.

Ann had a live-in partner who was the wife in this relationship. Janice — the Juliet to Ann's Romeo — was the one who stayed home and cleaned the apartment and cooked. She also managed the twenty-unit apartment building in which they lived that Ann had purchased as an investment years before. It was a huge square edifice with a shaded courtyard in the center. The swimming pool in the courtyard was just the right touch, especially on hot summer days, not to mention the fact that their apartment was on the ground floor poolside. Heck, as owners they had the right to the best place in the house!

Ann and Janice had been together for nearly four decades, and they were as content as any old married couple could be. One day as Ann was heading off to work Janice told her partner she didn't feel very well. "It's probably just that bug that's going around. I'll check back with you at lunch time," Ann said as she closed the door behind her. That day turned out to be a Murphy's Law day: if something could go wrong it would. So not only did Ann not phone at noon to check on Janice, she was also late getting home from work. When she arrived, Ann discovered Janice, unconscious and barely breathing. She called the paramedics, but it was too late. Janice was declared dead upon arrival at the hospital.

The combination of the grief and guilt nearly destroyed Ann. To say she went off the deep end would have been putting it mildly. The love of her life was dead and she felt completely and totally responsible. "If I had just stayed home," she raged at Franklin, her second in command at work. "Oh, if I had just cared enough to stay home!"

Franklin reasoned with her. "You thought it was just the flu, Ann. Nobody knew Janice had a heart condition, not even Janice. It was just her time."

"No! I should have gone home at lunchtime to make sure she was okay. If I'd just gone home, I would have called the ambulance then and she would be alive now."

There was no reasoning with Ann and she would accept no comfort.

She turned inward and her anger at the world morphed into a depression so deep that she finally decided to take her life and join her beloved Janice. But Franklin, his wife Julie, and Julie's sister Charlene, all Ann's *honorary* family members, had been on suicide watch ever since Janice had died. They knew Ann's grief was beyond anything she could handle and, sure enough, they found her in the nick of time shortly after she'd ingested an entire bottle of sleeping pills. Ann was rushed to the same hospital where Janice had died. However, while Ann had been praying for death, her prayers weren't answered. Her doctor, a staunch Catholic, had known Ann for years and had always looked askance at her homosexuality. So, instead of treating the patient for her depression, he decided she needed to be locked up in the psych-ward at the hospital for a block of time. "Let her get a load of what truly mentally ill people are like. That ought to make her sit up and fly right," he told Franklin. Franklin didn't agree with the doctor, but not being a blood family member he was in no position to prevent Ann's incarceration in the psych ward. Franklin figured it would just be a matter of time, Ann would finally be released, and then they'd take it from there. But little did Franklin know, the state of California was about to get involved.

The doctor and the social worker at the hospital decided that Ann, to use legalese, was going to continue to be a *danger to herself* and that something needed to be done to be sure she was kept under control. Enter Morgan Smyth. At that time, Morgan was fairly new at the business of conservatorship and so in this instance Morgan was only granted conservatorship of the person. Conservatorship over Ann's enormous estate was put under the control of her business, which was a corporation, and the corporation's accountant became conservator of the estate with Franklin overseeing him. So while Ann's corporation paid all the bills, Morgan made all the medical decisions.

In time the hospital released Ann. Morgan hired two caregivers: Lucy took the morning shift and Gwen took the evening shift. Morgan was adamant that someone was to remain in the apartment with Ann at all times; she was never to be left alone. Life fell into a routine and a decade flowed by. For Ann, time never moved forward but went around and around and around never progressing. That was her hell on Earth — the inability to opt out, to jump off the merry-go-round. The sameness of each day was her prison. Time had triumphed.

Over the years Ann had become so dependent on her caregivers that she had become childlike. Lucy literally fed her, bathed her, and wiped her huge butt. Gwen pretty much just watched her as she slept. And as Ann refused to exercise, sitting on the couch watching television being her only activity, her muscles grew weaker and weaker; so when she did go out to doctors' appointments, she needed a wheelchair.

Ann was always resistant to any kind of change. So when Hope first took over as case manager the year before, Ann resented Hope's intrusion into her life. Hope would arrive at the apartment for a visit and Ann would be rude and surly. She'd sputter and fume about Morgan. She recited with gleeful malice how much she hated Morgan detailing the various physically painful ways she'd like to pay Morgan back for her captivity — as she called it. Hope would just nod agreeably and say, "You and a lot of other people would like to boil Morgan in oil." No matter how rude Ann was, Hope just rolled with the verbal punches and didn't let this unhappy woman get to her.

At some point during the visit Ann would always ask Hope for a gun so she could shoot herself. "I just want to die," she'd say looking Hope dead in the eyes. And Hope believed her. After all, the unsuccessful suicide attempt was what had gotten her slapped with a conservator in the first place. Ann was the most miserable woman Hope had ever known. She wouldn't help herself and she refused any help from others. And yet, something about her was mysteriously appealing. Life had punched this woman in the gut with a sledge-hammer blow and knocked her down so hard she'd never get up. In the business world she had thrived on adversity, but after Janice's death she had simply given up. Yet, occasionally some of her old feistiness rose to the fore. For instance, when it was time for Hope to leave the apartment after her visit, Ann's parting shot was always, "Go play on the freeway! And don't come back!" In time those words became an expression of endearment.

With the passage of months, Ann became accustomed to Hope's visits to the apartment and looked forward to seeing her. "Have you got a boyfriend yet?" Ann started inquiring.

"Nope." Hope would shake her head. "Why would I want a man in my life? I like not having to answer to anyone."

Ann would say, "But you don't want to grow old alone, do you? Being alone, that's not good; a pretty woman like you should have someone." Hope never knew if that was a dyke's way of flirting or not. Nor did she care. She and Ann had finally come to a comfortable place in their relationship and that was all that mattered.

●●●

Today, Hope arrived at the waiting room of the hospital where the wound center was located and watched out the plate glass window for Ann and Lucy to arrive. Before they got there Franklin's wife Julie and her sister Charlene showed up as they always did.

"Isn't it exciting?" Charlene, the more demonstrative of the two sisters, gave Hope a little hug. "Finally after all these months, she'll have a clean bill of health!"

"It has been a long haul," Hope agreed.

When they saw Chester pull up with Ann and Lucy, they walked over to the door.

Chester wasn't on Morgan's payroll per se, but he was hired to drive many of Morgan's clients who were in wheelchairs to doctor's appointments, or to transport them to or from facilities as needed. Chester was a registered nurse who used to work in a nursing home. One day, after observing that so many of the patients just stayed in their rooms never even getting outside for fresh air, he decided the patients needed to get out more often. He would arrange little outings here and there and transport the patients on day trips. His little venture was a rousing success and soon became a business. As his transportation business flourished, he gave up the nursing. He now had a fleet of six medical transportation vehicles and had become a very successful entrepreneur in the process.

Each week when Chester pushed Ann in the wheelchair through the door of the hospital, the other three women would fall in with Lucy as they made their way down the hallway to the wound center. With this entourage, Ann resembled nothing if not a queen on her throne surrounded by her ladies in waiting and being escorted by her palace guard.

Over the past couple of months the girls had followed the ups and downs of Hope's relationship with Fred. As they continued down the hallway, Charlene sing-songed, "Say Hope, now that Fred's out of the picture, when are you going to get yourself another boyfriend?"

"Pffftttt!" was Hope's response.

"You know what they say?" Charlene wasn't about to give up.

"What do they say?"

"Gotta get right back up on the horse. We've got this really cute cousin, Dom. If he wasn't my cousin, well, I wouldn't mind getting up on that horse." She grinned at Hope.

"No, thanks, I prefer going it solo. Now can we drop this subject?"

Chester looked at Hope sideways and Ann turned her bulk around in the wheelchair and said over her shoulder to Hope, "You know something, you're too persnickety." Then, changing the subject, she added, "I don't want today to be the last day."

The four women just looked at one another over Ann's head and rolled their collective eyes. "Be careful what you wish for," Charlene said.

Ann's response was, "Pooh." Ann, creature of habit that she was, who detested most outings, had come to depend on the routine of her weekly visits to the wound center. Now that the wound was healed, well she'd just have to get used to not making this trek.

Before Hope had taken over as case manager, Ann had been diagnosed with skin cancer. Years of working under the baking sun had taken its toll, and now Ann was paying the price for not wearing a hat or sunscreen—well, they didn't have sunscreen back in those days so she couldn't be faulted for that. She'd had a few small facial and scalp cancers removed. But one cancer right on the top of her head resisted all treatment. So every couple of weeks the entourage would accompany Ann back to the dermatologist and the doctor would treat it some more. When Hope came on board over the course of about three visits to the dermatologist she noticed that not only wasn't the skin cancer healing, it was increasing. She called the doctor on it. He agreed that he had done about as much as could be done and that all he was doing now was basically just containment control. "Well, then it's time we find someone else who can do more," Hope told him. So Ann started going to the wound center at the hospital to see if they would have any better luck.

Enter Dr. Beth Adrian, and Dr. Adrian, so it appeared, was a miracle worker. She was a plastic surgeon who volunteered one day a week at the wound center and luck of the draw she ended up with Ann's case. Dr. Adrian realized the cancer had gone into the bone and surgery was the best treatment before the cancer migrated to the brain. Of course Ann fought against having any surgery, but Morgan was the conservator of person, so Ann's feelings weren't taken into account. Ultimately the surgery appeared to be a success and the healing process began. Lucy made sure Ann was ready every week for her visit to the wound center to make sure the wound was healing properly after the surgery — and what a long drawn out process that proved to be. Ann was diabetic so her wound did not heal rapidly. Literally months had passed since the surgery, but now, finally, the wound was healed!

Chester dropped everyone off in the waiting room of the wound center. "Just give me a holler when it's time to pick her up."

Before long, Ann and her ladies in waiting were ushered into the largest examination room and the nurse came in and did the preliminaries. "So today is it?" She wrapped the blood pressure cuff around Ann's meaty arm.

"What do you mean?" Ann always challenged anyone's comments.

"If everything's okay today, you're done. You won't have to put up with us anymore."

"I like coming here." Ann began to protest. "I'll keep coming."

The nurse patted Ann's arm. "But you will be all better, so you won't have to."

Sounding like a recalcitrant two-year-old, Ann almost whined, "But I want to." And on that note, Dr. Adrian entered the room.

"Okay!" The doctor clapped her hands once. "Let's get this show on the road."

She rolled a huge lit-up magnifying glass over and positioned it above Ann's head. During her cursory examination, she was all smiles. "Looking good," she nodded. Then, all of a sudden the nodding stopped and the smile disappeared. The doctor continued palpating Ann's head here and there. Charlene looked over at Julie. Lucy reached out and squeezed Hope's hand.

"Doctor?" Hope questioned.

The doctor turned off the light, pushed the magnifying glass away and sat down on the nearby stool. She took Ann's hand and glanced up at the top of Ann's head. "You've got something going on up there, Ann."

"What?" Ann's voice was barely a whisper.

"Just under the scalp, I can feel maybe three more growths."

"But...you got it all." Ann's voice quavered.

"We hoped we had it all."

"Be careful what you wish for," Charlene said so softly under her breath that it was more a thought than a whisper.

While the doctor indicated what was to happen next, Ann stared off in to space fiddling with a loose button on her plaid shirt.

Ann was no longer a candidate for surgery. Been there done that. Radiation was the next step. Dr. Adrian made the arrangements and told Hope and Ann that she would be passing the baton to Dr. Ruth Sims. Ann was to go for her first appointment in two days. They would do the preliminaries that day and set up a series of treatments following that initial appointment.

It was a somber group of woman who wheeled Ann back out to Chester's vehicle. "I'll meet you guys here for the appointment," she told Lucy. And with a heavy heart took leave of the others.

When she got to her car she picked up her phone as Morgan needed to be appraised of this latest development.

"Okay Hope, you go to the initial appointment with the radiation doctor and the following one to make sure things are running smoothly. It will probably be about a six week deal, every day, so once things are okay, just go once a week when she will be having the update with the radiation doctor. And meanwhile, I'll take care of the rest on this end."

Hope didn't ask what that meant. Sick at heart, she clicked off, sat back, and stared at the windshield feeling the sorrow well inside her like a tide. But, she knew she couldn't indulge in her sorrow for long; she still had a full day ahead of her. And she was hungry too. She started the car and headed over to In and Out Burger to get a double-double and some fries on the fly.

8

Wren

"The old gray mare she ain't what she used to be."
— American Folk Song by J. Warner

Wren's beautiful one-karat diamond engagement ring, that had been a family heirloom, had gone missing. The thing was no one knew when it had actually disappeared.

Wren was an eighty-something-year-old woman who had Alzheimer's. And as is the case with many Alzheimer's patients, she was often angry and out of control. She had gone ballistic one evening and broken all the windows in her home where she lived with Hector, her spouse of more than sixty years. A neighbor hearing all the commotion had called the police. Realizing they were not dealing with a coherent woman, and finding a man who was in no way capable of handling his wife or the situation, the police called the paramedics who quickly subdued Wren and whisked her away to a hospital. The next thing Hector knew, the court had appointed Morgan Smyth as their conservator.

Morgan saw to it that Wren was placed in a locked-down facility, then, against Hector's expressed wishes, Morgan placed a caregiver in the home with him. The eighty-nine-year-old-man had macular degeneration to the point that he could barely see, and yet he had been driving his car to the market every day. Morgan put an anti-theft steering wheel lock on the steering wheel of Hector's car so it could not be driven and told Hector that the live-in caregiver was to drive him where he needed to go from now on in her car. He was not to get behind the wheel of his car, nor would he be given access to the key to the lock on the steering wheel.

Hope's first assignment was to go over to the house, meet the new client and caregiver, and then get someone in who would replace all the broken windowpanes. When she met Hector she knew it was going to take a huge effort to win him over. Hector was about an inch or two shorter than Hope, who stood five feet seven inches in her stocking feet. He had a shock of white hair on his head and bushy white eyebrows that needed trimming.

He was dressed in black trousers and a stained white dress shirt buttoned at the frayed cuffs. His shoes had probably been kept polished back in the days when he worked for a living, but today they were very much the worse for wear. Hector had come around the corner of the hallway into the living room leaning on a walker. When he looked at Hope, he was frowning. Hope tried breaking the ice with a warm smile. She gestured to a picture of Hector and Wren on the fireplace mantle. "You make a lovely couple," she told him.

"When will she be able to come home?" Hector wanted to know.

"I'm not sure."

Hector shook a fist in her direction balancing the walker with the other hand. "And I want that damned thing taken off my car steering wheel so I can drive it. It's my car!"

"I'll have to talk to Morgan about that." Hope loved that she had Morgan to blame things on. Morgan was bad cop and she did her best to instill herself as good cop. She was, after all, the one who had to deal with the clients face-to-face so she needed to be good cop. But today, Hector saw her as the enemy and was as impolite as he dared to be. Hope understood him perfectly. This man had essentially become a prisoner in his own home, his wife had been removed and locked up in an institution, and the caregiver, Hope had never seen one with such hard eyes, was much like a warden. All she could do was her best and give Hector time to adjust. So that first day, Hope assessed the damage, called the window repair person, set up an appointment for him to come over and replace the broken windowpanes, and got the heck out of Dodge leaving Hector alone with the caregiver.

Hope got into her car which she had parked in front of Hector and Wren's cute little home with the welcoming sky-blue door. The lawn was neatly trimmed and surrounded with a white picket fence. There was a dozen or so flowering camellia bushes by the corner of the garage, in front of the living room windows, and along the back fence. The place looked like a fairy tale cottage. Feeling eyes on her, Hope glanced around and saw Iris, the caregiver, staring at her from the family room window. Yep, a fairy tale cottage complete with wicked witch.

Most of the caregivers that Hope dealt with were from the Philippines. They were the kindest and most caring people Hope ever had the pleasure of meeting. And so very polite; they always called her Miss or Ma'am. They took their jobs seriously and as a whole loved the elderly people who were their charges. She couldn't say enough good things about Lucy or Wendy or some of the others she knew. This was the first time Hope had met a caregiver who made goose bumps rise up on her arms. She was going to have to keep a close watch on this one.

●●●

The next stop, that long-ago day, was to visit Wren in the locked-down facility where Morgan had placed her. Hope signed in at the window and then waited until the attendant unlocked the door to the inner sanctum. The inside of the facility wasn't any different than others she visited. She asked at the nurses' station where she would find Wren. The nurse pointed in the direction of a woman parked in a wheelchair next to the wall. Wren was so drugged she couldn't even sit up straight. Hope decided to look at the medical chart first; it listed twelve different medications they had her on and most of them multiple doses to be taken several times a day. That seemed to be the way the system handled the patients they couldn't control, drug them into a stupor. If the patient didn't have anyone looking out for her, the people who worked in the system simply continued with the treatment that made the least amount of work for them.

Hope spent a few minutes sitting with Wren, but she was so drugged she was incoherent, so there was no point trying to communicate with her. And thus began the visits. Every week it was the same. The staff continued to give her the prescribed medication and Wren floated from day to day. And that's the way it would have gone on ad infinitum except for one thing. Wren had a loving husband. And Hector, while he did have macular degeneration and while he did walk with a walker to help him keep his balance, had his wits about him. His mind was as sharp as a scalpel and it had been in high gear ever since Morgan's intrusion into their life.

Hector, the quintessential good husband, who embodied and lived his marriage vows, came to visit Wren every single day. He would sit by her side and talk to her and tell her he was going to get her out of this place. And he meant every word he said. In time he got his court-appointed attorney to get him another day in court, and, small miracle that it was the attorney convinced the judge that Wren would be better off at home. Having accomplished this was no easy task. It was against the conservator's recommendations, and it was against the recommendations of Iris, the caregiver Morgan had placed in the house with Hector.

Iris had cornered Hope when she stopped by the cottage to make sure all was in place for Wren's return home in a few days. "She doesn't belong here!" Iris delved right in. "I can't take care of both of them, that's too much to expect of one person."

"Facilities with dozens of patients have only a handful of nurses and aides that are charged with caring for all of them. Do the math. I'm sure you will be equal to taking care of only two people."

Iris was shaking her head. "No. It's going to be too much."

"Hector pretty much takes care of himself," Hope countered. "He doesn't need help in the bathroom, or getting dressed. He fixes his own meals. All you've had to do up until now is to drive him to the store or to visit Wren. That's about the easiest job description any of my caregivers have. So, now your job is to take care of Wren."

Iris was shaking her head. "I was hired for Hector."

Hope had never had a caregiver challenge her before. "You were hired to help both of them."

"No!" Iris wasn't about to give any ground. "When I came here Wren was already in the facility. I am Hector's caregiver."

Rather than continue going around in circles, reminding the woman she should be damned glad she even had a job in this economy, Hope called Morgan and relayed Iris's issues. The upshot was that there would be two caregivers in the house — which would make logistics not only a challenge, but a living hell. The two-bedroom home had been set up so that the second bedroom was an office and an art studio. Wren had painted as a hobby and her artwork graced every room in the house. When Iris had been moved in to the home to care for Hector, he refused to allow her to sleep in the office/ studio. She had a roll-away bed in the family room off the living room. And because Hector didn't have dementia, Morgan had no recourse when it came to Hector's decisions about what went on within his home. However, as Morgan *did* have complete control over Wren's person and estate, when it came time to move her back home, Morgan did have say so. And that meant the office/studio was to become the bedroom it had been designed to be in the first place.

In preparation for Wren's return home, Hope had purchased two twin beds for the office where both Wren and the new caregiver would sleep. Hector was up in arms because he wanted his wife back in his bed. But Morgan was insistent that she be in the same room as the caregiver. Iris, never happy, complained because the new caregiver got a new bed and new bedding while she was still sleeping on the rollaway bed in the family room with a sleeping bag on it. Hope explained to Iris that while she had insisted on a second caregiver for Wren, her duties and circumstances regarding caring for Hector hadn't changed nor would they, nor would her living conditions. Hope wasn't proud of the feeling of satisfaction she got when denying Iris. Be that as it may, her theory was that uncooperative people would get what they deserved, and Iris certainly didn't deserve to be rewarded for her non-cooperation. That was for sure.

●●●

All was in place for Wren's return home. Hope pulled up in front of the cottage and was checking her messages on her phone when the medical transport van pulled up behind her. A jovial Chester bounded out the driver's door and sauntered up to Hope's car. She rolled down her window. With a wink Hope said, "We've got to stop meeting like this." That got a chuckle from Chester. Then she inquired, "How was the drive over?"

"No problems. Come on; let's get her settled back home."

Chester rolled Wren onto the lift, lowered it, and was wheeling her up the walkway when Hector bounded through the front door as fast as he could, pushing his walker in front of him. "Whoa!" Chester admonished, "Don't you go falling down. We'll get her settled alright."

Maria, the caregiver who had been assigned to Wren, was a pleasant, smiling Hispanic woman. She immediately took charge, thanking Chester and whisking Wren off to their room to get her settled, Hector following along in their wake.

Leaving the couple and the two caregivers to sort things out, Chester and Hope escaped. Hope was not the least bit optimistic about the arrangement. Hector had gotten his way and his wife was home. But she was still on massive doses of medications and as a result was basically non-communicative, non-responsive, and fully unable to help others help her.

"How long do you think that's going to last?" Chester wanted to know.

"I don't know."

Chester rubbed her arm. "You look a little unhappy."

"They can't win, not in the long run. Oh, Hector did succeed in getting Wren home, but it was a small victory; just a little skirmish with the system. He's going to lose the war. You know that."

"But for now she's home and by the looks of Maria, she's in good hands."

Hope shrugged. "We have an appointment with a neurologist in a couple of days. Who knows what that will bring?"

● ● ●

That was months ago. In less than three months Wren's neurologist had preformed a miracle. She was weaned off the over-prescribed quantities of the psychotropic drugs and was making phenomenal progress. At the same time, now that she was no longer drugged into a stupor, she was quite the challenge. As an Alzheimer's victim she had the classic "sundowner's" symptom. That is to say, when the sun went down the anxiety level rose. It was, in fact, that time of day when Wren had broken all the windows out of the house months ago that had started the whole relationship with the conservator in the first place.

As predicted, Maria did have her hands full with the active Wren, and Iris, who would attend only to Hector, was no help at all. In addition, because Iris had been in the household before Maria arrived, she took on the role of queen bee. Even though technically the two caregivers were in fact equals, Iris was having none of that. So a contest of wills commenced.

It was often mealtime when Hope stopped by the house for her visits. Wren would be sitting at the little dinner table with Hector. Hope would watch her eat her meal, nibbling with the delicacy of a little bird. When Maria would coax more food on her, sometimes Wren would take a few more bites. But other times, she would become agitated and start to yell, "No, no, no, no." Then add, "I want my mother!" Maria would take her away from the table and Hector would just shake his head and look so sad. Hope often left the house feeling helpless.

One evening Wren kept yelling and just would not be calmed down. Maria, in a desperate attempt to distract Wren, dipped her fingers in a glass of water moistening them then flicked her fingers at Wren. The unexpected sprinkle of water droplets on her face shut Wren up immediately. She looked around, looked up, couldn't find the source of the wetness that had sprinkled her and eventually settled down.

The next day Morgan received a call from the Caregivers' Association. Apparently Iris, who had been looking for any excuse to get Maria in trouble, had filled out an Elder Abuse accusation form against Maria. Morgan's reaction was to fire Maria immediately and hire a new caregiver to care for Wren. When Hope went over to the cottage to investigate the incident further, she got the whole story from Hector, but only after he'd sent Iris on an errand to get her out of the house. "She listens to everything," Hector said once the door had closed and Iris was on her way. Then he addressed the issue of Maria and Wren. "It wasn't anything bad," he told her. Personally Hope thought the sprinkling of water on Wren's face to calm her was brilliant. That Iris had manipulated the incident to get Maria fired angered Hope. "What about the new caregiver?" Hope asked Hector. "What's her name?"

"Vickie. She seems really nice."

When Hope left the house, she called Morgan back. "You fired the wrong caregiver."

"Give it a rest, Hope. It's over. Time to move on."

Hope did move on, but wasn't about to give it a rest. Like a wily spider Hope waited to strike. It didn't take long. She caught Iris in an infraction, contacted the Caregivers' Association herself, and lodged her own complaint. She had no compunction regarding getting Iris fired. *Live by the sword; die by the sword*, Hope mused. Or, to use another cliché, *what goes round comes round*. Iris got no less than what she deserved.

When a new caregiver, Mary Lou, showed up Hope sat both the newbies down to give them the ground rules. That Vickie and Mary Lou were already acquainted and had worked together before was a plus. "You are both here primarily for Wren. Both of you. Hector can take care of himself. Except for driving him to the store once a day, you will help Vicki with Wren—spelling each other now and then so each of you can have rest breaks and down time. That way nobody gets burned out and Wren gets the attention she needs. Got it?" They had it. And life in Hector and Wren's little cottage with the bright sky-blue door was, if not good, at least not hostile.

●●●

Vicki answered Hope's knock on the door. "Hi Miss." Vicki opened the door wider. "How are you today?"

"Fine Vicki. How are things here?"

"Not good. Hector is so upset."

"What happened?" Hope and Vicki stood in the entryway heads close as they spoke in low tones.

"He noticed a few days ago that Wren wasn't wearing her diamond ring. He hasn't accused me or the other caregiver of taking it, but he looks at us scowling all the time. But the thing is she never had a diamond ring. Not since I've been here."

Hope cast her mind back and realized that she had never seen Wren wearing a diamond either. She patted Vicki's arm as she went in search of Hector. He was sitting at the little dining room table drinking his afternoon cup of coffee. "Hector? Vicki tells me that Wren is missing a diamond ring?"

Hector got right to the point explaining he noticed it was missing a few days ago. Hope listened to him then said, "Hector, I have been visiting Wren for months now. I have never seen her wear the ring you are describing. She has always had the gold wedding band. But I never saw her wearing a diamond ring."

"I gave it to her more than sixty years ago." Hector voice cracked with anger. "It was my grandmother's."

Without mentioning his poor eyesight, Hope soothed, "I don't doubt what you say, Hector; but she didn't have any jewelry on except for the gold band when I first visited her in that lock-down facility months ago. Have you seen the diamond since then?"

Pausing to think, Hector closed his eyes, then shook his head. "I don't remember when I last actually saw it on her finger. It's always just been such a part of her, like her blue eyes, or her beautiful smile. Maybe it wasn't there, but because I expected it to be, I didn't realize it was gone."

Hope swallowed a little ball of anger knowing with a certainly that someone somewhere had stolen the ring. Her guess was that when the police had called the ambulance that fateful night so long ago, that Hector hadn't thought to remove Wren's valuable jewelry from her before they took her away. It could have been anyone who stole the ring: the paramedics, the staff, nurses, or even the doctors at the hospital where she first landed, or anyone in the subsequent lock-down facility when she arrived there. "We'll call the various places Wren was placed and see if any of them have something of hers in their safe, but I wouldn't hold my breath." Hope rested her fingers on Hector's forearm.

Hector stared off out a window for the longest time. "She never took it off. Not once since I put it there. Well, only once. She was having a miscarriage. I was carrying her in my arms up the hospital steps and as we passed through the doors and the nurses saw us and were hurrying up to take her, she took her rings off and gave them to me for safekeeping. That was the only time...the only time." His voice fell off into the barest whisper.

Hope peeked in the little bedroom where Vicki and Wren slept. Vicki was folding a laundry basket full of clothes and Wren was napping. "I've spoken with Hector. He doesn't think you or Mary Lou took the ring."

Vicki sighed in relief. "Good. He never said that, but he was very angry."

"Yes, but it wasn't at you." Hope nodded toward the sleeping Wren. "Maybe you shouldn't let her sleep too long in the afternoon, Vicki. You know how wild she gets at night. Maybe less napping now would help her to sleep better later on."

"I know, Miss. But if she doesn't nap when she's tired, she can be just as wild in the afternoon." The caregiver shrugged. "It's just the way it is."

9

Faith

> "I don't believe an accident of birth makes people sisters or brothers. It makes them siblings, gives them mutuality of parentage.
> Sisterhood and brotherhood is a condition people have to work at."
>
> — Maya Angelou

On her way to see her next client, Hope decided she needed a break and stopped by her sister's shop. Hope and Faith were as close as two sisters could be. There was another sister, Charity, but Charity who had absolutely no charity in her heart or soul whatsoever, in fact she embodied the antithesis of her name, no longer spoke to either Hope or Faith — a fact for which both were grateful. Not only didn't Charity love humanity, she charred everything in her path through life leaving a wasteland behind her. Her innumerable sins began in childhood and accrued with each passing decade.

At twelve years old, just before she moved from the elementary school to the junior high school, Charity attempted to burn down the junior high school simply because she didn't want to go there. She had dragged her eight and six year old sisters with her and made them stand nearby and watch while she struck the match and held the flame to some twigs next to a stack of lumber. Hope and Faith stood there, holding hands, with eyes that swallowed up their whole faces. They knew what Charity was doing was wrong, but were at a loss to know how to stop her. They had learned early on that to cross Charity was to regret it. The fire was discovered immediately and extinguished, and the culprit caught and punished. Charity managed to brush aside the whole incident, but the deed left an indelible scar on her sisters' souls. They knew there was something wrong with Charity but being so much younger didn't know how to deal with their knowledge.

During the ensuing years Hope and Faith witnessed Charity's lack of morality again and again and again with increasing sadness. Maturity hadn't had Charity cleaning up her act. She just became more devious, grievously vain, and hellishly selfish. She would no more put another's needs before her needs then she'd — well give to charities. Time only made Charity more intensely herself; she graduated from attempting to burn down a school to insidiously burning down people's lives. No matter what they did neither sister was able to get Charity to see the difference between what she saw as only selfishness and what the world saw as wrong. No one was exempt from Charity's disdain, her scorn, or her feelings of contempt, especially her sisters. Time, they say, heals all wounds, but the wounds Charity had inflicted on Hope and Faith were brutal and deep and everlasting. Not only wouldn't the wounds heal, but Charity had allowed the statue of limitations that would have allowed a fragile reconciliation to elapse. The gulf between the sisters grew wide, and it was a relief to both Hope and Faith when Charity no longer counted them as sisters

Hope parked her car and stepped onto the sidewalk in front of Faith's shop; a quaint and cozy little place called *Lovelier the Second Time Around.* The store which sold high-end gently-used clothing, shoes, handbags, accessories, and jewelry was the up-and-coming in-place to get outfitted and business was growing by leaps and bounds. Looking through the window she spied her sister putting the finishing touches on the manikin she had just dressed: a bold Kelly green scarf to accent the flowing dress. Faith looked up when Hope entered the shop.

"Hey, Sweetheart!" Faith almost sang out the words. "What's up?"

"This and that. Mostly...it's over with Fred."

Faith took a closer look at her sister. "You don't look upset about that."

"I'm not. He was just so..." She made a circular gesture with one hand. "So?"

"I think I'm just better off on my own. I don't get men. It seems each one has his own peculiar perversion."

"And Fred's was...?"

Hope laughed. "Actually he had several." Standing at the counter, she tried on some rings that were on display then held up her hand. "What do you think of this ring?"

Faith shook her head. "Too gaudy for you slim fingers."

"That's what I thought." Hope slipped that ring off and tried on another one.

Hope and Faith were as opposite in appearance as two sisters could be. Hope was a slim brunette with a few blond highlights in her hair who dressed conservatively in neat and trim business suits, blazer and skirt to the knee, with a feminine blouse to soften the harsher formal look of the suit. She refused to give up nylon stockings even through the culture in Southern California leaned toward bare legs. Hope just felt her legs were too white to go without stockings. She had that English, Irish, Scott's heritage that didn't really lend itself to a golden sun tan. Not that tanning was politically correct these days. So she wore stockings to give her that tanned look, plus she liked the silky feel of the nylon as she crossed her legs. And shoes, shoes were her downfall. Show her a pretty pair of shoes, especially a nice little pump with an inch or inch and a half heel, and she was sold. Faith, on the other hand, was a statuesque full-bodied true blond who had long hair and dressed like a gypsy. She favored flowing skirts or dresses and wore accompanying jewelry to accent the whole package. Bare legs and open-toed shoes, preferably sandals adorned her feet that had stylishly painted toe nails. Hope thought Faith was the most stunningly beautiful woman she knew. Conversely, Faith always told Hope that she was the pretty one. So while the two were hardly bookends, when together they did turn heads, each lovely in her own right and in her own way.

"I never did get what drew you to Fred in the first place." Faith had gone back to the dressing rooms and found some clothes that needed to be put back on the racks.

Hope held up one hand, looked at the ring, pulled that ring off, and slipped on another one. "Well, I'd had that long, dry spell since the divorce. But...you know what I realized? If it hadn't been for Gary, I never would have given Fred a second glance."

"Yeah? Well that Gary thing was really weird if you ask me."

"Tell me about it. I mean a man shouldn't be allowed to light a fire in a woman's furnace if he's not planning on tending to it. That's all I have to say on that subject."

Laughter bubbled from Faith's throat. "Honey, women have been doing that to men for ages. They call them cock teasers."

"I guess that would make Gary the male equivalent of a cock teaser, which would be...what?"

"You fill in the blank."

"He certainly got me going then left me high and...well...not dry. Then in walks Fred. I mean really! Fred! He wasn't at all anyone I would normally have looked at twice."

"Well, good for you, for getting out if it wasn't right for you. Remember, to rephrase a truism, time wounds all heels, so he'll get his. But there's one thing you should thank ole' Fred for. And Gary, too, for that matter."

"What's that?"

"Like you said, you'd had a long dry spell. Between the two of them, they—to mix a metaphor—broke the ice. Now maybe when somebody worthwhile comes along you'll be ready."

"Now you are beginning to sound like Darling."

Speaking of Darling, what's with her anyway? Why do you hang around with that crazy woman?"

Hope laughed. "She's not crazy. She brings whimsy into my life and with my job, believe me, I need as much whimsy as I can get."

"Which brings me to your clients. How are things there?" In answer, Hope groaned, sat down on a nearby settee, and dropped her head into her hands. After a moment, she felt Faith's fingers massaging the back of her neck. "Not good, I take it?"

Hope sat up straighter. "You know what I miss?"

"What?" Faith sat down next to her sister and held her hand.

"I miss my kids. I mean, I miss them being little boys. I miss living in that small town in North Dakota where Ross and I were raising them. It was a town and a time when everything was safe, you know?" Faith got up and continued hanging up clothes while Hope reminisced. "I never felt safer then I did there. Back then, we never locked our doors. And when the kids rode their bikes to the city park to go swimming in the afternoon, you never worried about if they would arrive there safely or get home safely. You just knew they would. And every pickup truck parked in the high school parking lot had a rifle in the rack across the rear window. But that was just the culture. Those kids were just farm boys who hunted. The rifles weren't anything more than what they were. So it wasn't a threat. They weren't even a status symbol. They just were. It wasn't a big toot. But moving back here to the big city after having been away a couple of decades, things are off. It's the same only different here. And it doesn't feel safe at all."

"So you miss your kids when they were little and the life you had back then, but what about Ross?"

"What about him?" Hope heaved a long sigh.

"I don't know. You were married for thirty years, divorced for five with no action, then this crash and burn with Fred. How did that happen anyway?"

"With Fred? He just kind of swept me off my feet and BOOM."

"Isn't that what you said you always dreamed of, someone to sweep you off your feet?"

"Yeah, well I heard someone today say to be careful what you wish for."

"So, if you were to ask for some specific thing in a man now, what would it be?"

Hope considered the question. "Ross was so judgmental and critical, disapproving really, of everything I said or did. I have no doubt that he loved me. But he really didn't like me. Or at least like to be with me and do things I liked to do. And to be fair, I didn't like his passions either: hunting and fishing. So as the cliché goes, we grew apart. If we liked doing things together, that might not have happened. So, if I were asking for something, I'd just ask to be liked. I'm thinking *like* is more important than *love*, at least at this point in my life. I just want to be liked for who I am. If a man can let me be me and not disapprove of my every word and deed then that would be nice." Hope stood up and stretched. "And now it's back to work."

"Sarah's monthly grocery shopping?"

"That's right. Lately I plan that shopping expedition on Thursday afternoons. That's Gary's day to go bicycling with his group. So the coast will be clear."

"I have to say, between Gary and Fred you managed to swing from one extreme to the other."

"No kidding. From now on, I'm taking my time. The way Fred came on to me like a runaway locomotive...I'll derail the next man who pulls that crap. Not being rushed; that's in stone. But, on a different note..." Hope walked over to the counter and picked up one of the rings she had tried on earlier. "I want to buy this." She slipped it on her left ring finger and admired it. "I just love the band and the setting."

"Faith rang up the purchase asking, "Shouldn't you be wearing that on the right hand?"

"Nah, right now, I'll stick with the left. It might keep the losers from trying to move in on me."

"But it might keep Mr. Right from making his move too."

Hope shook her head. "I need a break from men right now. So this can just be a nice, pretty little stop sign until I feel like taking it off again."

10

Sarah

The bright day is done.
And we are for the dark.
—Shakespeare, *Antony and Cleopatra* Act V

After getting into her car Hope called Sarah, and after twenty rings she began to mumble under her breath. Finally Sarah picked up. "Good grief, Sarah, you knew I'd be calling."

"Well, I was in the bathroom."

"I'll be there in about twenty minutes to pick up the grocery list. Make sure it's ready for me." Hope clicked off and took a few deep cleansing breaths. After Sarah's she was treating herself to a margarita at Joselito's. After all, every good deed deserved to be rewarded.

Sarah, in her mid-fifties, was a night owl. She stayed up all night doing God-knows-what, then slept most of the day away. She was also an agoraphobic who never left her apartment for any reason whatsoever. In fact she rarely answered the phone. When Hope needed to alert Sarah to the fact that it was time for her to pick up the shopping list, she often had to call a dozen times in a row, letting the phone ring and ring and ring each time. Sarah would eventually get tired of the ringing and pick up the receiver. She never said, "Hello." Hope would just start talking before Sarah hung up. "Hi, Sarah," Hope would hurry on. "It's Hope. I'll be by this afternoon to pick up the shopping list and get your groceries."

Sarah would always put Hope off. "Oh, no," she would stammer. "I'm not ready. You'll have to come later in the week." One way or the other they would set a day and time and Hope would then stop by at the appointed hour to get the shopping list. After Hope had climbed the stairs to the second-story apartment, Sarah then wouldn't bother to answer the door. The screen would be locked too. So Hope would stand out on the porch with one finger on the buzzer just holding it in while simultaneously holding her phone to her ear. So while the phone in the apartment rang and rang and rang, the doorbell buzzed and buzzed and buzzed. Between the two of them, Sarah eventually responded. After what was sometimes ten or fifteen long minutes, Sarah would finally open the door, full of surprise that Hope was there. That was the pattern and while it worked for Sarah, it drove Hope nuts!

Sarah flirted with the peripheries of sanity and insanity. She had probably stopped growing emotionally around thirteen or fourteen remaining the perennial immature girl who believed that the darling buds of May were everlasting. Time, however, had stamped itself on her features. But Sarah wasn't paying attention to the tell-tale heralds of aging such as her moustache or her wrinkles. She was so myopically shortsighted that she didn't even see the strands of gray in her longish hair which was always stringy and usually unwashed.

Sarah had lived alone with her father for years. The apartment had been her childhood home and after her mother passed away, it was just Sarah and Ward. He was a tall and handsome southern gentleman. Very religious, he insisted they go to church every Sunday. That was the only time Sarah ever left the apartment. During the week, Ward would do the grocery shopping, but other than that the two of them were just real homebodies. In time Sarah's knees started giving her trouble, so she had an excuse to forgo the churchgoing that Ward had insisted upon, as she simply couldn't make it down the stairs and up again on Sundays. At that point, Sarah became a complete recluse. Ward spent most of the day reading his Bible, and Sarah, an introvert of the first water, lived in her head. And what an interesting that place proved to be! Evidently it wasn't just children who had imaginary friends.

When Ward had his heart attack, Sarah didn't know what to do. Ward lay on the floor for hours while Sarah just slowly paced from one room to the other in confusion wringing her hands. When she finally heard her neighbor, Gary, bounding up the stairs to his apartment, which was next to Sarah and Ward's, Sarah opened her door and asked him to come in. From the front door Gary saw Ward laying on the floor, half in the bathroom and half in the hallway. He flipped open his phone and called nine-one-one while ascertaining if Ward was still alive. As the fire station was right around the corner, the paramedics came roaring down the street sirens wailing before Gary had even closed his phone. He stood out on the upstairs porch and waved the paramedics to the right apartment. Then, having done all he intended to do, he went into his apartment and popped the top off a beer.

After stabilizing Ward and getting him on the gurney in preparation for the trip to the hospital, they realized Sarah was a bit of a loose screw and that leaving her alone in the apartment was not going to be a good thing. She kept insisting that no, she wouldn't be going to the hospital, that she couldn't make it down the stairs because she had bad knees, and she would be fine; they could just call her when her father was settled in the hospital. The two paramedics looked at one another. If she couldn't make it down the stairs to get to the hospital then she wouldn't be able to get down the stairs to get groceries. To solve the problem of what to do with Sarah, they put her into a fireman's carry and toted her down the stairs, into the ambulance, and off to the hospital with her father. Enter Morgan Smyth.

Morgan's lawyer was the personification of the clichéd ambulance chaser. When likely clients arrived at the hospital the on-site social worker would give Morgan's attorney the high sign, the attorney in turn would then get on the horn to Morgan. The two of them, after slipping some largess to the social worker, would then double team the ailing person when he was at his lowest ebb, and before he knew what was happening, he had signed on the dotted line.

That was what happened with Ward. Morgan's lawyer pointed out that if he died there would be no one to take care of Sarah (whether this was actually the case or not, they didn't bother to ascertain), and that Ward needed to sign a temporary power of attorney so that they could see that everything went smoothly for Sarah if the worst happened. They always emphasized the words *temporary* and *revocable* so as not to get the potential client's guard up. Ward listened to their practiced speech and signed the power of attorney.

Ward bounced back quickly and the nurses had him up and walking within days. He was doing very well and looking forward to getting home. Sarah, meanwhile, had undergone some psychological testing while at the hospital, and, loving their labels, the authorities now had on record that she was a paranoid schizophrenic. Sarah had the gift of gab and didn't realize that telling these nice therapists about Charles, her FBI boyfriend who lived overhead in the attic of the apartment, would be a bad thing. When they were convinced that Sarah thought Charles was indeed a real person and not a figment of her active imagination, they had her number and wrote it all down in her chart. The truth was that Sarah was harmless, but labels are labels and as Morgan knew how to work the system better than most, the end result was a foregone conclusion. The lawyer and Morgan quickly trotted the recently signed power of attorney to court and, due to Ward's incapacitation and Sarah's mental issues, received a conservatorship over both Sarah and her father. As quickly as that, both father and daughter had their own control over their lives stolen from them.

After Ward improved enough to leave the hospital, Morgan moved Ward in to a nursing home, telling him that when he was stronger he could certainly go back to his apartment. And Sarah, well Morgan had fifty-seven-year-old Sarah placed in an elderly retirement facility where she had a bedroom and a bathroom and was given three meals a day.

Ward, instead of flourishing in the nursing home as he had at the hospital (and as he would have continued to do had he been in his own home surrounded by his own things), caught a viral pneumonia that, in his weakened state, he was completely unable to shake. When Hope came to bring him the Bible he'd asked for, she was shocked at how quickly he'd slid from a man on the mend to this chronically dilapidated wisp of what he had been. He lay in bed covered with only a sheet. He'd lost so much weight that he barely made a mound under the light cotton. Any expenditure of energy was more than Ward could bear. Each breath was torturous, labored, and seemingly the last one he'd ever take—until the next labored breath. Hope didn't know when she'd watched anything more painful. She left the Bible next to the radio she had brought him from his apartment the week before and promised to drop in again in a few days.

The upshot of Ward's illness was that he was dead in a matter of weeks. Sarah appeared to take the loss of her father in her stride and, at that point, decided it was time for her to go home. Not necessarily being of sound mind, but not having dementia, she contacted her court-appointed attorney, convinced him she was capable of caring for herself, and fought the conservatorship. They took Morgan to court, but discovered that once you have fallen down the rabbit hole of the system, you were pretty much stuck; there was no way back out. So while the court did allow Sarah to move back into her apartment, and did allow her control over her person, they figured she still needed a *parent figure* to take care of her as Ward had done. So, Morgan was granted continued conservatorship over Sarah's estate. Morgan was to pay her bills and, of course, that meant Morgan's monthly fee too. And as Sarah never intended to leave her apartment once she got back into it, it also meant that Morgan was responsible to see to it that Sarah had a fully stocked larder. That was where Hope came into the picture.

Hope saw Sarah as a cautionary tale personified for those who thought conservatorship could never happen to them. If Sarah had lived in a more rural area, the church community would probably have taken Sarah under their wing after Ward's heart attack. One of the parishioner's good deeds might have been to get Sarah's groceries for her and check up on her periodically. But for some reason no member of the church she had been attending stepped in to help. Which was fine by Morgan as Morgan didn't brook interference in the business by anyone or anything. Complete control, was Morgan's motto.

●●●

Hope had met Sarah early in the nightmare in which Sarah found herself. She had just been placed in the retirement home and was confused as to why she couldn't go back to her apartment which had been her home since she was a little girl. Here in the facility she was surrounded by all kinds of people; and not being a people person, Sarah was about as unhappy as she could be. Plus, here she was in an unfamiliar environment with only the clothes on her back that she had been wearing when the paramedics whisked her to the hospital along with her father. So Hope's first task was to go to the apartment and get additional clothing for both Sarah and Ward and drop the clothing off at their respective facilities.

The apartment building was an older four-unit edifice with two apartments on the ground level and two upstairs. It was constructed so that the apartments weren't side by side but at an angle to one another. So one set of upstairs and downstairs apartments faced south and one set faced west. Between the two wings were a sloping lawn as well as flowers and shrubs which were surrounded by a concrete walkway. Sarah had the upstairs apartment facing west and her landlord, Gary, had the upstairs apartment facing south. They shared the front porch which was reached by the outside staircase. When Hope arrived for the first time to collect clothing and other essentials like tooth and hair brushes, she first knocked on Gary's door. She wanted to let him know who she was and what she was doing in the neighboring apartment.

When Gary opened his front door, the words "Holy Shit" almost popped out of Hope's mouth. In fact she wasn't sure they hadn't. But as Gary didn't react, she figured she had kept them to herself. Or maybe he was accustomed to women reacting that way around him. Gary was, hands down, the most beautiful man Hope had ever laid eyes on. Picture Mel Gibson in *Braveheart* only way more handsome and much, much sexier; and with deep brown eyes instead of blue and you'd have a vague idea what Gary looked like. If Hope were to have conjured the perfect man out of thin air, he would have looked exactly like Gary.

Gary at this point in his life was a very youthful looking not-quite-fifty-year-old bachelor. He had purchased the apartment building outright in his twenties when he'd inherited a pile of money from his doting but recently deceased grandmother. He promptly moved into an upstairs apartment while collecting monthly rents from the other three tenants covering the utilities, the insurance, and the taxes with enough left over so he didn't have to hold down a job—which suited him just fine. Gary was an artist. He'd converted the second bedroom of his two-bedroom apartment into a studio and spent the greater part of each day either painting at his easel or at the computer designing T-shirt art. He made a nice chunk of change from his freelance T-shirt business, and as far as the painting, that was just a means of expression for him. He sold the occasional painting, but mostly just gave them away for free.

After that first visit to Ward and Sarah's apartment to get clothing, Hope didn't see much of Gary, but when Sarah moved back into the apartment, they did cross paths on occasion. Gary might be taking off on his bicycle, just giving her a wave as he zoomed down the street, or he might be doing yard work and, glistening in the sun, stop his raking for a brief visit as Hope was heading back to her car. And after each meeting, Hope would sigh and tell herself to chill. But, damn! He was a good-looking man! One afternoon when Hope was dropping off groceries, Sarah told her that Gary had a crush on her. Hope's response was, "What? No way."

"He thinks you're sexy. He told me so."

"Hummm?" was all Hope could think to say. So they both thought each other was sexy did they? On the way home that evening, she did find herself wondering if that was the case then why hadn't Gary ever acted on his feelings. Maybe Sarah was just making that up. Or maybe not. Or, maybe Gary was waiting for her to make the first move. Hummm, again. Is that the way this man-woman thing worked? She had been out of circulation for so long that she really hadn't a clue.

The next time after she had dropped off Sarah's groceries, on her way past Gary's apartment, she impulsively knocked on the door. He pulled it open and just looked at her, waiting for her to speak first. For a moment her breath backed up in her lungs. He was wearing low-riding blue jeans, a sweatshirt with torn off sleeves, and a bandana around his head. His long dark hair was pulled back in a ponytail. He held a paintbrush in one hand and had a streak of chartreuse across one cheek that probably hadn't been shaved for a couple of days. She watched as his eyes did one full sweep of her person, first down then up.

She swallowed then nodded her head toward Sarah's apartment. "I swear that woman drives me to drink. I thought I'd stop by Joselito's on the way home and get a margarita. Want to join me?"

They'd had a fun visit and two margaritas later, Gary suggested Hope sit for him. She laughed in his face. "What? Model for a painting?" He just nodded. She politely declined. But when he asked a second, then a third time, she began to realize he was serious. Not keen on committing to something like posing for a painting, Hope steered the conversation in a different direction.

Gary had told her that the elderly woman in the apartment below him had passed away recently and he was in the process of getting it ready to rent.

"Wow, first Ward and now this woman. What's going on?" When he just shrugged, Hope added, "Well, let's hope it's not going to be one of those things that happen in threes."

"No kidding."

"Do you have any tenants in mind?" Hope wanted to know.

He shook his head. "Not yet."

"Then why not move Sarah down there?"

"Why would I do that?"

"Because of her bad knees. She wouldn't have stairs to contend with, so she might actually get out on her own sometime. Plus she could wash her clothes in the laundry room instead of her kitchen sink. And..."

"Stop!" Greg held up his hand like a traffic cop. "No, no, and no."

"Why not?"

"Because I don't want her bedroom beneath my bedroom."

Hope wasn't sure how to interpret that, so left it alone. Although, come to think of it, if she and Greg ended up using his bedroom as a rumpus room, maybe she didn't want Sarah downstairs either.

That night she tossed and turned and couldn't sleep. Damn that man was gorgeous. And she had gotten a nice little hug after their drinks before she headed home. But that had been that, there had been no suggestion of getting together again some other time for dinner or whatever—only his request to paint her. She told Faith about that the next day.

"So sit for him," was Faith's response. "What do you have to lose?"

Hope admitted to herself that she didn't have anything to lose. So one afternoon after dropping off Sarah's groceries, she stopped by Gary's once again and said, "Okay, if you want to paint me, it's now or never."

"I'll need to you to sit more than just this once."

"How often?"

"I don't know, a few times."

He poured her a glass of wine, set her on a stool by the window in his studio and went to work.

Gary began by sketching on the canvas. He worked in fits and starts, stopping suddenly to study her and then focusing intently on the canvas. When she had first slid back on the stool her skirt had ridden up high on her thighs; she immediately tugged her skirt back down toward her knees. Gary simply said, "Nuh nuh," and slid her skirt back up her thighs a bit. Beyond that he never touched her except to reposition the angle of her head or arm then went back to work. And one sitting blended into the next.

Most of the time he was completely intent on her as an object he was painting, but seemingly oblivious to her otherwise, so Hope felt free to focus on him. She was glad he always offered her wine as it gave her something to sip on while he painted her. The warmth, the slow, subtle arousal encouraged by Bacchus's nectar flowing through her veins, coupled with the energy emanating through the room, awoke her hormones, set them percolating. Gary would stop and stare at her, then return to painting, his brush flying over the canvas.

It hadn't taken her take long to discover Gary wasn't much of a conversationalist. They talked a little bit about Sarah. And he talked a little bit about his T-shirt business; he did a lot of work for the different bands that wanted to sell shirts at their various venues. He also did some work for a T-shirt shop in Santa Monica. And now and then he talked about the bicycle group he was a member of that toured here and there across the city on Thursdays. But mostly he didn't have much to say. He just painted.

One day his mother stopped by the apartment to drop off some food she'd made for her son. Gary introduced Hope to his mother as a model and that was the extent of it. When his mother left, Hope said, "Well, now I know where you get your good looks. It is certainly genetic. I think you mother is probably the most beautiful woman I have ever seen." And she was. That she had to be around seventy was shockingly unbelievable. "She's who I want to be when I grow up," Hope thought. That day while Greg painted he spoke a little about his mother and his growing up years, and Hope started intuit why the man had never married; or, for that matter, made a pass at her. Oedipus Rex was alive and well in Southern California.

One time he talked about the apartment building and how he stored some things in the attic that ran the length of the building above both his and Sarah's apartments. Hope laughed. "So, there really is a man in Sarah's attic. Only the racket you made up there, instead of spooking her, became her FBI boyfriend."

He chuckled at that too. "So you know about Charles do you?"

"Lucky Sarah, she must feel very much protected knowing an FBI agent is living in her attic. She tells me he comes down into her apartment to visit quite often."

"Yeah," Gary stepped back from the easel and studied it. "She does a lot of giggling sometimes — at night, of course. I always wonder what she's up to as she doesn't watch TV. Maybe she and Charles are doing it doggie style on the kitchen floor."

"With her knees?" was all Hope could think to respond.

"Oh yeah, I forgot about her knees." They both cracked up, but then Hope felt a ping of disloyalty. Mocking Sarah did rub Hope the wrong way. The woman was who she was and there was no reason to make fun of her. So Hope changed the subject and they talked about something else.

But mostly they didn't talk much. Gary just focused on the painting. One day, however, when the painting was nearly finished, he did say something shocking. "You have no idea how many times I've jacked to your image." He added another brush stroke to the painting.

Hope wasn't sure she had heard him correctly. "What?"

"You really are one sexy babe. And what makes you even sexier is that you don't know it. Yeah, I think of you a lot when I jack off."

Okay, she thought as she sipped her wine, he *was* attracted to her. That was a good thing, she supposed, as she was attracted to him too. But? Jacking off? One of her greatest disappointments was that, other than the goodbye hug she always received, painting her was the closest he ever came to any form of intimacy. Her fantasy was to be under him, naked and sweaty, and writhing with pleasure. His hard body, that Samson hair falling across her face and breasts, his long, sustained thrusting...but Gary, darn him, turned out he'd rather take matters into his own hands than share the experience? What was that all about?

"Done." Gary put the brush down and stood back studying the painting.

"Does that mean I can finally see it?" Hope asked.

"Have at it." He stood back and gestured for her to come over and see the finished product.

Hope skirted around the canvas and got her first look at the painting. "Ummm?" She looked over at Gary. "I'm nude."

"Yeah." Gary was nodding.

"But," she looked down at what she had on. "I was wearing clothes when I posed."

"So? I paint what I see."

"You see me naked?"

"I always see women naked."

Hoped looked around the studio and pointed to a scattering of pictures here and there. "Those aren't nudes."

"You wouldn't *want* to see them naked," was Gary's response.

Hope turned back to the painting. It was certainly her face, but the similarity ended there. The woman was seated on a large, flat rock beside a tumbling brook that flowed through a lush forest. The woman had beautiful long, russet hair that fell over one shoulder covering one breast then cascading lower blanketing her lap. Only one of the woman's plump round breasts was showing; the rose-petal pink nipple erect.

So this is what he did, Hope thought. He painted erotic pictures and, what, whacked off to them? She was beginning to realize that he had no reason to get her naked in reality.

"So?" Gary was so close to her she could feel his breath by her ear. "What do you think?" She turned and looked him full in the face. His dark eyes caught hers and stared deeply into them. Her respiration slowed.

"You made me look...fabulous. But, it's not really me."

"It's you, babe, the real you." She turned to look at the painting again. He added, "I call it *Nymph in the Woods*."

As she studied the painting, she realized Gary had, in fact, discovered her, touched her more deeply than a hand or fingers ever could. He'd penetrated her aura; connected with her essence more intimately than any sexual encounter. The funny thing was if he had asked her to pose in the nude, she probably would have. But she had to admit, his imagination was a lot better than the reality would have been.

In time, Gary had the painting framed and he gave it to Hope. And that was the end of it. He wasn't interested in a relationship. He was content with his life the way it was, and having a girlfriend didn't fit in with what he wanted. But, damn it, he was so attractive. And in fact, maybe that was the rub; maybe, because of his good looks, women had been throwing themselves at him all his life; and he was just tired of the whole thing. Easier to take things in hand when the urge struck and be done with it then having to put up with a woman he didn't really want. And then there was his mother. It was such a shame that he had all those Oedipal issues. Although, truth be told, those issues were also likely why he had initially been attracted to Hope in the first place as she was several years his senior and hence a good candidate upon whom to focus his complex.

One evening Faith and Hope stood in Hope's bedroom looking at the painting that she had hung opposite her bed. "Why you shameless hussy!" Faith was laughing.

"Hey! I didn't *pose* nude. That clearly isn't me." Hope's defensiveness only made Faith laugh more.

"Actually it's a damn good painting." Faith had been an art history major so Hope felt that her sister's assessment must be an accurate one.

"It doesn't really look like me."

"It most certainly does. There's no doubt that it's you."

"What? What part of that is me?"

Faith pointed. "That's your nose."

"Well, we have the same nose. So the painting could just as easily be you then."

"It's more than just the nose. It's your face."

"But the gorgeous long hair, that's so...Julianne Moore. I don't have hair like that. And that woman in the painting is...voluptuous. That's not me."

"Oh, please..." Faith patted her sister's cheek. It's a beautiful painting and why the guy didn't end up jumping your bones I'll never figure out."

"Me either." Hope knocked back some wine. "But far be it from me to put a crimp in his style."

"You should have just grabbed him by the dick and led him into the bedroom. That's what some guys need. The direct approach."

"This is how a woman who has been happily married for over twenty years talks?"

"How do you think I stay happily married?"

"Seducing your husband?"

"You got it. Didn't you ever seduce yours?"

Hope thought back then shook her head. "Not really, no."

"You're kidding. Why not?"

"We didn't have that kind of marriage. Sometimes I'm fully convinced my kids were a product of Immaculate Conception. But lately, well Gary sure got my juices going. After half a century, I finally know what the word *horny* means."

"The guy's an idiot to miss out on you. That's all I have to say."

"You know what I think?" Hope topped off both glasses of wine. "I think that apartment building was built over an old Indian Burial Ground. That's what I think. That's why all the people who live there are a little," she twirled her index finger around in circles by her ear, "you know, squirrely."

Faith tapped her wine glass to her sister's and toasted. "Then here's to you not spending too much time there. We don't want you going around the bend on us."

"Well, as I just pointed out, one good thing did come out of all this. If it hadn't been for Gary I never would have had a full understanding of the word *lust*." Faith laughed and just shook her head. "Unfortunately," Hope continued, "as it now stands, here I am ready to roar and have no place to focus all that passion."

"Don't worry, doll-face, something's bound to come along."

That was months ago now, and Fred had been the one to come along. But Fred had not been Gary. Hope still lusted after Gary, and she always shook her head every time she walked past his apartment door. What a waste, she'd think then go on about her business.

●●●

Today as Hope unloaded groceries in Sarah's kitchen Sarah, once again, complained about being under conservatorship. Hope placed the yogurt containers on the refrigerator shelf and said over her shoulder, "How would you get your groceries if you didn't have a conservator overseeing things?"

"Charles told me he'd do my shopping for me."

"What if he forgot?" Hope put the ice cream in the freezer.

"He wouldn't forget. He tells me I don't need a conservator. That I have to go back to court and fight it."

Hope leaned against the counter and crossed her arms. "And you'd leave the apartment to go to court."

"Why not?"

"Why not, indeed." The two women just looked at one another for a moment. "On a different note, Sarah, when are you going to clear out all the stuff in Ward's bedroom? It's been months since he died. It's time to deal with all that."

Sarah shook her head. "No. I have to go through everything and decide what to sell and what goes to Good Will."

"Sarah, nobody's going to want his old socks and underwear. Let's go in there right now with a big garbage bag and just toss the things nobody will want. It will take less than twenty minutes and you will have at least started on that chore."

"No, not today. I have too many other things to do."

"Such as?"

"Just things."

Hope gave up and headed out the door. Over her shoulder she said, "Next time I call, will you answer the phone right away, pretty please?"

Part II

The Sands of Time

"A time to be born and a time to die."

— Ecclesiastes 3:2

"The art of living well and the art of dying well are one."

—Epicurus

11

Shirley

"What day is it?"
"It's today," squeaked Piglet.
"My favorite day," said Pooh.
— A. A. Milne

Before Hope had taken on this job working for Morgan she had only understood aging in the abstract. It was something that happened to other people. But now, aging and dying were things she faced every day. In time Hope realized that growing toward death was just another kind of growing up that humans experienced. And by and large most of her clients, even those deep in dementia, were growing old gracefully and coming to understand death not only as a part of life but also as a blessed rest at the end of a long, long journey. Unfortunately those in charge of the elders of our society Hope came to see as *adolescent adults* who were so afraid of death that they refused to allow the elders a serene passage at the very end of their lives. Instead of letting the individual withdraw to do this work alone in a peaceful environment there was all kinds of interference; the dying elders were usually subjected to technological intrusions and blaring sirens racing them from one bed to another bed, all of which is anathema to a dying person. They just wanted to be left in peace. Speaking in soft voices, doing nothing abruptly, no rough handling, these are kindnesses to the dying that are ignored in today's society. But every now and then, a lucky soul snuck past the galumphing intruders who were determined to try and halt the inevitable, and Hope saw that as something to celebrate.

Shirley Miller, a gem of a woman, passed away in her sleep one night in the nursing home where she had been placed. Nursing homes, of course, don't like it when that happens. When they get an inkling that the end is near, instead of just leaving the person alone, except to make them as comfortable as possible, they call the ambulance and try to get the person to the hospital to die. That way they don't have it in their records that they have had X number of deaths on site. The lower the percentage, the better it looks. Conversely, if a client is in the hospital and looks close to the end, often the hospital sends the person back to the nursing home for the same reason. As this is a quantitative society, all thoughts are on statistics; so if you can stick the other institution with the negative numbers so much the better. But as Shirley was a quite and non-disruptive patient, her passing in the nursing home had gone unnoticed until the morning changing of the staff. As sad as Hope was to see Shirley go, she celebrated the fact that the woman had managed to slip past everyone's guard and glide into death. If Morgan had had a clue that her time was near, Morgan would have moved heaven and earth to get her hooked up to every life support system know to man. After all, when the person dies, the conservatorship dies and that's no way keep making money off the person's estate. But Shirley, who was tired and worn down from the radiation that was supposed to have extended her life, moved on to the next dimension to join her husband and son, who had gone on before her, without fanfare or any advanced warning to all and sundry who cared for her.

Hope, who had spent the afternoon at the mortuary arranging Shirley's funeral, now sat on her balcony in the chase lounge with a glass of wine at her elbow and a sigh on her lips. Although September was usually as hot as Hades, temperatures had dropped on this cool and blustery fall evening. Hope had an afghan that her mother had crochet years ago tossed over her legs. She was staring at the faint outline of the hills, but not really seeing them. She was remembering Shirley as well as thinking of all her clients. With only one or two exceptions, all of her charges were in the throes of living the closing chapter of their lives. A week ago, if someone had asked her which one would be the next to die, Shirley would not have topped the list. Ann, who had also undergone radiation therapy for her cancer, was in much worse shape than Shirley had been. Poor starving Ellen was only hanging on by a thread. Sweet Bonnie had gone from being a spry ninety-something to a wheelchair-bound ghost of herself. And Wren, too, was failing. And then there was her pet, Mr. G. He was deteriorating before her eyes and she was helpless in the face of the inevitable. No, Shirley definitely would not have topped the list, but the universe has a way of doing things in its own time and its own way. And so the process of laying this lovely lady to her final rest had begun. Hope's thoughts turned back the clock...

●●●

Shirley was a card to use an old-fashioned term. She had a wonderful sense of humor and a love of life. Her dementia was such that she did repeat herself a lot, but so did most of Hope's clients, so that was nothing new. Shirley had been one of those few unspoiled souls. Her wit was always sharp and quick—something her dementia hadn't taken from her. Before she had failed to the point that she needed to be in a nursing home, Shirley lived with a friend who had *taken her in* when her mental capacity had diminished to the point where she couldn't care for herself. Shirley was in her early nineties at the time, and her friend, a feisty Puerto Rican woman, was still in her youthful eighties. They two of them lived in Magda's little one-bedroom house located on her son's property behind his much larger house. The property was a beautiful place, almost an old-fashioned estate, with a wall around the yard that was full of beautiful flowers and two large dogs. Magda always had to lock the dogs up before Hope arrived for her monthly visit.

Hope's job was simply to see that Shirley was fine. Shirley was abundantly healthy, took no medications, walked and bicycled every day, and danced whenever she could. She loved Magda's spicy cooking and the two women were a joy to visit. Hope would spend a pleasant hour checking up on her client and getting a kick out of how the two woman interacted; their conversation would occasionally be interrupted by the parrot who like to insert an, "I love you, Shirley," into the conversation whenever he felt like it. The brightly colored bird did have a cage, which he perched on top of, as the cage door was always open. Hope was leery of birds, especially big birds, but this one mostly behaved, and Magda keep the floor scrubbed on a daily basis so there was never any tell-tale sign of bird poop anywhere. Good thing or Morgan would have had something to say about that.

Shirley had been a housekeeper in the film industry when the film industry was at its heyday. She worked for the studio cleaning the bungalows inhabited by Lucille Ball and the other greats of the fifties and sixties and seventies. And while she had been a blue-collar employee it was during an era when blue-collar workers could earn a fine living. It was also a time when house loans were of the fifteen-year variety and refinancing was almost unheard of. The homeowners paid off their mortgages and celebrated when the last payment was made to the bank. They then owned their modest houses outright while they were still young enough to keep working and salting more money away for their old age. The savvy middle-class citizens of that era knew how to avoid debt and enjoy life to boot. Shirley and her husband worked hard, raised a strapping son, and went out dancing every weekend. They had a zest for life and lived it the way they wanted to. When her husband passed away of a sudden and massive heart attack, she and her son purchased a double plot so that when Shirley died she would be with her dearly beloved for eternity. It wasn't a side-by-side plot but a one-on-top-of-the-other plot. Magda always used to make fun of Shirley saying, "You no go pee pee on your husband when you are there." Those words always made Shirley laugh with glee.

As Shirley's son had never married, he had moved back into his childhood home with his mother to keep her company after his father's passing. And life went on and all was well. Until, sadly, Shirley's son died of an undetected aneurysm so she was left alone in her little house with not much more than her memories. And the formerly light-hearted and carefree woman fell into the pit of despond. Oh, Shirley had her pension and her savings, and luckily for her the motion picture industry had wonderful insurance for its employees so this woman was set for life as far as finances and healthcare. But she had lost the two most important people in her life and depression set in.

Magda found her one crisp, fall day wandering the streets far from home without a sweater or a jacket to ward off the cold. Shirley was confused, lost, totally disoriented, and at the point of tears. Magda had asked her, "What are you doing so far from home?"

"Waiting for a bus," was the reply.

"You want to take the bus somewhere?" Magda had inquired.

"No. I'm going to throw myself in front of it so I can be with my husband," was the sad answer.

It was then that Magda took her home to live with her. They went back to Shirley's house, packed a few necessities, made sure the house was locked up, and that was that. The two got along famously and Magda's son and his family embraced the new member of their household. Even the dogs liked her. And the parrot, well, it had learned to say, "I love you, Shirley."

So she was accepted all around and life was good again, at least for a few months.

It was usually greed — one of the seven deadlies — that ended up getting Morgan involved with a client. And that bore out in this case. Morgan ended up being appointed conservator because Shirley's nephew, her only living relative, felt that this upstart Puerto Rican woman was stealing his aunt's assets — assets he felt he should eventually inherit. The nephew, of course, hadn't bothered to visit his aunt in years and was not so much interested in her person as in her savings. He told the court that his aunt needed to be placed in a nursing home (which he knew would be paid for by her motion picture industry insurance) and taken away from these people who were stealing from her.

Fortunately, Magda and her son had kept meticulous records and were able to prove to the judge that not only hadn't they stolen anything from this demented woman, but that they had in fact done much for her out of their own pockets. Shirley, her dementia notwithstanding, was also able to take the stand and tell the judge that she wanted to continue living with Magda. The nephew raised additional objections saying that the two women slept in the same bed and there was something decidedly *wrong* about that. Magda explained that she had a one-bedroom house and a king-sized bed in the bedroom. When she was a little girl she had slept with her sisters as had Shirley. So it was just like sleeping with a sister and there was nothing wrong with that. The judge, a woman in her sixties, had apparently had to sleep with her sisters too when she was a child, so she agreed with Magda, that there was nothing wrong with their sleeping arrangements.

The judge, however, did feel it prudent to put Morgan in charge over both Shirley's estate and person, but cautioned Morgan that in this case to leave the client where she was, with Magda. It was a situation that had been working out for nearly a year and there was no reason to disrupt the status quo at this point. In addition, Magda was to be paid a monthly fee for her services. The nephew, naturally, was furious because now not only was Magda to be paid out of his aunt's estate, something that hadn't been happening before, but now yet another person, the conservator, would also be paid out of his aunt's estate, and that would mean a lot less for him when she did die. And if Morgan had anything to say about things, the estate would be bled dry before that eventuality occurred. Oh well, Hope thought, the universe does often have ways of biting a person in the ass who deserves it.

Morgan, of course, worked hard at trying to find reasons to remove Shirley from Magda's care and to put her in a facility. That was just Morgan's modus operandi—to put a client in a facility, then when she started to fail to the point of not wanting to eat, which doesn't take long after being incarcerated, insert a PET tube, and then keep on collecting the monthly fees often for years for doing basically nothing. But luckily Shirley had her support team in Magda and Magda's son not to mention the judge, so Morgan's hands were pretty much tied in this case.

For Hope the visits were always pleasant. And while she heard the same stories over and over again, she didn't mind. Shirley would reminisce about how she had met her husband. "We both worked for the studios," she explained. Then she would wink. "We had a dalliance going on and nobody had a whiff of it." She'd laugh before confiding, "That man's kisses made me dizzy. We'd be hiding out in the back lot kissing and kissing and one day, before I knew it, he popped the question. I didn't even have to think about it. We were married right away and never looked back."

Oh, life had indeed shat upon her when her husband had died and then her son. She had briefly tumbled into the abyss. But she'd climbed out of it with Magda's assistance and regained her zest for life. She'd wrestled with the dark side and instead of succumbing, moved back into the light. Not one to snivel over the past, she viewed it philosophically. Time would march on, carrying her with it, and eventually she'd join her loved ones.

When she was younger Shirley had been an avid reader, but in recent years she had to give up that passion due to macular degeneration. Ironically, she kept a book in her basket-like purse which she carried with her at all times. It made Hope smile that a woman who couldn't see to read carried a book around with her.

"What's the book?" Hope asked her one day when Shirley had pulled it out of her purse when looking for her handkerchief.

"Here." She handed it to Hope. "It's the best book I ever read. I keep it with me to remind me."

"*The Power of Now* by Eckhart Tolle," Hope read off the cover. "What's this about, Shirley?"

Shirley may have had dementia, but she remembered reading that book and remembered what it was about, which she shared with Hope in detail. She told Hope that book had changed her life, teaching her to live in the moment, and that it was the most important book she had ever read. And Hope believed it. Other than that short period of time after her husband's and son's deaths when she had been so depressed, Shirley had lived the message of this book. "I carry it with me every day even now when I can no longer read anymore just to remind me of its significance," Shirley had told Hope.

"Quite the testament." Hope turned the book over and read the blurb on the back.

"I'd lend it to you, but I don't want to be without it. But you can have it when I die."

Hope chuckled. "Rather than wait that long, maybe I'll go to the library and check it out and read it."

"Okay."

Shirley put the book back in her purse with a smile on her lips as the parrot sang out, "I love you, Shirley." And life was good.

Things, however, as they are wont to do, took a turn for the worse when a small sore showed up on Shirley's cheek. Hope, who only visited the women once a month, noticed the sore and asked, "What's this?"

"Oh, I just scratched myself," Shirley said.

Hope looked to Magda for more information. "I don't know how she got it. We noticed it one day. I've been putting this on it to make it go away."

Hope looked at the tube of some over-the-counter cream and made a notation in her notebook. "So how are you two doing other than this?" She handed the tube of ointment back to Magda.

"We're just a couple of old relics, but we do fine."

The next month when Hope visited, not only had the sore not gone away, it was bigger. "Time to get to the dermatologist," she told the women.

The upshot was that Shirley was diagnosed with skin cancer. It was a serious cancer and it had already gone pretty deep. The doctor claimed that surgery would not do any good, that radiation was the only way to go. As the sore was high on the cheek and close to her eye, her vision would become an issue, but with Shirley's macular degeneration already nearly blinding her, her possible loss of sight in the one eye wasn't really factoring into the doctor's decision to go the radiation route. Hope was heartsick when she heard the verdict. Ann had undergone radiation for her skin cancer and, like a modern-day technological vampire, it had drained Ann of every ounce of energy that she had. Ann was so worn down she landed in the hospital, where she had contracted a viral pneumonia and was now almost completely bedridden. That Shirley would soon be traveling this same path was almost too much for Hope to bear.

As with Ann, the daily radiation treatments which lasted for weeks sapped Shirley of her life force. The woman who had exercised by walking or dancing almost every day of her life could no longer get out of bed without help. Her energy level had fallen off so dramatically that Morgan was finally able to get her placed in a facility without much of a battle from Magda or her family.

Each time Hope visited her, Shirley had lost ground. But she still retained her sense of humor and had that zest for life that Hope admired. Lying in her hospital bed, she pointed out the window one day and said, "See that fraternity house across the street. Those boys are always having parties late at night, making so much noise. I went over there last night to tell them to pipe down and they invited me to join them. I never had so much fun, drinking beer and dancing to what they call music. It was a hell of a night."

The fact that there was no fraternity house across the street notwithstanding, Hope humored her going along with the tale; knowing that it had happened only in Shirley's mind made Hope admire Shirley all the more. *Partying with the frat boys, how much fun was that!* "You go, girl!" she told Shirley.

Out of the blue one morning Morgan called Hope, told her that Shirley had died in the night, and asked her to go over to the facility and collect her things. Hope made it the first stop of the day. There wasn't much to collect, but one thing more than incensed her. She had looked in Shirley's purse and discovered that *The Power of Now* was not there. "Where's the book?" she asked the nurse's aide who was helping her pack up the clothes and other effects.

"What book?"

"The one she kept in her purse."

The aide just shrugged. She didn't know or really care. Hope then inquired at the front desk about the missing book and got the same response. No one had a clue what had happened to the book. The administrator inquired, "Are you sure she even brought it with her when she came here? She had macular degeneration, you know."

The missing book did nettle Hope. It wasn't the first time a client had things go missing in a facility. Sarah's father, Ward, had a radio stolen. Wren's engagement diamond never surfaced much to her husband's dismay. Unfortunately, it was just to be expected and clients were warned not to have valuables with them as they would be stolen. That people were more dishonest than honest seemed to be the case. As far as *The Power of Now*, it was only a book, Hope said to herself. But she sure would have loved to have it as a reminder of this remarkable woman. And besides, Shirley had essentially bequeathed it to her.

The funeral was a graveside affair with only a handful of people present. The temperatures had soared once again. It was a blistering September day, so that might have accounted for the lack of attendance. Then again, when a person was in her nineties, how many friends would still be alive to go to the funeral? Hope looked for the nephew who had tossed the monkey wrench into his aunt's life. No sign of the interloper. Nor had Morgan bothered to show up. When the funeral was over Hope and Magda stood side by side looking down at the coffin that rested on top of her husband's resting place. "You no go pee pee on your husband," Magda told her one last time. Then she turned away with a bowed head and rounded shoulders and walked toward her son who stood waiting by his vehicle to take her home.

Alone with Shirley for a moment, Hope smiled a small, sad smile. "Well, you got the best of Morgan, old girl. You didn't end up with a PET tube and now you are with your husband. Good job." She blew Shirley a kiss and headed for her car.

●●●

When Hope exited the freeway at Pennsylvania Avenue she smelled the smoke before she saw the fire. In the distance her beloved hills were ablaze. The fire was cutting a swath near the top; she could see by the charred path that it must have been burning for hours. Hurrying home she stepped through her French doors onto her balcony, already dusted with a fine coat of ash. A helicopter dropped fire retardant and she could see fire fighters swarming like ants pushing the fire up the rise and away from the homes below.

It wasn't the first time that fire had stripped the hillside. And it probably wouldn't be the last. Hope stood mesmerized as she watched the flames lick at a few sturdy yucca plants. The brush surrounding them had already been destroyed. All of a sudden another burst of fire seemingly materialized further along the crest of the hill. Hope could hear the "oomph" of the new blaze as it ran amok teasing the fire fighters to come and get it before it started down the other side. Watching the fire she understood why they said a fire consumed; she was seeing with her own eyes that it gulped and swallowed everything in its path. Its hunger diminished her own — food was the furthest thing from her mind. What if the wind shifted? What if the fire jumped the boulevard? What if it landed on her balcony and swallowed it whole? She stood there until it was full dark and nothing but the glowing red fire could be seen in the distance. It wasn't until it was mostly beaten back that she realized how exhausted she was. She went to bed, fell instantly asleep, and dreamed of flames being doused by a helicopter above. But instead of fire retardant, what was thrown from the copter, one after the other, were her clients — all falling into the unquenchable flames.

Hope woke up early, almost as exhausted as she had been when she'd gone to bed, and hurried out on to her balcony. The dark had pearled into gray and there were a couple of rays of sunlight brightening the horizon. The fire was out, but her hillside was completely denuded. Wisps of residual smoke curled upward from the carnage. The few homes she could see down by the foothills had escaped the fire, but were now at risk for mudslides. Such were the joys of living in Southern California. She continued to observe her hills as the sun grew bolder and the day allowed itself to be born. Looking down, she ran her finger along the balcony railing leaving a streak of white through the black ash. When she looked further down, she wished she'd thought to put slippers on. She could see her footprints leading from the French doors, across the balcony, to the railing. Lifting one foot and looking at her sole, she confirmed what she already knew—it was black from the ash and soot of the fire. Boy oh boy, clean up wasn't going to be fun. Turning to head back in she spotted a spider's web glistening with dew drops that looked liked jewels in the golden wash of morning. Turning her eyes once again toward the rising sun she smiled, suddenly remembering the verse her father used to recite to his daughters when it was time to rise and shine: *Awake! for Morning in the Bowl of Night / Has flung the Stone that puts the Stars to Flight: / And Lo! the Hunter of the East has caught / The Sultan's Turret in a Noose of Light.* It was from *The Rubaiyat of Omar Khayyam* and that she remembered it from so long ago amazed her. She spent a few moments looking inward and belatedly thanking her daddy for the lovely memory.

After a moment, looking back down at the spider's web sparkling in the dawn, she silently acknowledged that, yep, it was pretty, but she didn't want to share her balcony with a spider. Time to give the balcony a good going over.

12

Beatrice

> "I want to warn potential victims. Many of them
> are women, and many of them are battered women.
> It's a cause for me. When I look back, though, so
> many of the books I've written are about wives
> who just couldn't get away."
>
> — Ann Rule

With Morgan you never knew which way the grenade was going to be tossed. In one case a wife was separated from her husband and shouldn't have been — that was Bonnie. In another, the reverse happened; the husband and wife should have been separated and weren't — this was Beatrice. In this case the wife ended up dead, not that Hope's clients didn't end up dead in the long run anyway that was the nature of things in this business, but this client in particular broke Hope's heart.

Beatrice was a battered wife married to a womanizer. It was a second marriage for Beatrice who had remarried in her mid-sixties after a messy divorce. Beatrice had been having an affair with Duke and, as usually happens, the truth did out. She had been wealthy in her own right before her first marriage, so the divorce didn't leave her broke, far from it. And Duke, always one with his eye on the money, immediately scooped Beatrice up and married her. Her children claimed that Duke, the somewhat-over-the-hill tennis pro at the club, had done his homework: knew her worth, seduced her, made sure that the affair became public knowledge, and then ran off with the prize before anyone was the wiser.

The honeymoon didn't last long. Soon after her marriage to Duke, Beatrice became *accident prone*. Broken bones and black eyes that weren't easily explained away got her grown children concerned. Beatrice attempted to calm the kids down telling them she was fine, that she loved Duke, and that all was well. They never believed her. Her words hadn't carried the strength of conviction. Reading between the lines, they sensed fear. Years passed. Beatrice was in her seventies when she had a stroke; that the stroke may have been the result of physical violence was never proven, although Beatrice's children had done their best to do so. Their mother could no longer walk and could only speak with difficulty. With their mother in such a helpless state, they were frantic.

Not long after her stroke, because Beatrice needed so much hands-on care, she and Duke moved into a retirement home where they had a nice one-bedroom apartment, went down to a dining room to be served three meals a day, and had an aide come in several times a day to distribute medications and to help Beatrice get dressed and into the wheelchair or undressed and into bed depending on whether it was morning or evening. It concerned her children that they were never allowed by Duke to see their mother alone; he never left the room when the kids were there. Beatrice always indicated that everything was fine, but her eyes spoke volumes. In addition, Duke supervised her phone calls by making sure the phone was on speaker.

In desperation her children hired a private investigator to do some sleuthing. The investigator discovered, when Beatrice was safe in bed at the retirement home, Duke could be found back at the house that had not been sold *entertaining* a friend. He was not only abusing their mother physically, but living a double life while spending her money. The children as a last resort got the court to appoint a conservator over their mother hoping that would prevent their step-father's continued abuse of her and her assets. The only catch was the court didn't give Morgan Smyth full conservatorship over Beatrice.

Duke was young, relatively speaking, and in good health. He could also talk a good story. He told the court that he and Beatrice had been married ten years, and in all that time had gotten along just fine. It was only since her stroke that her grown children had felt the need to interfere. He was more than outraged that he couldn't be trusted to care for his wife. "We vowed to be with each other in sickness and health," he reminded the court. On top of all that, the wily Duke, years before when the marriage was young, made sure his name was put on all his wife's assets including the house. So as far as the community-property state of California was concerned, all assets belonged to husband and wife together. So while the court would consider granting conservatorship over the person in this case, it was not going to pull the financial rug out from under Duke by granting conservatorship over the estate to Morgan when Duke was very clearly of able body and able mind. The upshot was that Morgan was granted co-conservatorship of the person *with* Duke. The two of them had to come to terms before any decisions could be made regarding Beatrice's care. That didn't set at all well with Morgan or Duke. It was a hostile partnership with neither one willing to give an inch.

When Morgan insisted that Hope go over to the retirement home and see how things were, she felt a bit like she was bearding the lion in his den. She stood at the door holding her briefcase wishing it was a whip and a chair.

Hope knocked on the door at the appointed hour and waited. No response. She knocked again; still no response. Knowing she was in the middle of a tug of war between two strong wills, she was about to call Morgan when the door finally opened. A dapper Duke, like Iago, stood there all smiles. Hope realized the delay tactic to answering the door was a ploy; this guy had control freak written all over him. He swept the door open ushering Hope into the apartment. "*Welcome to my parlor said the spider to the fly,*" Hope recited in her head.

"I wasn't expecting such a pretty girl."

On the downhill side of fifty-something, it had been a long time since Hope had been called a girl, but in the interest of diplomacy she didn't contradict the man. She merely acknowledged the compliment with a nod. Looking around she noticed Beatrice on the living room couch. "Pleased to meet you, Duke." Hope extended her hand. "May I call you Duke?"

"That's my name." He grinned a feral grin and shook the proffered hand, holding on to it just a bit longer than he should. "I can't believe those kids got the courts involved in all this." Duke gestured to a chair. Hope ignored him and walked up to the woman leaning over on the couch. You couldn't call it sitting because she was mostly tipped over toward one side. The position looked incredibly uncomfortable. "Hello, Beatrice." Hope waited for a response. The woman was looking at her but not answering. "Can you hear me? Should I speak louder?"

"Just sit over there, nothing wrong with her hearing." Duke continued to gesture in a shooing fashion. "She can hear you from there."

Not one to rock the boat on a first meeting with a client, Hope did sit down and then addressed a comment to Duke. "Morgan prefers that I see the client alone. So if you don't mind taking a little walk...?"

"I'm not leaving her alone with you." Suddenly the smile was gone and in its place was a thin-lipped, narrow-eyed glare. "Morgan may have temporary conservatorship over *my* wife, but it's a co-conservatorship and I am equally as responsible for Beatrice as Morgan is, if not more so. Beatrice is *my* wife, after all, and I know what's best for her. Plus she can't talk, so I have to be the one to answer your questions."

Hope knew when someone was trying to cow her and she wasn't about to be cowed. "Quite the contrary, I have it from both Morgan and her children that she can talk."

Duke turned to his wife. "You don't feel like talking, today, do you sweetie?"

The way Beatrice was leaning on the couch her hair fell over her forehead so only one eye could be seen. And Hope didn't have to be clairvoyant to see that that eye was saying, "Fuck you." But the words, of course, were never spoken.

Hope shivered in the unseasonably air-conditioned room. She noted Beatrice was wearing a short-sleeved blouse while Duke wore a long-sleeved shirt and a pull-over sweater. "Would it be possible to turn off the air?" Hope rubbed her jacketed arms. "It really is quite chilly in here."

Duke's eyes swept her with a crude once-over. "She likes it cold," was his irritable response. Then he steered the conversation along the lines he preferred. He went into unnecessary detail about the relationship he and Beatrice had indulged in while she was still married to her first husband.

"I don't know that ancient history is relevant here." Hope was watching Beatrice as Duke was expostulating and she sensed the women's discomfort at having this dirty linen exposed.

Duke immediately went on the defensive. "I just wanted you to see that what we have here is a love affair, with love being the operative word. We fell in love at first sight and nothing would keep us apart. Not even her first marriage. You see," Duke went on, "the women at the club always liked me. I always had women." He leered then continued. "But Beatrice was..." Hope mentally filled in the pause: *richer than the others...* Then Duke finished the sentence, "...she was the one for me." Beatrice looked at Hope mutely, but her eyes spoke loudly and clearly. Hope shivered once again. It might have been the coldness from the air conditioning, but it might also have been revulsion.

After a while Duke excused himself to use the little boy's room, as he called it, and left the room. Hope got up from the chair she'd been relegated to, sat next to Beatrice on the couch where Duke had been, and placed her hand on Beatrice's bare arm. Her flesh was quite cold to the touch. "Are you chilly, Beatrice?"

"Yes." The woman's whisper was a rasp coming from unused vocal chords.

Hope spied an afghan on the back of the couch behind them. "Here." She tugged it loose from where it was tucked in to the sofa cushions. "This ought to warm you up." She covered Beatrice with it. "There, is that better?"

"Yes. Thank you."

Hope looked over her shoulder in the direction Duke had gone. He was still in the bathroom, so she took advantage of his absence. "Why didn't you ever allow your kids to help you? I understand they tried and tried."

Her whisper was so low Hope more likely read her lips than heard her say, "Redemption."

Confused, Hope asked, "You were looking for redemption?" Beatrice didn't answer, just nodded a slight nod. "Why?"

"Why indeed."

"Is there an answer?"

In a quiet, shaky voice unused to speaking she said, "Of course there is." They both heard the toilet flush and knew their conversation was about to be cut short. Beatrice continued in her whispery voice. "I think we'll save that weighty discussion for another day."

"What do you think you are doing?" Duke was still zipping his pants when he re-entered the room.

"Beatrice was cold." Hope made a point of straightening the afghan around the woman.

"I told you, she likes me to keep the apartment chilly. She doesn't want that blanket over her." With that pronouncement, he whisked it off his wife and put it back where Hope had found it. "There, sweetie, that's much better, isn't it? Some people just don't get it, do they?"

The pretense of concern was so obviously counterfeit it literally brought bile to the back of Hope's throat. "God, but this man is a piece of slime." Poor Beatrice, Hope thought to herself.

Hope stuck around until it was lunch time. At twelve o'clock straight up, Duke had pushed a button ringing a bell somewhere that signaled they were ready for the noon meal. Within two minutes an aide came into the apartment to help get Beatrice into the wheelchair so they could head down to the dining room. In a scolding tone, Duke said, "It's about time you got here; I rang that bell fifteen minutes ago." Duke tapped his watch, looked over at Hope and mouthed, "Rolex." Then smiled over at the aide and added, "Just kidding." Turning to Hope he smiled some more and said, "They love it when I tease them." The aide, with his back to Duke, mouthed the word "asshole" and rolled his eyes at Hope then tossed her a conspiratorial wink. They both had Duke's number which was probably six six six. Hope found herself rubbing a point over her right eye. It had literally been years since she'd had her last migraine, but she was pretty certain one was trying to blossom. Rolex! Good lord! Hope wouldn't have know a Rolex from a Timex, but that Duke had found it necessary to point it out just made Hope dislike him all the more.

Duke focused on Hope and smiled at her; she returned a wan smile of her own and in her mind said, *Fucker*. But out loud, and with one eye on the door as she was anxious to be out of there, she merely thanked him for the time and once again offered her hand.

"Now we're going to be seeing a lot of each other in the near future so none of this handshaking business." He opened his arms and, before Hope could react, moved in on her and embraced her. She kept her arms at her sides and over Duke's shoulder she saw Beatrice looking at her husband's back with disgust. Well, Beatrice wasn't the only one who could feel disgust. Hope felt as if she had been coated with slime and wished she didn't have to see another client as she wanted to go home and scrub herself clean.

Hope sat in her car and thought about Beatrice's cryptic comment regarding redemption. Certainly a few years back that woman's journey through life had taken a sudden left turn. Was it remorse over her failed first marriage that made her talk about redemption? Did she think that staying married to that monster, Duke, was a way of paying back some retribution

127

for her actions that had landed her in such an unhappy circumstance? Not just unhappy for her, but for her children too. Duke's deliberate seduction rendered her a victim as well as a fool. And ten years of an abusive marriage had given her plenty of time to nurse her remorse. Maybe she felt that her abusive second marriage was her just desserts. Perhaps she even took a perverse delight in her punishment. People who felt guilty about their actions often behaved in strange ways. Actions have consequences, as we are all taught by our parents—or we should be Hope thought. Some might say Beatrice was now lying in a bed of her own making, but Hope didn't look at it quite like that. People make mistakes and deserve to be forgiven for those mistakes. But forgiving someone else and forgiving one self are two very different things. Hope suspected that Beatrice had never been able to do the latter.

●●●

It wasn't long after that visit that Morgan called Hope to let her know that Beatrice was in the hospital and wasn't expected to live.

"What happened?"

"She took a tumble out of bed trying to get into her wheelchair."

"That doesn't make sense." Hope's mind was in top gear." She didn't have the mobility to get herself out of bed to the wheelchair. She always needed help. I saw the aide getting her from the couch to the wheelchair when I was there. There's no way she could have attempted that by herself."

"Well, according to Duke, she fell, hit her head on the corner of the night stand, and it doesn't look good. She was on blood thinners and because it took so long to call the ambulance after the fall, well, the hemorrhaging is quite extensive."

"And why did it take so long to call the ambulance?" Hope wanted to know.

"Apparently Duke was out for the evening. The staff there says that happens quite often."

Hope could paint by numbers and it didn't take much for her to fill in the picture. Smiling Duke had probably staged the accident then left to see his honey. When he got back several hours later, he probably called the front desk of the retirement home in distress. His wife had fallen out of bed trying to get to her wheelchair. Blah, blah, blah.

Morgan's voice was buzzing in her ear. "The doctors say it's just a matter of time before she dies. Days, maybe even hours."

"It's a crime, Morgan. She didn't just fall."

Morgan paused, then said, "You don't know that, Hope."

"I do know that. She didn't just fall and when she dies, Duke will have gotten away with murder."

"Hope, you know as well as I do that our clients die. That's what they do. It's just another day at the office. Now snap out of whatever kind of snit you are in, and just do your job."

Hope, always stunned when Morgan displayed insensitivity, gasped. "I never want to get to that place where death and dying are just another day at the office."

"It's not like I don't grieve over our clients who die."

Hope bit her tongue, but couldn't stop herself from saying, "There is a difference between real grief and pseudo-grief."

Morgan paused and thought about what Hope had just said. "That was rather ungracious of you."

"Sorry." Hope didn't sound the slightest contrite. "I have to get going; as you just pointed out, I have a job to do." Hope hung up the phone and rubbed that point over her eye that had begun to throb.

●●●

Beatrice died and the conservatorship died with her. The court had only given Morgan co-conservatorship over the person in this instance, and as the person was no longer living, that was that. Duke, not needing to be in a more controlled environment now that his invalid wife was dead, moved out of the retirement home and back into the house he had lived in with Beatrice since he married her; his name, of course, had legally been added to the deed shortly after said marriage.

Duke played the role of the grieving husband to the hilt. So even though the children called foul and tried to get the authorities to see that this was murder, that a woman's life had been cut short, no charges were ever pressed. The last Hope heard, the kids had gone to civil court and filed a wrongful death suit against their step-father. Hope wished them well.

13

Ellen

"How sharper than a serpent's tooth it is to have a thankless child."

—Shakespeare, *King Lear* Act I

Fall drifted toward a close and winter was gearing up for its opening act. The weather had been cold and rainy all week, and Hope's clients all seemed to be on the downhill slide. Ellen in particular was as close to the end as she could be. There were all kinds of suicide, Hope mused, but starving oneself to death had to be because one had no other option.

Ellen was one of Hope's most heart-breaking clients. A mere twelve months before Ellen had been a feisty, headstrong, and vibrant eighty-two year old woman. Today she was nothing more than a bag of bones in a hospital bed waiting to finish wasting away and die. Beyond that she was on so many psychotropic drugs that she had no concept of what was real and what was hallucinatory. Hope sat by the bed holding Ellen's thin hand while Ellen rambled on about how her son was now working in the nursing home, and how he was making sure that she was being cared for properly. "I knew he wouldn't let me down," Ellen kept repeating until she fell into a fitful sleep.

When Hope heard the door swish open, she looked up. There stood Steffane, Ellen's daughter. Hope put a finger to her lips then got up and the two of them walked down the hallway to the lobby.

"How is she today?" That Steffane actually seemed to care at this point was at least some improvement.

"About the same. She thinks your brother is working here and taking care of her."

"As if..."

Hope didn't want her to get going on her brother again so interrupted by saying, "Morgan is still insisting on the PET tube."

Steffane shook her head. "I have mother's DNR and will right here and she clearly states no to that."

"Morgan's going to tell the court the only reason you don't want her to have the PET tube is so you'll get your inheritance sooner as opposed to later."

Steffane's head dropped so all Hope could see was pinkish scalp through thinning hair. When she looked up her eyes glistened with moisture. "I guess at one point, yeah, I was guilty of that. But Morgan has pretty much spent all mom's assets on," she looked around her, "this." Then a tear or two did fall. "I didn't expect it to come to this. I just wanted to stop her from throwing good money after bad. That's all I wanted."

"Yes, I understand that. But actions have consequences and you were old enough to know that. What's happening now is just a culmination of what you started."

Steffane looked as if she had been slapped. "Are you saying that my mother's starving herself to death is my fault?" The shrillness of her voice had nurses and aides looking in their direction.

"When I met your mother she was full of spunk. But that was robbed from her along with her teeth. What followed after that..." Hope literally heard Steffane's own teeth grinding together and she realized she should say something to defuse this woman's anger, but, damn it, Hope was angry too. She had overheard many conversations between mother and daughter over the months and Steffane had never held back from plunging sharp pointed words into her mother forming a wound so deep it would never heal. Hope took a deep calming breath. "I'm sorry. It was tactless of me to suggest such a thing. Her refusal to eat gets to me too. I'm just...sorry."

Steffane's head dropped lower. "We can't even get Ensure down her anymore."

"And yet you rejected Morgan's PET tube idea."

"Mother's made her decision."

Well! Hope thought that was a comment that certainly had more than one interpretation. But Hope did agree that Ellen has been wrestled into a place where such a decision, to starve herself to death, seemed like the only alternative to her; her prior DNR decision just helping to pave the way. If life was no longer worth living, was it just and/or moral to force someone to keep on keeping on? That was a question that just kept popping up.

On the one hand, Hope felt badly for Steffane, but on the other hand, she felt more deeply that Steffane was getting what she deserved. The sullen woman-child had started a process in motion that had taken on a momentum of its own. She couldn't stop it now if she wanted to; all she could do was witness the horror that her greed had wrought. Hope knew she shouldn't have chastised her, but she couldn't help herself. After Steffane went back to her mother's room to sit with her, Hope left the facility while listening to her stomach grumble. It was too early for lunch yet, but she was ravenous. Watching a person starve herself to death just made Hope hungry, she couldn't explain it; it just was.

Hope's thoughts turned back to when she had first met Ellen. It was in the lock-down psych-ward of a hospital. And as Morgan was never fully forthcoming about things when briefing her on new clients, it took Hope time to gather all the puzzle pieces and put them together into a picture that made sense. And at first, the picture made no sense at all. Ellen had no dementia. She was not psychotic or schizophrenic. She was as sound of mind as anyone Hope had ever met. And yet here she was. It was rage that had precipitated the incarceration. The fact that Ellen was as outraged as a scalded cat and was striking out at anyone who got within range explained why she ended up in the psych ward. Once Hope did start putting the puzzle pieces together, she could not fault Ellen for her outrage.

"Look what Morgan did to me!" Ellen pointed to her healing mouth with both hands.

Hope was completely confused. "What did Morgan do?"

"My teeth. All my teeth have been pulled!" And Ellen began to cry.

"There must have been a problem with your teeth?" Hope questioned.

Between sobs Ellen said, "I'd been to my dentist the week before. He'd just started me on antibiotics for the one tooth that was abscessed. Then this whole mess with Steffane and Morgan."

Hope realized she needed to find out more about what had happened in the case before she was going to be of any help to Ellen.

Ellen's daughter Steffane, as it turned out, had recently been asked by her eighty-two-year-old mother to help straighten out her affairs. Ellen's attorney, who was also her accountant, had recently passed away and Ellen needed to get back on top of things and then find another advisor. In the interim, she turned to her daughter for help.

It was during the process of going through her mother's financials that Steffane discovered to her immense dissatisfaction that her mother had been giving her son, Steffane's brother, thousands of dollars a month for literally years. That she had received none of her mother's largess did not sit well with her and she told her mother in no uncertain terms that the flow of money to her deadbeat brother was going to stop. Ellen begged to differ. The daughter, in an outrage that would be matched by her mother's in a short time to come, was not thinking clearly and proceeded to get a court-appointed conservator involved to oversee her mother's estate, thinking, and rightly so, that such an action would stop the flow of money to her brother.

The fact of the matter is, the court will never say, "No, we don't think we need to be involved." It will always give the petitioner the benefit of the doubt and "take matters into consideration" and grant a temporary conservatorship until things are straightened out. Often, as in cases like Ellen's, the conservatorship is granted just over the estate, but Morgan, of course, never content with handling only the estate, also often managed to get the court to grant temporary conservatorship over the person as well. It was Morgan's gift of gab that sold the judge a bill of goods that was usually to Morgan's advantage.

Hope knew that Steffane had no idea that by trying to save her inheritance from being given away to her brother she had just handed it over to Morgan. And Morgan wasn't about to give it back. There was sure to be nothing left for the daughter when the time came. And when Steffane got her first statement indicating just what Morgan charged the estate on a monthly basis, well, good luck trying to get the court to reverse itself. Steffane had just screwed herself and nothing could be done to fix her faux pas. Beyond that she had also single-handedly sentenced her mother to a hell on Earth as well.

After receiving the power of conservatorship, Morgan's first obligation was to visit Ellen. During that visit, Morgan noted that not only was she furious at having control over her assets taken away from her, she was also in considerable pain. Morgan later claimed that the women had a serious infection in several of her teeth. Things had gone too far, Morgan insisted, so instead of getting a dentist to start repairing the teeth, Morgan arranged to have all of Ellen's teeth surgically removed so she could, at some later time, be fitted for dentures. And it happened quickly. Before Ellen knew it, she was in a nursing home recovering from oral surgery. Twice she was caught hauling ass down the street in the middle of the night in her nightgown and slippers heading for her home. Twice she was picked up and escorted back to the nursing home. When it became apparent that the nursing home couldn't handle this determined woman, Morgan had her locked up in the hospital psych ward.

After her first visit to Ellen, Hope sat in her car trying to get her mind wrapped around what she had just learned. This was probably not the first time a perfectly sane woman had been placed in a psych ward, but that didn't excuse Morgan's decision. Today was actually the first time Hope had been in such a place. After gaining admittance, she headed to the nurses' station to find out where Ellen's room was. On the way she passed one doorway and peeked in when she heard whispering. A woman in a wheelchair was facing the corner of the room fingering her stringy hair that even from a distance Hope could see needed a shampooing. "Shush, the baby is sleeping. Shush, the baby is sleeping," the woman intoned over and over again. She then plucked a few strands of hair from her head and started wrapping them around two fingers. "Shush, the baby is sleeping." Turning from the room, Hope then saw the *dancing woman* doing pirouettes down the hallway. The cliché almost made her snicker. The only thing that stopped her was the realization that this was really happening and that the woman actually was hearing music in her own head and the dance was pretty and not hurting anyone after all. But there was no desire to snicker after her visit with Ellen. Hope was angry and, turning the key and firing up the engine, she decided she needed to let off steam and blast Morgan.

Hope stormed back to the office, brushed past Tanya, and charged into Morgan's domain. Morgan, however, was in court, which was probably a good thing.

Back in the outer office Tanya received the brunt of Hope's outrage. "How," Hope wanted to know, "does someone who was perfectly fine a week ago, someone who had never had a psychological problem in her life, end up in a psych ward?"

Tanya, clearly having spent too much time under Morgan's wing, was showing no sympathy whatsoever. "These people need to realize that at a certain point it's time to pass the baton and let other's take over."

"These people!?"

"You know what I mean." Tanya's voice was defensive.

"Tanya, this woman isn't demented. She is perfectly capable of making decisions. And if her daughter didn't agree with her decisions, too bad."

"Well, the court saw things differently. And if our clients aren't going to be compliant, Morgan needs to take action to make them compliant."

"And yanking out her teeth is going to make her compliant?"

"Everything was infected."

"No it wasn't. One tooth had an abscess and she had a dentist taking care of the situation."

"Not according to Morgan. Morgan had no alternative. Things had gone too far. There was no choice but to pull all her teeth; her health was being compromised." Hope was just shaking her head. "Morgan has to account to the court..."

"Oh stop!" Hope knew the drill. She could see she was getting nowhere, so she turned on her heels to leave.

"Do you want to leave Morgan a message?"

Well, she did, but it was best not to have it in writing. "No." Hope pulled the door closed behind her.

The actions of both Steffane and her boss left Hope feeling rather ill. And having all Ellen's teeth pulled! Hope was appalled. Oh Morgan's reasoning was so convincing, at least to Morgan, that it was for the woman's health and that no other option was available. But Hope knew that on some level removing the woman's teeth had been a deliberate act of showing Ellen who was boss.

Hope slammed her car door and just sat for a moment. Then she picked up her phone and punched in Darling's number. "Hey, there," Hope was glad it hadn't gone to voice mail, "want to meet me at Emilio's for a late lunch?" She glanced at her watch. "Ouch, I mean an early dinner? I can be there in about half an hour."

"It might take me forty-five," was Darling's response.

"Perfect. See you then."

●●●

As usual, Hope arrived at the restaurant before Darling. She told the hostess that a friend would be joining her then ordered a glass of wine. Enjoying the spicy aromas wafting from the kitchen along with the old Frank Sinatra songs in the background, she closed her eyes while sipping the icy cold pinot grigio and tried to relax. Emilio's had such a quaint old-fashioned feel to it. Dark wood paneling, white linen tablecloths, flowers bursting out of a little vase on each table, and the waiters in cute bow ties all combined to make a dining experience here one to remember and want to repeat. Hope drank in the ambience along with her wine and was on glass number two when Darling came breezing in zigzagging around tables making her way toward Hope's booth.

"What the heck are you doing out this way this time of day?" Darling wanted to know. She plopped down in the booth and grabbed Hope's glass of wine and took a long swig.

"Morgan had this client's teeth pulled. Just...yanked them out."

Darling just stared at her for a moment before asking, "And? They weren't, like, rotten?"

"One was abscessed, but the rest were fine. All she needed was some antibiotics, which her dentist had just recently prescribed. And she had the follow-up appointment to have it taken care of on the books when Morgan stepped in and took over."

"Well, it does sound like Morgan went overboard."

"Not just overboard, Darling. Think about the bigger picture."

"What bigger picture?"

"Well, that's what I was thinking about over my second glass of wine. It's the symbolism. The teeth are a primate's most deadly weapon. And we, underneath all our civilized veneer, are primates."

"Well, girl, this is the first time someone name-called me a monkey."

They both chuckled, but Hope wasn't to be deterred. "Shut up and listen to what I've been reasoning out. This is why naturalists tell you not to smile at a primate in the wild. The primate will think you are bearing your fangs and will go on the attack. The teeth can rip, tear, sink into an enemy and cause an enormous amount of damage. To have your teeth removed is to take away your means of self-defense; even if, for the human primate, it's just a psychological defense. It removes not only the weapon but the will to fight, because the person now knows he or she can no longer win the fight."

"Huh huh. And you think Morgan reasoned all this through before doing the deed?"

"Of course not. I'm sure it was all on a subconscious level. At the same time, pulling her teeth was an amazing and nefarious tactic. I mean, we are dealing with a woman who does not have dementia—or any psychosis either for that matter. So first the system strips her of her assets. And then pulling her teeth, well, that stripped her of her one primal defense against the enemy. Talk about psychological warfare in the battle to control people who have wills of their own."

Darling was gently waving her hands in front of her. "Whoa, there, Hope. You are starting to scare me. Pretty soon you're going to be breaking into one of those sixties songs—*We shall overcome*—or some shit like that."

"I would think you would celebrate a person's right to protest something like this."

"Well, of course I do. In theory."

"Theory! Let me tell you about theory. In theory conservatorship, like communism, is a good thing. On paper it all makes sense. But when putting it into practice, like communism, you come to realize it just isn't the best way to handle people. If a person has reached a place in his or her life where he or she can no longer make sound decisions, if that person has dementia of some kind, then certainly, the government and the court system should be stepping in to help. But you have the human factor in play and more often than not greed is also factored into any decisions; so overstepping the bounds of what the court sees as proper is what is now happening. Here with Ellen is yet another client who has had her life stolen from her. And the fact that a citizen of the United States of America can have her life stole from her at the snap of someone's fingers should make the populace sit up and take notice. The fact that this can happen isn't broadcast, so nobody knows it's happening every day. It's scary stuff. Gestapo scary. Even if you think you've protected yourself, you haven't. The big fish eat the little fish, that's the law of nature."

"Here." Darling plucked up Hope's wine glass and proffered it. "You need a swig."

Brushing the glass away, Hope continued. "Don't you get it? The terrifying thing is, if this can happen to Ellen, it can happen to anybody."

"Oh." Darling sighed as she perused the menu. "Your poor little old people."

Hope took a long sip of her wine and said in a considering tone, "In times past elders of the village were revered for their wisdom and sought out when advice was needed. But in modern times, in fact perhaps for the first time in the history of mankind, the village is no longer caring for its elders. Instead they are being drugged into stupors and warehoused until finally — to the immense relief of their families — they die."

Darling put up two crossed fingers like she was warding off a vampire. "I know you like your soapbox, girlfriend, but I need some more libation before I'm in the mood to put up with that."

"Okay, enough shop talk." Hope took another sip of her drink. "Take my mind off all that. Tell me about what's going on with Mr. Derek. Have you given him the heave ho yet?"

"Oh, that Mr. Derek. He keeps sniffing around. He just can't get enough of me, you know. He goes on and on about how guilty he feels, about how he's not going to keep on with me. But then he keeps coming back. That wife of his hasn't given him any in years. So...but he won't divorce her; I need to find me a *new* boyfriend, one who will put a ring on this finger." She waggled her finger for emphasis.

The waiter came by and they ordered an appetizer and more wine. "And for the entrée?" he wanted to know.

"Who knows if there's going to be an entrée," Darling informed him. "Just bring us the munchies and the wine and we'll be happy. And happy customers leave decent tips."

"Yes, ma'am," he said.

"That Derek is so horny all the time. We were having breakfast at the House of Pancakes the other day and he kept wanting me to reach under the table and stroke his fly. What's up with that?"

"So did you do it?" Hope wanted to know.

"Hell no! I told that man, 'Hell to the no' I wasn't going to behave like that in public. I ain't no hooker. Which reminds me. Here we were in my car sitting in this parking lot in Bel Air one night, just talking, you know, and he keeps wanting me to touch him and play with him. Now this place has video cameras all around, plus the security guard kept kind of wandering over toward where we were parked. Well, believe you me, I kept both hands on the steering wheel where that guard could see them. I didn't want him thinking I was giving this ole' white boy a hand job or anything. Sheesh!"

The wine and calamari had arrived and, once again, the waiter asked if they would like to order an entrée.

"How about we split the lasagna?" Hope cocked an eyebrow at Darling. "It comes with a salad. So we could order an extra side salad and we'll be set."

"Good. Got that?" Darling asked the waiter.

"Yes, ma'am."

When the waiter walked off Darling watched him go. "Was he condescending to me?"

"I don't think so."

"Well, I think he was. But, no matter, he has a cute little butt, doesn't he."

"I didn't notice."

"You really are off men, aren't you?" Darling held out her hand, palm up. "Let me see that ring you're wearing." Hope slipped it off and handed it to her. "Humm, interesting band. What's this stone? Topaz?"

"Gold zircon, or something like that."

"Never heard of *gold* zircon. You sure it's not topaz."

"No, I'm not sure. What difference does it make? I bought it for the band anyway. I like its unique design."

Darling shrugged. "It just isn't your color, that's all."

"Well someday when I hit the lotto I'll replace the stone with an emerald. How does that sound?"

"Explain to me again why you are wearing this on your left hand?"

"I don't know. I just thought it would keep some jerk from trying to swoop me up the way Fred did. Like I told you, I need a break from men."

"Amen to that, sister. But not too long a break. You broke up with that Fred Fucker months ago. You don't want to start drying up inside like the Sahara."

"Whatever."

●●●

Hope now recalled that evening with Darling from months ago, and all she had shared with Darling about Ellen. At that time she had just met Ellen and the woman had been able to function and communicate in every way. In the beginning, as week flowed into week, when Ellen first thought she had a chance of getting her life back, she and Hope shared a few long talks. Ellen had been a precocious and independent child. She moved out of her parents' home at an early age and gotten a job as a waitress in a little mom and pop café in Glendale. One day a studio executive was in the café having lunch. He flirted with the pretty teenager and asked her out. Ellen brushed him off. He kept coming back and she kept telling him no. He was a nice enough man, but old enough to be her, well, her uncle. One day he told her they were making a movie about a girl and her horse. It was called *National Velvet* and they needed someone who could ride a horse to be a stunt double for the little girl who was playing the lead in the movie. The exec told her she looked remarkably like this young actress. "You're certainly a couple of years older than she is, but you're tiny. And doubles don't have to be dead ringers." As it turned out Ellen wasn't much of a horsewoman and so didn't get the part of Elizabeth Taylor's stunt double in *National Velvet*. But she had impressed the executive enough that she did go on to do some backup dancing in a few musicals and then later married the man. Ellen had done well. Now she had come to this!

In the beginning, Ellen reminded Hope of a caged lion who stood at the bars of her cage and roared her displeasure. Ellen was nothing if not a fighter. But, ironically, because she was a fighter, the system decided to control her in the only way at their disposal—though medication; this, of course, with Morgan's full sanction. And when Ellen realized all vestiges of her control were being removed from her, she just gave up and stopped eating. Today, such a short time later she had been reduced to a bag of bones in a bed. She even needed help to turn over from one side to the other to prevent bed sores. Early on Morgan had convinced the court that she was mentally incompetent to look after her own affairs. The irony was that at this point the incompetency was due to medications, but no one ever brought that up in court; that if the medications were stopped, Ellen would have been fine. Ellen had no advocates who were working in her best interest.

Hope knew that the history of mankind was replete with examples of those with power crushing those who are powerless. And, AARP notwithstanding, the elderly of this country had become the new powerless. And when the powerless tried to fight back, they were punished in the most insidious ways. If the powerless refused to allow their wills to be broken, they had their teeth removed, or were doped up with drugs, or had feeding tubes inserted through their abdominal walls, or a combination of all of the above.

Her poor clients, they really had no advocates. To hell with their court-appointed attorneys and their court-appointed conservators; they literally had no one who would stand and fight for them and the wrongs being done to them. And the scary part was that more and more people without dementia were becoming victims of this system because a sibling or a child or even a friend was jealous of their assets and just wanted to get his or her hands on the money. It's all greed driven, Hope thought to herself. And, sad to say, Ellen wasn't the only client whose life had been destroyed because of sibling rivalry. Bonnie's had too.

Working for Morgan was like being in league with the devil. But, Hope tried to reason with herself, someone was going to have this job, and she, at least, was trying to make a difference by working from within. But more often than not, she felt like the little Dutch Boy with his finger in the dike. The dike was full of cracks and was about to disintegrate unleashing a tidal wave of horror over the unsuspecting populace. She couldn't do it alone. Well, Boomers, Hope thought, decades ago you succeeded in driving the machine right into the sexual revolution of the sixties and seventies. Maybe today it's time to get back into the driver's seat and, power to the gray-haired people, fix this mess before the impending disaster carries a whole generation away.

When she got home that evening, after visiting Ellen, Hope felt chilled to the bone. It wasn't just the weather, the rain and the wind. It was a visceral ague of sorts. She felt as if her insides were on the verge of crumbling. A cup of hot tea didn't warm her, nor did burrowing under her comforter when she went to bed that night. She could hear the wind whining then picking up momentum until it literally wailed. And Hope shook under her covers not from fear but from shame. She was ashamed that she was so helpless, so unable to do the right thing for her clients. She had recognized Ellen's rage. It was a rage that ebbed and flowed, a rage that waxed and waned, but was always present in one state or another. She recognized it, she had felt it, and she had basically been unable to do anything about it. The wind howled and sounded shrill through the walls of her condo. Hope pulled the covers over her head and found that she was weeping. She realized she was grieving for a woman who hadn't yet died. And as with all grief, there was no way out except through it.

Ellen, like Shirley, slipped away in her sleep. The struggle was over for her, but others like her still lingered on. There were always others who would fill the void.

14

Wendy

"The most satisfying thing in life is to have been able to give a large part of oneself to others."

— Pierre Teilhard de Chardin

Hope had been cruising down Ventura Boulevard heading toward the hospital to see Wren when her phone rang. She pulled over and glanced at the readout before answering. Of course it was Morgan, who else would it be? She put the car in park and answered. "What's up?"

The conversation shook her to her soul. She was to head out to visit three VA-approved nursing homes as Mr. G was going to be moved in to one of them within the next few days. To say Hope was stunned would have been an understatement. "What happened?"

Morgan was all business. "What happened is that Mr. G missed his last appointment at the VA. And *what* was that all about? I'd like to know! He was to go in for blood tests and when that didn't happen, they decided to send an investigator over to the house to see what was what. Apparently the place was a filthy mess as was Mr. G, and it was also apparent that Mr. G hadn't been eating his meals. The VA people are making threats..."

"Wait, wait, wait," Hope interrupted. "Mr. G was in the hospital when he was supposed to go to the VA for that blood test. I called, canceled the appointment, and told them as the hospital was taking blood tests, I'd have the hospital fax the test results over to them so they'd be up to date and save us a trip over there when he got out of the hospital and they said, fine."

"Well, apparently that didn't happen. His VA doctor..."

"She's not a doctor. She's a physician's assistant."

"Whatever. She called the office yesterday in a rage saying that Mr. G was not being brought in to his appointments and was missing scheduled testing etc. She said she'd sent investigators over to the house and you know the rest. I'll have Tanya text you the addresses and you go check out the facilities. Now!" Morgan clicked off.

Hope stared out of her windshield but wasn't seeing a thing. Poor Mr. G had been in and out of the hospital twice in the past month. He was refusing to eat much and had a low-grade fever the source of which had not yet been determined. He was completely bedridden at this point so it had been necessary to procure a hospital bed and have it delivered to the house. That he only had a short time to live was apparent. But promises had been made to both Mr. G and his daughter. He was supposed to be allowed to die at home. And now that was not to be. What exactly had happened? Damned if she wasn't going to find out. Hope shifted her car into drive and pulled out into the stream of traffic. Before heading out to the valley to investigate the VA-approved nursing homes, she was going directly to Mr. G's house for some straight talk.

It was evident that Wendy had been crying when she answered Hope's knock, "You've spoken with Morgan?" Wendy just nodded. "What the heck happened?"

"I don't know, ma'am. Some people from the VA came over yesterday and it was not good. Mr. G had just pooed and I was trying to clean him up, but then the knock on the door, and I left him for a minute to answer it, and then when I got back to him he'd gotten poo poo smeared all over and under his fingernails, and they said I wasn't keeping him clean. I keep him clean, but he'd just pooed, and I hadn't finished helping him when they knocked."

"Okay, okay, I get it." Hope soothed the caregiver who was starting to wax hysterical. "It was just really bad timing all around."

"And he hadn't been out of bed for the past couple of days. And he hadn't finished his lunch. It was still on the plate on the bedside table and they were upset because they could tell he hadn't eaten."

"I get it." Hope spoke softly while mentally kicking herself. She had known Mr. G was nearing the end, and she had intended to speak to Morgan suggesting they get hospice involved. She had only held off because she knew Morgan's philosophy, and that was to avoid hospice at all costs. Now it was too late.

"So what is going to happen?" Wendy wanted to know.

"Apparently that physician's assistant over at the VA contacted Morgan and said either Mr. G is put in a facility or they will be challenging the conservatorship. So Morgan has lined up three places that I have to check out this afternoon. This is going to happen fast."

Wendy mopped her streaming eyes and blew her nose into a handkerchief. "It's all because of Ma'am Peggy, isn't it? She doesn't like us."

Hope didn't want to cast aspersions, but she'd been thinking the same thing. "Some people don't get mad, they just get even."

"Ma'am?" Wendy inquired.

"Never mind."

The sound of mumbled prayers in Hebrew floated down the hallway and out to the living room. "He prays all the time," Wendy said. "He prays to go to God."

Hope sent up a silent little prayer of her own asking that Mr. G's prayer be answered and the sooner the better, because what was about to happen was not going to be good, or nice, or pretty.

Hope looked around the cute little living room — the décor a step back in time — furnished with items Mr. G had made with his own hands. He'd been a fashion designer as well as a furniture maker and owned one of the most upscale shops in the Hollywood area back in Hollywood's glory days when stars were stars — most of whom had been his clients. He'd made things to last and took pride in his work. He was a craftsman, an artisan, a dying breed. He drew strength being surrounded by his own creations, and Hope knew taking him away from his home was the first note in his death knell. She sat on the sofa and brushed her hand over the material. Talking to herself, she said, "He told me this cost him a hundred dollars a yard. And that would have been decades ago." After a moment she said, "I'll just go in and check on him."

Mr. G looked over as soon as Hope entered the bedroom and smiles wreathed his withered face. "Oh thank you, thank you for coming to see me." He was always so happy to see her.

Sitting in the chair by the bed, Hope rested her hand on his forearm. "How are you doing, Mr. G?"

"I want to go to Israel."

"I know you do."

"I want to see Adam and Eve."

"Yes," was all Hope could say.

"I will go to Israel and walk on the holy ground. Do you know that you have to take off your shoes when you walk on the holy ground? I will take off my shoes. Will you take me to Israel before I die?"

Tears filmed Hope's eyes but she refused to allow them to fall. "You have to get stronger before we can take a trip like that," she told him. "You haven't been eating much and so you are not as strong as you should be."

He sighed. "I am not hungry. I'm tired. Not hungry."

"I know."

"I think I want to sleep now."

"Okay." Hope stood to take her leave. "I'll come see you tomorrow."

"Yes, tomorrow you will take me to Israel."

Hope walked over to the coffee table in front of the living room couch and pulled a Kleenex out of the box that rested there. She dabbed at her eyes and turned to look at Wendy. The two of them, in silent communion, shared a moment of pure sadness.

"What should I do?" Wendy broke the silence; she was literally wringing her hands.

"Nothing different. Fix his meals, keep him clean. I'll go check out the facilities and report back to Morgan. Morgan will let you know what happens next."

Wendy stood in the doorway, waving goodbye to Hope, her tears unchecked. It was a very different picture from the first time Hope had seen her in that exact same place.

With a fist pressing down on her heart, Hope made the rounds of the three facilities. Really, no one of them was any better or any worse than the other two. They were all horrible albeit adequate. She sat in her car looking out the windshield toward the last of the three facilities. The first one she had dubbed Auschwitz and the second Dachau. She couldn't think of the name of a third extermination camp, so this last one didn't get labeled. And in fact, this one was in a nice neighborhood. Shade trees lined the sidewalks. And it was far enough away from the main thoroughfares that traffic noise was at a minimum. On the plus side, if Mr. G rallied, this would be a nice area for Wendy to take him for walks in his wheelchair. That is if Morgan was going to keep Wendy on the payroll. That might be a non-issue come to think of it. Some facilities didn't like patients with their own caregivers.

Hope suspected it was because they didn't want ears and eyes around that weren't under their thumbs.

Hope held the phone in her hand, but hesitated calling the office. She knew once the call was made, a series of events would be set into motion that would remove Mr. G from all that was known and comfortable and place him in a sphere of the unknown and the frightening.

A few months before another client, Virginia, had been taken from her home and placed in a facility as she neared the end of her life. Instead of letting her go peacefully she was raced back and forth between the facility and the hospital. And the constant poking of needles to either draw blood on the one hand or provide IV fluids on the other hand had bruised the woman's arms to the degree that they were a deep purplish red from her finger tips to way above the elbows almost to her shoulders. Her paper-thin skin was breaking down from the constant abuse. And each time they put the blood pressure cuff on she cried out in pain when it tightened on her arm. It didn't make sense to keep taking her blood pressure, to keep poking her with needles. What made sense was to let her die in peace, but that was not to be allowed. And what was about to happen to Mr. G was just going to be a variation on that theme.

On a sigh, Hope reached for her phone and called the office to report her findings. Then, with fingers crossed, she broached the subject of hospice. "It really would be the better alternative in this case."

After a little throat clearing Morgan said, "Not in this instance, Hope. It's too late. Beside's he's not about to die. He's made it to ninety-nine years old. There's no reason to think he won't make it to one hundred or beyond."

"You promised he would never be moved into a facility." She knew she sounded petulant.

"I never make promises like that. I simply told his daughter that we'd see about those considerations when the time came. Well, the time has come and that's that."

"But..."

"No buts, Hope. I did honor his daughter's wishes by keeping him at home as long as I did. It would have been much easier if we had put him in a facility years ago."

Yeah, easier for you. But Hope didn't say those words out loud. Instead she begged, "Can't you..." her voice broke. "Can't you let him die at home? It won't be long; he has such a small amount of time left."

She could hear Morgan breathing on the other end of the phone. Morgan finally said, "No, Hope." Morgan's edicts: were they merciful or malicious. Who knew?

Hope's head was bowed, but beyond that...nothing. She didn't even have the energy for tears. She was simply once again reminded of the one immutable universal truth: those with power impose upon the powerless. She asked her boss, "So what's the timeline here?"

"If the one you recommended has a bed, we'll fill it by tomorrow. If it doesn't, I'll probably just go with one of the other places. We have to get him placed ASAP."

Hope sat in her car staring at her phone that no longer connected her to Morgan. How easy it would have been to say, "I quit." But what about her clients? She didn't want to abandon them. She needed to be there to help cushion the blows—which, of course, meant she suffered the blows too. It was a no-win situation, but like Sisyphus, she had no choice but to keep on keeping on.

Dropping her head into her hands she pressed her fingertips into her forehead. The sudden throbbing hadn't given her any warning. "Oh, ouch!" she said out loud, "Please, not these again!"

●●●

"Thanks for getting me in on such short notice, Dr. Lee."

Dr. Lee removed the blood pressure cuff. "Pressure is up, Hope."

"That's probably the pain of the headache; you know pain drives blood pressure up."

"That's true." She glanced at Hope's chart. "It's been over five years since your last migraine."

"I know. I haven't had once since my divorce." *Well, I did have a preview of coming attractions a week or so ago. And now this.*"

"So what brought this one on? Any ideas? You sounded absolutely dismal on the phone."

"Well, I feel absolutely dismal. They're putting Mr. G in a facility tomorrow."

"I'm so sorry to hear that. I know he is one of your favorites."

For a moment the two women remained silent. It wasn't the time for words. Then Hope opened her palms toward the heavens and shrugged. "His God better hurry up and take him, or..." She didn't exactly sob, but shook her head to swallow the sound that tried to emerge from her throat.

"Last time you were here we talked of the stress of your job that it is getting to be too much."

"Yes, the sudden migraine is a kind of tip off.

"So what are you going to do about it?"

"Nothing. At least not for a while. One by one my clients are dying. I've told Morgan I won't take on any more clients. When all my people are gone, I'm going to quit. But until then, I guess I'll need a prescription to kick my headaches." She brushed a tear off her cheek. "I can't believe I had to find a facility for Mr. G."

The doctor placed her fingers lovingly on the back of Hope's hand. "Just remember, Morgan's the asshole. You're just following orders."

"Yep, that's me, just following orders. Which puts me on a par with what's-his-name? Oh yeah, Eichmann. No, your honor, I'm not guilty of all those war crimes, I was only following orders."

"Shush, you're not supposed to be getting yourself riled up during a treatment. Try to think of something nice. Go to your happy place." Dr. Lee simply rubbed Hope's temples first before inserting the needles. "If you could be anywhere right now, anywhere in the world, where would it be? A lush rain forest? A cabana on a sandy, deserted beach? Where?

Hope sighed with her eyes still closed. "I'd be on my balcony on a summer's eve, gazing at the stars and..."

"Are you alone?"

Hope paused and thought a moment, "I guess I am."

"Is that what you really want, Hope? To be alone on your balcony? It sounds kind of arid or even stagnant to me."

Hope paused and thought for another long moment. "You're a sly one, Dr. Lee. Real sly."

"Oh?"

"Don't play coy with me." She had opened her eyes and was looking at her doctor. "You pose tantalizing questions then blast home the zinger. I call those subversive tactics. Real sneaky."

"Shush, now." Dr Lee turned down the lights and left the room, admonishing Hope to go to her happy place.

Her happy place, as she'd told her doctor, was her balcony. So she closed her eyes and imagined standing there looking at the sparkling diamonds in a night sky. It was so big, and wide, and forever—and it was making her really dizzy. Hope opened her eyes and focused them on the ceiling of the treatment room. But still thinking of the night sky she wondered, was there really a God up there somewhere? Or was that just an idea that puny humans thought up all on their own. "Please let Mr. G die tonight," she whispered. "Please, please, please."

●●●

After the treatment Dr. Lee handed Hope a prescription and asked, "Is there anything else going on in your life, other symptoms for example besides the migraine that point to the stress of this job?"

Hope thought a moment and made a self-deprecating grimace. "Well, I find I cry more than I used to—in my car between visiting clients, or at night when I'm home. And I guess, I should admit, I seem to be drinking a bit more than usual: wine and margaritas. Not to the point of getting drunk, just trying to numb myself, I guess."

"So, I'm thinking our next acupuncture treatment should be to give your ole' liver a boost." Hope looked sharply at Dr. Lee who added, "I'm not kidding,"

Hope put her hand on her side. "Great, now my side hurts. Is that where the liver is?"

"Not exactly. Now, before we digressed you were sharing with me things that are pointing to your stress from the job."

"It's time for me to face the facts that I need to change my life. I can't do what I'm doing anymore. It's too hard. But at the same time, I love my people. I can't abandon them."

"Here's a thought. Instead of doing what you do, being a case manager, why don't you become the conservator? Why don't you make the decisions for these people? You know as well as I do that you would certainly put their interest first."

Hope thought deeply for a moment then shook her head. "I can't. I don't want to have to be the one to make decisions like conservators make. I want to help my people, not have them hate me."

"Do they really hate Morgan?"

"I've had some of them burst into tears, literal tears, at the mere mention of Morgan's name. So, yes, I'd have to say they really do hate Morgan."

"So are you just going to...quit?"

"Oh, God, Dr. Lee, part of me wants to quit right now. But, no, I'm not ready to quit yet."

"I think your head is telling you that you are ready."

"Not yet."

●●●

Mr. G, relegated to the nursing home late the next day, was assigned a room and taken there in time to be fed his supper. He was tired, confused, and didn't feel like eating. Wendy helped put him to bed, then left for home. Morgan told her that she would finish out the week working days with Mr. G to help get him settled. Friday her responsibilities would be at an end.

Wendy had been with him for years. A childless woman, Mr. G had filled that void in her life and had become her child. Being a caregiver wasn't just a job to her, it was something that defined her essence. Like so many others in her profession she was from the Philippines which is where she had received her training. Years before she had taken an extensive comprehensive training course consisting of both lecture and laboratory work—then the all-important on-the-job training. In just a few short months she had received her caregiver's license and was good to go. The Caregiver Schools in her country all had to comply with certain standards. There were all kinds of core competencies that had to be realized. And when the students received their certifications, they knew they were qualified to be hired anywhere in the world. Most people in the industry knew if you hired a Philippine caregiver to care for your elderly client, you were getting the best in the business. As far as Hope was concerned most of her caregivers were saints or angels. She could never say enough good things about them.

When Hope stopped in to the facility the following day to see how Mr. G was settling in, for the first time ever, he did not recognize her. He squinted at Hope in perplexity. "Do I know you?" he asked a bit concerned, even fearful, facing an unknown entity.

"Of course you do." Hope hoped her matter-of-fact voice would help sooth him.

He finally said, "Myrna?"

Hope looked over to Wendy, who was unpacking a suitcase and hanging clothes in the closet, and mouthed, "Whose Myrna?"

Wendy shrugged. "He called me that name too. I never heard him say it before."

Hope looked around the room that was right around the corner from the nurses' station. It was generous, lots of space, a huge closet, a bank of windows facing south, and he didn't have a roommate. Yet, while it was roomy, it wasn't homey. The linoleum floor was cold and scarred, the industrial green paint on the walls was unappealing, and there were no pictures or nick knacks on a nearby shelf. "Why don't you bring him some pictures from home?" She gestured to the empty walls. "Something familiar for him, as well as some little doodads for the shelf."

"Yes, ma'am."

"I want to go to bed." Mr. G was sitting in a wheelchair dressed in slacks and a short-sleeved shirt.

Wendy said, "They won't let me put him to bed. They say he cried all last night and they don't want to put up with that. So I have to keep him awake all day long so he will sleep at night."

Hope looked at the old, old man sitting tipped over in the wheelchair staring at a point on the tile floor. He had a small driblet of drool sliding from between his lips and down his chin. That was a first. "And so the nightmare begins," Hope said to herself. It was then that she spied the uneaten breakfast on the tray. She walked over to the plate with congealed eggs and cold, fatty bacon on it and picked up the piece of bacon. "What the hell is this?" She shook the piece of bacon at Wendy.

"His breakfast ma'am." Wendy shrank back when Hope grabbed the plate and marched out of the room.

Hope slammed the plate down on the counter at the nurses' station. Three people looked up. "Which one of you is in charge here?" They looked at one another but no one answered. "None of you. Okay, call someone who is in charge. I'll wait."

A no-nonsense middle-aged woman strode down the hall in Hope's direction. "May I help you?"

"I would like to know why there is bacon on Mr. G's breakfast plate?"

"Is there a problem with the bacon?"

"Only that he's eaten kosher for the whole of his ninety-nine years and there is no reason for him to be served bacon at this juncture."

"He doesn't have to eat it if he doesn't want it."

"Must you put it on his plate? It is kind of an insult. Can you put in his chart that he is allergic to pork so no pork products will be put on his meal plates?"

"It's actually a non-issue."

"What do you mean?

"Because his conservator, actually his doctor, has ordered a stomach tube put in tomorrow. He'll be taken to the hospital first thing in the morning..."

Hope felt as if she had just been sucker-punched in the solar plexus.

"Is there anything else?" The nurse looked at her watch.

"Yes." Hope could hardly speak for the lump in her chest. "The man is a war hero. He was shot six times in the service of his country. He should be treated with dignity and respect."

"They're mostly all war heroes here." The nurse looked at her watch again. "This is a VA-approved facility."

"He's tired of sitting up in the wheelchair; he wants to go to bed."

"No can do, if we put him to bed now he'll sleep all day then be awake all night. He's a screamer, as we discovered last night, and we don't want to have to put up with that. So he stays up until we feel like putting him to bed."

Hope went back to the room that was so unlike Mr. G's nostalgic home and sat with him holding his gnarled hand. "Myrna, you came back."

"Yes, I came back." Hope felt so helpless.

"You look the same." Mr. G had a faraway look in his rheumy eyes. "Time stands still when I look at you."

They sat side by side in silence for a time. After a while Mr. G focused on his hands. He turned them front and back looking at them as if seeing them for the first time. They were an old man's hands, gnarled with swollen knuckles. The fingernails were yellowish and cracked. Staring at them he said, "*I wasted time, and now doth time waste me.*"

Hope gave a surprised little laugh. "You know your Shakespeare?"

"Of course." He smiled at her. "I am an educated man." Then, "I want to go to bed now."

"I know you do."

"I'm so very tired."

"I know. You can go to bed soon," she soothed.

That night on her balcony Hope cursed the universal energy that most call God. She cried until she was weak, then went to bed to toss and turn, and didn't fall asleep until dawn. The phone woke Hope from an exhausting dream. She had been running and running. Whether to something or away from something, she didn't know. "Yeah?" she managed.

Morgan said, "I didn't want to call you last night. Mr. G passed away. The ambulance couldn't get him to the hospital in time."

Hope could only feel that maybe for once a prayer — albeit her angry prayer — had been answered.

●●●

The funeral was not well attended — perhaps because it was a cold and blustery December day or more likely because Mr. G at ninety-nine had outlived all of his cronies. His daughter and grandson were there as were Morgan and Hope and a few others. "Where's Wendy?" Hope whispered to her boss.

"Guess she didn't get the message," was the only answer she got. Hope just shook her head. Morgan probably hadn't even given Wendy the message as to time and place of the funeral. And why wasn't she surprised about that. That Morgan was cheating Wendy out of her chance to share a last good-bye with the man she had taken care of for years was unspeakably cruel. Hope started to say something, then bit it back. She wouldn't disrupt Mr. G's funeral. He deserved a fine and peaceful send off.

The rabbi's sermon was comforting, although Hope listened more to the cadence of his voice than the words. She could hear the traffic from the nearby freeway whizzing by. And the chilling breeze was also a distraction. When the plain pine coffin was placed in the ground, each person in attendance was invited to shovel three shovels full of dirt into the grave. As Hope sprinkled the coffin with clods of dirt she felt as if she was tucking Mr. G into bed for a long restful sleep. "I hope God flies your spirit over Israel before He takes you to Heaven," she whispered to him as her last shovelful of the dirt hit the pine box with a thud. She passed the shovel to Morgan and turned and walked across the grass and toward her car.

She had started the engine to give the heater a boost and was checking her messages when she heard a tap on her window. Morgan motioned for her to roll it down.

"I have a new client you need to check on in the next couple of days. His name is Eugene and..."

"Morgan, I told you no more clients. Give him to Leslie."

"I'm placing him in The Crescenta Arms which is only a couple of blocks from where you live. So it doesn't make sense for Leslie to take him. And what's this about no more clients? I thought you were just in a snit when you told me that. I don't get it."

"Really? You don't get it? Or are you just being obtuse? I'm burned out, Morgan. I've started getting migraines again. I haven't had them for five years, but the stress of the job is just too much. I cry myself to sleep. I can't do this anymore, it just hurts too much."

"Well, then," Morgan's brow creased in thought. "When you do decide to officially quit, I'll be very sorry to see you go. You and I may have philosophical differences, but you are really good at this job, Hope. Maybe you just need a leave of absence and after a rest you'll reconsider your decision to quit."

"Well, one thing's for sure, I won't quit as long as Ann and Wren still need me. And speaking of Wren, I need to go visit her."

"Then I won't keep you longer. Just don't forget to check in on your new client too."

Hope put the car into reverse and as she rolled up the window she said, "Will do."

15

Eugene

"I'll tell 'ya how to stay young. Hang around with older people."
— Bob Hope

Eugene's life had been a fascinating journey. He was a tall, rugged, Hemingway-esque man who wasn't handsome, but he had a presence about him reminding one of Charlton Heston in his prime. Eugene, or Gene to his friends, was photo journalist who had traveled extensively spending most of his time in Mexico. He was also a diver who took underwater photos and had won numerous prizes and awards for his work. He lived hard, played hard, and spent his money as he made it. When he reached his fifties he thought maybe he needed a home base so he did manage to buy himself a small house at the edge of the San Fernando Valley. It was sparsely furnished as he didn't spend much time there, preferring to sleep on a beach in Baja, but as the years passed he spent more and more time at his house, and as most people do, accumulated a houseful of furniture, books, and what-have-you. As he grew older he travelled less often and eventually not at all. He still lived the manly life. He belonged to a gun club nestled in the foothills not far from his home and, never having married, his buddies there were as close to family as he'd ever gotten. Life went on. Interested in politics and well read, he was a man who could hold his own in any conversation. Then, at seventy-three, he had the misfortune to break a vertebra in his back and it was a downhill spiral from there.

At first he thought he'd just sprained a muscle. He rubbed some Bengay on the painful site and knocked back some Jim Beam to help provide some relief. But instead of getting better, things got worse and pretty soon he was almost unable to move. A buddy came by to find a stinking drunk Gene in so much pain that all he could do was grimace. A phone call to nine-one-one brought help and Gene was on his way to the hospital. Back surgery and then rest and recuperation were on the agenda. Not long after the surgery a social worker showed up in Gene's room with a clip board and a sunny smile. She asked questions, he answered them, she wrote things down on her clip board and finally she left. Next thing Gene knew he had received papers saying that his case was being brought before a judge.

Against doctor's orders he showed up in court in a wheelchair pushed by his buddy. The judge examined the papers and looked at Gene over his half-glasses. "Says here you are a risk to yourself."

"How am I a risk to myself?"

"Says here you have thoughts of suicide."

Gene looked only momentarily confused then heaved a breathy sigh. "Your honor, a social worker came to visit me. We had a conversation. During the course of that conversation she asked if I had ever thought of killing myself. Now, be honest, judge. We're men of the world. Who, at one time or another during the course of his life, has not thought of, to use a quaint old-fashioned expression, putting a period to one's existence? It was just a conversation. You know, chit chat. Theorizing. If I'd known she was a literalist, I'd have talked down to her instead of mistakenly treating her like my intellectual equal."

"Hummm. Is that right?" The judge didn't appear to be listening to Gene as he kept scanning the papers in front of him. His next question flew out of the clear blue. "You an alcoholic?"

"What?"

Lifting up a page the judge intoned, "Says here you were drunk when taken to the hospital."

Another breathy sigh. "I had been in considerable pain. I was taking a nip now and then to kill the pain, that's what that was all about."

"Hu huh."

"Judge, that was an aberration. I am perfectly capable of taking care of myself and my affairs."

Once again the judge looked at him over his glasses. "Seems to me that you aren't good at taking care of yourself. The doctor said not to get out of bed yet, and here you are in a wheelchair in front of me. Social worker says you're a danger to yourself." The upshot was that Gene was to be assigned a conservator for the period of time he was to be in rehabilitation for his back.

"I don't want some stranger poking his nose in my business," was Gene's pronouncement.

"Is that right?" The judge glanced over at Gene's buddy sitting next to him. "What about him?" The buddy, being in the right place at the right time, or wrong place as the case may be, was given the job as conservator of the person and the estate until such time that Gene could prove to the court that he was "no longer" a danger to himself.

"How the hell am I going to prove something like that?" The judge ignored Gene's question and pressed on.

Gene wanted to move home during his rehabilitation time but the judge was having none of that. "Judge, any facility where you place me will be overly expensive. If I am sent home, I can just have my housekeeper come more often. Or hire..."

The judge interrupted him. "You'll need more care than a housekeeper can provide." The gavel symbolically came down. Instead of being allowed to go home, he was assigned to a six-pack where he would live until the judge's next review six months hence.

During those six months several things happened. Instead of living at home in a house that was completely paid for, it cost thousands of dollars to keep Gene in the facility. His social security check didn't come anywhere near what the expenses added up to. As a result his meager savings disappeared in record time. Next his buddy, to raise money, sold Gene's three vehicles to pay for expenses. When Gene found that out he was livid. "You didn't think to ask me before selling my stuff?"

"Hey, the judge gave me discretion to pay the bills."

"But all three? You couldn't have left me one car? How am I supposed to get around when I get out of here?"

The buddy just shrugged. "Buy another car."

"With what? You've spent all my money!"

Next thing Gene heard was that his house had been broken into and all his belongings had been either stolen or trashed. Gene listened to his buddy relate this bit of news. He'd already heard it from the cops, that empty houses are targets yada, yada, yada. The cop had also said that interestingly no windows were broken, and the door hadn't appeared to be locked. The vandals/thieves walked right in. The neighbors hadn't heard a thing.

He asked the cop, "You think maybe they did it?"

"Don't have any way of knowing."

"Fingerprints?'

The cop had scoffed. "Yeah, right, on this city's budget?" And that was that.

Now his buddy stood in front of him with his jaw jutting out just a bit. "It happens," was the way he ended the tale of woe about the house.

Gene didn't say a thing, just looked at his so-called friend and waited. It was an interview technique he had perfected during his years as a journalist. People love to fill a void and sometimes they do so with interesting bits of information they might not otherwise say. His friend, as it turned out, didn't feel the need to say anything else. But his body language was telling Gene that there was a lot more to the *break in* story than he was hearing. Gene's thought was: with friends like this no one needed enemies.

Gene had spent the six months not only getting well, but also writing to his congressman and his senator, for all the good that did him, and planning how to reclaim his life — now that he had no savings, no car, and no furniture. But the judge still wasn't convinced that Gene was ready to tackle life on his own.

"Judge, the guy you appointed to oversee my affairs mismanaged things so badly I am now all but destitute. If you had just let me go home, I was doing fine getting by on my social security."

The judge, who never really listened to anything Gene said, removed the buddy as conservator and appointed Morgan Smyth to take over. Morgan was not pleased as this was a guy with no estate to charge. The only thing left to liquidate was Gene's house and he was fighting that tooth and nail. So for now, it was going to be pretty much pro bono work and that was not Morgan's style.

Morgan did move Gene from the six-pack where he'd been stuck for six months and placed him at The Crescenta Arms, a facility that was a hybrid between a nursing home and what they used to call an old-age home. Half the facility housed bed-ridden elderly who needed lots of care; the other half of the facility was for mobile seniors who still had lives of their own. They could come and go as they pleased; some even still had their own cars. Since Gene could get around without a wheelchair now that his back had healed, he was relegated to the wing of the facility where he had his own studio apartment. But he still had to account to, Sasha, the facility's administrator as far as his comings and goings. He also had to sign a paper stating that he would not drink any alcohol while living there. The facility provided three meals a day in the dining room, and if the client didn't like what was being served, there was also a menu that could be ordered from—things like burgers and fries. In addition, there was a Happy Hour on Friday afternoons where the clients could enjoy a glass of wine and crackers and cheese. Gene was told not to attend Happy Hour.

During their first visit, Hope asked Gene how he liked The Crescenta Arms. He exclaimed, "Are you kidding! The place is full of old fogies. I don't belong here."

After that pronouncement, Gene had asked her to pop across the street to the liquor store and get him a bottle of Jim Beam. Hope had literally laughed in his face. "You want to get me fired?"

"What fired? I just want something to wet my whistle."

"You are on record as being an alcoholic," Hope reminded him.

"I am not an alcoholic. I just like a little nip now and then."

"I'm not judging you, Gene. I am just not going to get fired because you want me to bend the rules. Not going to do it."

After a moment he said, "You're probably wondering why I don't get it myself."

"Actually I wasn't, but I can guess. It's right across the street; anyone might see you and snitch on you."

They sat in silence for a while. Gene was the first to speak. "So am I like your other clients?"

"Not in the slightest. Most of them have dementia or Alzheimer's. Because of that, if I want to get the full picture of who they are, I have to piece the stories of their lives together like a puzzle."

"Is that right?"

"With you, I could just ask and you could tell me. I wouldn't have to build a story."

"So...without me telling you a lot about myself, could you come up with a story about me?"

Hope took a good look and observed a man who hadn't shaved in a couple of days; on him scruffy looked good. "Oh, it would have to be an adventure story. Full of action. I can see you bellied up to a bar in some exotic locale with a Mynah bird perched on a swing saying, 'Pieces of Eight' or something like that."

Laughter reached his eyes. "It's parrots who say that."

Hope shook her head. "Too clichéd. I'm sticking with the Mynah bird."

"Okay, Mynah bird it is."

Hope then asked, "So tell me, why didn't you ever marry?"

"Is this a proposal?"

"Not hardly."

"Ouch. Okay, I'll answer your bold question; I didn't want the encumbrances."

"In other words, none of my business. Got it." To change the subject Hope looked at the spine of book sitting next to Gene's laptop. "Spinoza? You're freaking kidding me?"

He laughed at her reaction and winked at her. "Bet most of your clients don't read Spinoza."

"Sucker's bet."

"So my turn to ask you a personal question: why this job?"

"Oh lord, you get right to the heart of things. So many times I've felt the need to bail out of this job. But it's not an easy decision."

"Why?"

Hope pondered before answering, "Because I can't abandon my clients, and because quitting would be the easy way out. But there are times I want out so badly. I'm just so tired of it all."

"I'm hearing defeat. But you wouldn't feel defeated if you didn't feel passionate about this. You need to realize that once you move from passion to action, then the answers will become clear for you."

"That doesn't sound easy."

"Of course it won't be easy, Hope. The attainment of the noblest things is always the hardest. And to reach that end, I think you should start rebelling and go get me that Jim Beam."

"Nice try." She laughed out loud.

Once again she changed the subject. "So tell me this, Mr. Philosopher. I was reading an article by this British physicist who claims time does not exist, or if it does in fact exist, it is not linear. He says all time is 'now.' And all nows exist at once. One of my clients who died a while back, Shirley, she would have said the same thing. So my question is..." She laughs. "I guess I don't know what my question is."

"Your question is: is all time now and if so how is that possible? It was Plato who explained time as a moving picture of eternity."

"So the next question is, what is eternity?"

"It's all the nows rolled up into one."

"And this sounds like a circular argument to me."

Gene laughed. "Now I get to ask you a question. Do you ever think that keeping unhealthy people alive is ethical?"

"Depends on how you are defining unhealthy."

"I'm thinking of all those vegetables in the other wing." He jerked his thumb in that direction. "The ones begging to die. Personally, I think Darwin is probably spinning in his grave. No more survival of the fittest. All that prolonging the life of people who would have naturally succumbed long ago means not letting nature take its course. That, in my view, may very well be abuse of the species."

"And on that note," Hope told him, "I am going to bid you a fond farewell until next time."

"Let me walk you out." Gene was set up to have three-month reviews with the court system to determine if he could move on with his life sans conservator. He knew he needed to come up with a plan. The judge that he'd been assigned throughout this whole horror story was just not listening to him. So step one in his mind was how to get assigned to a new judge. He broached that subject with Hope as they rode the elevator down to the first floor.

"That shouldn't be a problem," Hope encouraged him. "First you need your own attorney. But be wary of any court-appointed attorneys. You want one working in your favor. There are actually a couple who have offices within walking distance of this place."

"Any ideas how to hire an attorney when you no longer have any money?"

"Pro bono?" Hope shrugged.

Gene just waved good-bye and headed back up to his apartment.

In Hope's mind, there were only two good things about The Crescenta Arms. One was that it was less than half a mile from her condo so getting there to visit Gene was a cinch—no freeway gridlock to deal with, no real planning, just pop in and do her job. The second really good thing about The Crescenta Arms was that, in the opposite direction from her condo, it was only a couple of blocks to Joeslito's. Hope had arranged her visit with Gene to be the last of the day. That way, when she was finished, she could then head on over to her favorite watering hole and have a late lunch and a margarita.

●●●

Hope had just put her last bite of chicken enchilada into her mouth when her phone rang. Something clutched at her. Had someone else died? "Yes, Tanya, what's up?"

"Morgan needs you to go over to Sarah's." She proceeded to fill Hope in. Someone had been calling and calling Sarah, and Sarah wasn't answering the phone. So that person called the police and said they needed to go check on her. The upshot was the police were there at the apartment, but the screen doors—both front and back—were locked as presumably were the regular doors and no one was answering the doorbell as well. The cops were ready to force entry so Morgan wanted her to haul ass over there before it went that far.

"Morgan explained to them that Sarah was fine, that she just never answers the phone or the door," Tanya was telling Hope. "But they are insisting they talk to her to make sure all is okay. So Morgan said for you to get over there. ASAP!"

"Okay, call the cops back and tell them I'm on my way." Hope eyed the last third of her margarita. Damn, she didn't dare knock it back if she was going to be dealing with cops. She signaled the waiter, paid her bill, and headed off to do her job.

Parking in front of the building behind the police car she looked up at Sarah's apartment and saw that Sarah had finally answered the summons and was standing on the porch talking to the two police officers. Hope, breath mint in her mouth and briefcase in hand, joined the group, greeted Sarah, and introduced herself to the cops. One cop took Sarah inside the apartment to keep interviewing her in private and the other cop kept Hope out on the porch to talk to her. Separating them as if they were criminal conspirators, Hope thought.

"I see she finally answered the door."

"It took a while," the cop filled Hope in. "She's been telling us that she is really upset with this conservator she has. She wants us to help her get out from under the conservatorship. What does this Morgan do for her anyway?"

Hope explained the situation and her job while surreptitiously taking peeks through the open front door into the living room where Sarah talked to the other cop. After all, Hope thought, Sarah is mine and I don't want this man, hummmm? this really, really handsome man, upsetting her. Multitasking was one of Hope's strong suits, so she was able to keep an eye on Sarah and the cute cop while talking to the other cop on the porch. "I essentially do all the grocery shopping for her and make sure that there is food in the fridge and in the cupboards."

"Yeah, we already checked on the food situation before you got here. We saw she wasn't going to go hungry."

"She's just a loner, doesn't cause any harm," Hope explained to the officer while still scoping out the other officer talking to Sarah, then she frowned and focused on her cop. "Say, how did you know to call Morgan?"

The cop pointed toward Gary's apartment. "The landlord told us about the situation."

"He did, did he?" She wondered why he hadn't just use his key to open the place up and let the cops see that Sarah was fine without calling Morgan. The locked screen wasn't really an issue. There was a tear in the meshing next to the frame right near the inside lock button and all Gary would have had to do was slip a finger in and unlock the screen then use his pass key to open the door. In fact Gary was the one who had slit the screen mesh in the first place so he could get in to check on her when she didn't answer.

The cop was handing Hope his business card with numbers for both the precinct and for his cell phone. "It looks like everything is fine, but if things start to get out of control here, don't hesitate to give a holler."

Hope nodded and slipped the card in her briefcase just as the other cop and Sarah came back out onto the porch. The cops bid them a good afternoon and retreated down the stairs and headed back to their car. Sarah was saying, "I told them to get Morgan off my back."

But Hope wasn't really listening to her. She was watching the cop—not the one who had spoken with her, but the one who had taken Sarah into the apartment. Broad of shoulder, narrow at the hips, taller than the one she had conversed with. He had a very distinguished head of steel gray hair. And no pot belly! Not bad. It was usually firemen who caught her eye, as they were all pretty buff. Cops tended to put on pounds with age. But this one was very nice on the eyes. "Okay," she jerked her attention back to Sarah. "What did you say?"

Sarah just grinned at Hope. "He was kind of cute, wasn't he?" Both the woman chuckled. Then Sarah added, "I said, I told them to get Morgan off my back."

Hope sighed. They'd been over this so many times. There was no way Sarah would go out to get groceries and the local stores did not deliver. But Hope wasn't about to reiterate all that. She simply said, "So what was their reaction to that?"

Sarah shrugged. "I don't know. I think if Charles goes and talks to them that would help."

"Yes, I expect it would," Hope agreed. "Why don't you get him to do that?"

● ● ●

Hope and Faith were lounging out on Hope's balcony gazing at the stars and enjoying a nice, chilled white. Hope was speaking of Gene. "Then he just sort of threw down this gauntlet of sorts."

"To go buy him a bottle of booze."

"Not just that. I think the Jim Beam was symbolic. He was challenging me to look beyond the man-made rules toward what was just and right."

"Oh, I don't think so."

"I do. If I went out and bought him a bottle of the forbidden beverage, it would be symbolic of stepping through a previously closed door. It would be a gesture that said, 'If you can't buck the system overtly, it's time to begin covert action.' The honorable tradition of Robin Hood stealing from the rich and giving to the poor comes to mind."

Faith sighed and shook her head. "Sounds to me like you are trying to rationalize, Hope. Do you really want to play Eve to this guy's Adam and bring him the forbidden fruit? We all know what happened the first time around."

It was Hope's turn to sigh. "I know. I just don't want this guy becoming another Ellen." They enjoyed their wine in silence for a while.

"This really is a lovely spot, sis." Faith's voice was relaxed. "It gives you perspective, it kind of removes you from the madding crowd, it's as close to perfect as there is."

"It is. And the rains this winter have already started greening the hills up again. In another month or so no one will even know there had been a fire in September."

"Time flies. Winter's shot. For all intents and purposes it's already spring." Faith replenished her wine on a contented little sigh, "Between the hills for backdrop and the starry canvas of the sky at night, you really lucked out living here."

"I know. I dreamed about being out here on my balcony the other night. Well, sort of. It was my balcony but it wasn't. And it was me, but it wasn't me. And I wasn't surrounded by the city as I am here. It was in a wooded area with no people anywhere around. So peaceful, not like now." She pointed to the night sky where a police helicopter was speeding by with a searchlight scanning for some perpetrator below. "And I could hear water, like a brook or, no, it was more like waves lapping at a shoreline. Like I said, so peaceful and yet different and...I was out on that balcony nude."

"Oh?" Faith took on a German accent. "Tell Dr. Freud all about it."

"The funny part was, at first I thought I was awake, but I wasn't. It was like I woke up and looked at the clock. It was three and I felt wide awake. I got up and looked out the French doors and there was this yellow wash of moonlight almost turning the night in to day. And the woman was me, but not me. In fact it was as if the woman in Gary's painting had stepped out of the canvas, but at that point wearing a bathrobe. And like I said, there was no city surrounding me. And it wasn't winter," she tugged the afghan she had tossed over her legs up more snuggly toward her chest, "but fall, a New England autumn. It was like this:"

•••

Picture a cool, crisp night in mid September. A barefoot woman stands on the balcony overlooking her backyard looking up at a Full Moon. Her home is in a rural, isolated part of the community, so she is completely alone—a solitary observer of the surrounding woods and the heaven above.

Chirring night sounds had stopped when she first came out of the house, but after a short time, the soft sounds recommence. She absorbs the night. The bay, not far away, adds a hint of moistness to the air. Closing her eyes, she turns her face upward and at first just feels the light of the Moon kiss her. Slowly she opens her eyes and looks at it; the mysterious orb so much more powerful than people really suspect. Round, huge, glowing golden and rich, splashing down light reflected from a powerful life-giving Sun, the Moonbeams drift on the soft sea-misted air. Wearing nothing beneath her lightweight bathrobe, she slides it from her shoulders letting the garment pool at her feet. Gentle invisible fingers of the night air caress her breasts, nipples, thighs. She has never done this before, stood outside stark naked. She stands motionless absorbing sensations that are new, yet also somehow familiar. Skyclad, she slowly raises her arms in supplication to the Goddess that is the Moon, cupping her hands so they may be filled with the soft dancing light. Little does she know that one Full Moon away, a mere twenty-eight days in the future, her life will be forever altered.

●●●

"Wow!" Faith was looking at her sister who had been relating the dream in an almost trance-like voice. "How is her life going to be altered?"

Hope shook her head. "I don't know."

"Do you think it was some kind of prophetic precognitive thing?"

Again shaking her head. "I doubt it. I mean it was fall in the dream and a month from then is still going to be fall or early winter. And it's now almost spring. So, no, I don't think anything precognitive was going on."

"God, you are so literal!" was Faith's exasperated rejoinder. "Open up a little bit like that woman in the dream was opening up." Hope just made a rude sound with her lips. "Okay, change of subject, back to that yummy cop you were telling me you met. Was he wearing a ring?"

"Give me a break, Faith. Why would I have even looked to see if he was wearing a ring? He just had one of those eye-catching bodies is all. Plus those sexy blue eyes."

"I was just saying..."

"I know what you were saying. I'm taking a hiatus from men. Or did you forget that part?"

Faith's response to that was to reach over and tap the business card that sat on the patio table next to the open bottle of wine. "Call his partner and ask if the guy's married? Also ask his name while you're at it."

Inhaling the sip of wine she just taken, Hope began to sputter. When she cleared her throat she said, "Yeah, like that's going to happen."

"Do it!" Was Faith's command.

"Did anyone ever tell you that you are a pain in the ass — sideways? I'm not going to..." She reached out and snatched up the card just a nanosecond before Faith got her hands on it. "And you're not going to butt into my business."

"Party pooper," was Faith's only observation as she picked up the bottle of wine instead and topped off both glasses.

16

Edna

"Big sisters are the crab grass in the lawn of life."
—Charles M. Schulz

Things had not been going well for Ann. The radiation treatment for the skin cancer on her scalp had been a success. There were no more growths; nor was there any hair on her head, although the doctor claimed that would grow back. No, the cancer was beaten, but the radiation had taken its toll on Ann; she had been completely sapped of energy. And not being the most energetic person to begin with she had begun to fade away, slowly at first then more quickly as the days and weeks passed. She was, once again, back in the hospital for the third time in two months. Each time her hospital stay was longer. She'd contracted a viral pneumonia along the way and had been unable to shake it. She was so congested that she needed a suction-tube treatment several times a day just to get the phlegm out of her system. Lately the container holding the suctioned material was laced with bloody strings. The prognosis was not looking good. It was the opinion of both Lucy, her caregiver, and Hope that Ann was not long for this world.

Whenever Hope would visit her, Ann would look at her with pleading eyes and whisper, "I want to die."

A helpless Hope patted her hand and made chit chat that resulted in Ann's closing her eyes and feigning sleep. But in truth, all Ann wanted to do was sleep. And that meant she didn't want to eat, and that gave Morgan an opening. Morgan was of the opinion that it was time for a PET tube insertion and Edna, Ann's until recently estranged sister, was one hundred percent in agreement with that.

Hope had called Morgan and cut straight to the chase. "Ann does not want to be hooked up to one of those devices to linger. She just wants to die. She's ready to go. Why can't you respect her wishes?"

"Edna wants..."

"Who cares what Edna wants? You are the conservator..."

"That's right, Hope, I'm the conservator, and if Ann doesn't start eating, we'll take measures to feed her. Period."

"What if Edna comes around and decides she's willing to abide by Ann's wishes?"

"Then, I'd have to think about it. But that won't be happening. Edna wants us to do everything in our power to keep Ann alive."

Yes, Hope thought, power being the operative word.

Edna had suddenly shown up on the scene the day of Ann's first radiation treatment months ago and had been a thorn in Hope's side ever since. Hope had gotten to the hospital early the day the treatments were to commence, and made sure all the paperwork was filled out. Of course paperwork was a misnomer as everything was done on computers now-a-days. Regardless, she got all the documentation in order. She had copies of the client's insurance cards and other necessary papers in her brief case, so everything was ready when Ann arrived with Lucy pushing her in the wheelchair. The minute Hope saw them, she knew something was amiss. She had never seen Ann looking so pale.

"Ann? What's the matter?" Hope knelt next to the wheelchair and took the ashen woman's hand."

"My sister."

Hope could barely hear Ann's voice. "Your...sister?"

"Yes," came the desperate whisper. "Edna."

"What about her?" Hope wanted to know.

"She's here."

Hope looked around the waiting room and didn't see anyone. "Here?"

"She's coming. They're parking the car." Lucy began to fill in the blanks as Ann could barely talk.

It turned out, Ann did have one actual bona fide family member still living, an older sister. But Ann and her sister, Edna, didn't get along. In fact, Ann had literally paid Edna off to go away and never come back into her life: a cool million dollars and a one-way ticket to Miami. That Ann was completely and utterly through with Edna was the one small satisfaction of her life.

But apparently Morgan had notified Edna that Ann was about to undergo radiation treatments for her cancer and the woman flipped out.

She hadn't even been told about her sister's cancer to begin with and now this! She jumped on the first plane to the west coast and the pot then began to bubble, bubble, and boil.

When Edna walked into the waiting area with Julie and Charlene, all it took was one look for Hope to know that this prim woman was going to try to steamroll all of them. And, in fact, that was exactly what happened. Even Morgan kowtowed to every one of Edna's demands. She had been furious that no one had kept her in the loop to this point regarding her baby sister's cancer and she never failed to express her displeasure over that.

Julie had sidled over to Hope that first day while Edna hovered over her sister. "She's making Franklin pay for everything," Julie whispered. "Her airfare, her hotel room, her rental car."

"Why doesn't he just refuse? Maybe she'll go home."

Julie sniffed. "She won't go home. Edna's going to stick like glue until the bitter end now. Money, you know. She knows that Ann is loaded and as the only living relative, she figures she's going to get it."

"Is she?" Hope wanted to know.

"No, she was paid off years ago and written out of everything. It's all legal. The business goes to Franklin. Period. But no doubt she'll play on Ann's sympathy and get a chunk of something before it's over."

"Leach," Hope whispered.

"What are you two whispering about?" Charlene's whisper had them turning and including her in the conversation.

Things had devolved from that point on. Hope began to think of Edna as the *wicked witch from the east* and now the more so as she and Morgan together were conspiring to have a PET tube inserted into Ann's abdomen.

●●●

Sunday afternoon found Hope flat on her back on her living room floor. She was stretched out on her yoga mat listening to *Phantom of the Opera* and doing gentle spinal twists. Her lower back had started to protest over the number of hours she spent sitting in the car going to and fro from client to client. So rather than risk her back giving out on her, she had started making yoga a part of each day. Her flexibility had greatly improved in the first week and by now she was feeling as fit as could be. When her iPhone rang she knew it couldn't be ignored; any one of her clients might be needing her. Releasing her stretch she reached for the phone she'd placed nearby.

"Hope, Franklin. I hate to bother you on a Sunday, but it's important. Do you have a minute?"

"Of course, what's up?"

"I was just speaking to Morgan. Apparently he and Edna had a pow-wow and he's decided to go ahead with this stomach tube thing. He wants to schedule it for this week."

"For Pete's Sake!" Hope stood up in one fluid movement and started pacing through her condo.

"Don't they realize that this woman has simply wanted to die for over a decade now? Why not just let her go peacefully? Ann doesn't want this crazy feeding tube. She just wants to be left alone."

"You know as well as I do that her wants don't count when there is a conservatorship in place. And now that Edna has Morgan's ear..." Hope just sighed as her sentence trailed off.

"Can't we stop them?" Franklin's question had a hopeless ring to it.

Once again Hope sighed into the phone. "Not likely."

"There are times I wish we'd never found her, after she'd taken the pills." Franklin's voice nearly cracked. "It's been a horror story ever since; if I'd only known then what I know now."

Hope stood looking out the French doors beyond her balcony to the hills. The drizzle spitting from the sky mirrored her mood. She was about to reiterate to Franklin that no, there was nothing they could do to stop the process, when a ray of sunlight broke through the clouds and a rainbow shimmered over the hills. "Damn it! Let's try," Hope told him. "I'll meet you at the hospital tomorrow morning and we'll have a meeting with Edna and Lucy, you, me and whoever is there—an intervention of sorts. We'll see if we can get that wicked sister to realize Ann doesn't want a feeding tube."

"Morgan? You going to invite Morgan to this meeting?" Franklin asked.

Hope made a rude sound. "Not a chance," was her response. She knew Morgan was going to end up crucifying her, but she had to try to stop this madness.

On Monday the sun had won the battle and had completely chased yesterday's clouds away. When Hope arrived at the hospital the place was busy and crowded as usual with nary a parking space to be found. After driving around and around, she finally found a spot in the bowels of the parking garage. She had to squeeze in next to a concrete pillar that helped support the upper level from crashing down on the level below. As it was, she was barely able to get out on the driver's side because the car next to her had hogged over the line and was partially in her space. "Probably a bed hog too," she muttered as she squeezed out the door.

Franklin was pacing in the hospital corridor when Hope arrived. Together they peeked through the doorway into Ann's room. Edna, as usual, was hovering over Ann. Lucy was holding a basin while the bedridden woman urped something up from the depths of her being into it. Lucy looked over at Hope and just shook her head. To add to the mix, a young on-call doctor showed up to do his rounds. Franklin took the initiative and invited the doctor to join them for their meeting in the lounge. He checked his watch and said, "Sure, I have a few minutes." Hope, Lucy, Edna, Franklin, and the doctor all exited the room and headed to the lounge. Along the way, the social worker got wind of something interesting in the air and she joined the group.

Franklin, accustomed to being in charge as he ran a multimillion dollar business, started the meeting. He expressed his feeling about the situation. "I've know Ann for years, decades. She is one of the most important persons in my life, and I know her as well as I know myself. She would not want to be hooked up to a feeding tube. She has said as much many times. I just can't respect going against her expressed wishes."

When it was Lucy's turn to speak her voice cracked with emotion and unshed tears. "I love Ann. I have been with her over ten years. She is so unhappy and so miserable and she just wants to be released. She doesn't want any tube. She doesn't want..." And the tears broke through and ran down her cheeks.

"I can't believe you people!" Edna was full of wrath and fury. "I can't believe what you are saying. This is my sister! MY sister! I won't lose her. I'm not ready for her to go. She's younger than I am. I'll do everything in my power to keep her alive."

The social worker looked at the doctor, who cleared his throat and said, "Have you been listening to what everyone is saying, Edna? They are all saying what Ann wants and what is best for her based on that, her wants. All I am hearing from you is I me and my. It's all about you and not about Ann. Maybe you should think about that before making any decisions here."

Edna stubbornly shook her head. "I won't allow her to die. She gets the feeding tube."

"Edna," Hope began, "Ann has explicitly expressed in writing that she wants no extreme measures at the end of life."

"This isn't the end of her life."

"Oh, Edna," Lucy's voice pleaded, "you are here every day. You know it is."

"It isn't! Beyond that, she has a conservator who can override her," she made little quotation marks with her fingers, "*expressed wishes*. We all know that Morgan is the one who makes all ultimate decisions regarding Ann's person."

Hope, still in fighting mode, said, "She's miserable now, Edna, the insertion of this tube will make her even more miserable."

"You don't know that. You can't know something unless you experience it. And you've never experienced it."

Hope had to acknowledge that touché but she stood her ground. "Nor have you."

"I know my sister."

Hope stopped herself from saying, "No, you don't."

Lucy was shaking her head sadly. Her tongue made a little "tech, tech, tech," sound behind her teeth.

Hope knew better than to argue further, but was thinking that one of her own sisters didn't know her any better than Edna knew Ann. And she sure would never want Charity trying to take control of her end-of-life situation as Edna was doing in this case.

When the meeting broke up everyone except Edna left the lounge. In the hallway Hope turned to the doctor before he got too far away and asked, "It sounded like you were on our side in there. Would you be willing to tell Morgan that the PET tube is not in Ann's best interest?"

He pulled on his upper lip before answering. "There are...guidelines in place, and if the Conservator and the next of kin think it's the best decision..."

"Even if it flies in the face of every bit of common sense?"

He reached out and gave Hope's upper arm a friendly little squeeze before heading on down the hall to look in on his next patient.

Franklin lingered in the hallway with Hope and Lucy. "Why is it that the people who care the most about her aren't allowed to honor her wishes and make the decisions?" Franklin's question was basically rhetorical so there was no need to answer it.

Feeling something prickly between her shoulder blades, Hope looked behind her. Edna was standing in the doorway of the lounge glaring down the hall at her. If a look could scorch, Hope would have been beyond burnt. Then, once she had Hope's attention, a smirk slid over her face and, cell phone in hand, Edna punched in some buttons.

"Oh, oh," Hope told Lucy and Franklin. "Looks like little miss tattletale is calling Morgan. I'll probably be getting my own call in a little while."

"Will Morgan be angry with you?" Lucy worried.

"Yeah, Morgan will pretty much hand me my own ass. But I had to try."

"Yes," Franklin agreed. "We had to try."

While Edna stood in the doorway of the lounge on the phone, Hope popped in to see Ann. She took the cool hand and said, "Hey."

Ann's eyes fluttered open. "Hey," she whispered back.

"How you doing?"

"I've been better." Hope just nodded. "Have you got yourself a new boyfriend yet?"

"No, not yet."

"Better hurry up. You're not getting any younger."

Hope leaned down and kissed Anne's cheek. "You are the most exasperating woman I have ever met, and I love you dearly." Suddenly tears sprang to her eyes and when one fell on Ann's arm, Ann just shook her head.

"Stop crying and go play on the freeway," Ann whispered as she patted Hope's cheek with a clumsy hand then she closed her eyes signaling she wanted to be left alone.

•••

Hope slipped into the silent hospital chapel and sat in a pew feeling the chilly wood against the back of her thighs. She wasn't really praying, just thinking of all her clients. In the face of the immense system they were what—peasants, peons, victims, collateral damage? Poor Ann, she had wanted nothing to do with her sister to the degree that she had paid her a million dollars to get her out of her life. And now said sister was calling all the shots.

Once again her thoughts turned toward Charity. What a horror story it would be if that woman were to be the one to call the shots for Hope. What right would that woman have to dictate...and yet, Hope knew, that's exactly the type of thing that controlling Charity would do. She decided she and Faith had to get together and get some legal documentation in writing that would prevent that eventuality. Maybe that's why this was happening, to let her know it could happen to her. Oh Lord, she felt so sad and so weary. She had been oscillating between rage and depression over Ann's situation for so long. At this moment the fiery rage was banked and the depression tiptoed to the fore. Tears stung her eyes, but she refused to let them fall.

She crossed her arms on the back of the pew in front of her and rested her head on them. She let her mind go blank and might have dozed, she wasn't sure, but a small noise had her looking up. At first it seemed like no one was there, then she saw him—a young priest or at least she assumed so as he was wearing the clerical collar. She sat up straighter and he came and sat beside her.

"Are you alright?"

"No, not really."

"Is there anything I can do?" His voice was soft and inviting.

"Is there a saint who protects the elderly?" Hope wanted to know.

He looked thoughtful for a moment. "It would probably be Saint Anthony of Padua."

"You sound like you aren't sure."

"Well, he's the saint who is most particularly concerned with the poor and the oppressed and thus, I would make the educated guess that that includes many of the elderly."

"Ah," Hope tried to smile at the man. "A multi-purpose saint?"

He smiled back at her. "Is this elderly person you are concerned about here in the hospital? Stupid question, huh?"

"Actually there's more than one. I have several elderly clients. One here who is my immediate concern, but others as well. One in particular is my pet, Hector. His wife recently passed away and when he, in his depression, started refusing meals, my boss, Hector's conservator, ordered him to be put in a facility and had a PET tube, a feeding tube, inserted so he could be force fed. Now my boss is making the decision to do this same thing to my client here in this hospital, and it's not the right decision for her. It's hard."

"It sounds like you carry the burden for many."

"Yes, I do."

When her phone rang, Hope excused herself and exited the chapel before answering. She didn't even have to look at the readout to know it was Morgan. All efforts had failed—Ann would be subjected to a feeding tube. "You are a loose cannon, Hope. You can't keep flying off the handle. You have to work within the system as I do. I do my best, you know. I am doing..."

"Yeah, I know, God's work. If you actually believe your own propaganda, Morgan, if you actually believe you are doing something noble then heaven help you."

"No, heaven help you if you step out of line again, Hope. The buck stops with me, not you, and you need to remember that."

"She's not out of her mind like most of your clients, Morgan. She should be allowed to make her own decision."

"Not according to the courts."

"She will be so angry with you. She won't be able to bear it."

"People are never given more than they can bear."

"Oh for Christ's sake! Do you even hear what you are saying? Visit any hospital or psych ward and tell me that again. That sort of pronouncement is pure nonsense and you know it." When Morgan didn't respond she added, "Just because you can do it doesn't mean you should do it."

"What?"

"Didn't you ever take an ethics course in school?"

"Probably."

"Do you understand that sages and philosophers say that harming others is worse for the person who does the harm than it is for the one suffering?"

"And your point is?"

"That your profession, unrestricted by moral obligations, turns a conservator into a tyrant."

"I'm not doing harm, Hope. I'm the last best hope for our clients. Ann will have the PET tube inserted tomorrow. End of discussion." The arrogant tone of Morgan's voice reignited Hope's rage, but she had nowhere to focus that rage. She hit the end button hanging up the phone and stalked off toward the elevator.

The PET tube was, well, one of Morgan's pets. Morgan loved the simplicity of it; the way it enabled control over clients in the most basic way. When Morgan had wanted to have a PET tube inserted in Wren when she had started to fail, Hector had not allowed it. Morgan might have had conservatorship over Hector's wife, but as the husband the doctors had taken Hector's side. Something Morgan would neither forget nor forgive. So when the opportunity arose, he jammed a PET tube through Hector's gut. And now with this new opportunity to have a PET tube inserted in yet another of his clients, Morgan would not be thwarted. In this instance the next of kin, Edna, and Morgan were on the same page; unfortunately, Ann would suffer the consequences.

Hope hated the fact that for the most part capitulation was her clients' only option. They were old, worn out, tired, ill and most had some degree of dementia. They could no longer fight their own battles and rare was the person who would take up the sword for them. Certainly not their conservator. It was not a cliché to call death a blessing for most of her clients. But the motif of death as the grim reaper pales in comparison to a conservator's control over prevention of a natural death. Talk about sacrificial lambs who were lead to the alter of medical science's intervention only to be held there in limbo for years waiting for the scythe to finally fall and release them.

As she waited for the elevator, Hope glared out of the third-story window of the hospital at the nearby hills. She felt her blood boiling and tried taking a few deep breaths to calm herself but she was too angry about Morgan's ruthlessness, riding roughshod over the wants, needs, and desires of the client. Stepping into the elevator, she jammed the down button so hard she was surprised she hadn't punched a hole in the wall. Fury continued to swamp her as she stormed out of the elevator that swished open into the lower level of the parking garage. She plowed right past the person waiting to get on not even bothering with an apology or an excuse me. A primordial anger pumped through her system as she charged between two rows of parked cars then stopped and looked around trying to recall just where she had parked; she had no idea where her Honda was, plus she couldn't even see a damned thing. That's what happens when one goes from bright daylight to a dim underground garage, plus she was still so angry she was literally seeing red. God! She just wanted to beat someone to a pulp. Preferably that someone would be Morgan Smyth. Damn! Where was a punching bag when you needed one?

"Let's have the purse and the brief case, lady." That snapped her back to the present.

A mugger stood in front of her with knife at the ready, and a quick glance left, right, and behind her, revealed to her that they were the only two around. Adrenalin rushed through her system, but fear was not the emotion that accompanied it. The thought in her head was singular and focused, "Thank God, someone to take it out on." And before she knew it, some muscle memory from her judo and karate class way back in 1968 took hold. She kicked out at her opponent's wrist, and was completely satisfied to see the knife sail out of his hand and clatter on the concrete.

"You want a piece of me?" The wrath in Hope's eyes was also written across her features as she threw her brief case at him and started charging. The thief's own eyes widened in complete shock that this fierce woman in a business suit would presume to take him on. Hell, maybe she was a cop or something. The brief case barely glanced off his shoulder when he turned to run. Ironically, he was so startled, and in such a hurry to escape the angry, screaming banshee, that he didn't bother to look where he was going. He ran smack into a concrete pillar separating the two parking levels knocking himself right out. Hope stood over the unconscious man while punching in nine-one-one on her phone.

"You Idiot! You Moron! You Fucker," she screamed at the prone man, and kicked him in the ribs for good measure. "Ouch!" Funny, this kick hurt her foot worse than the first one when she disarmed the assailant. Feeling something warm and sticky between her toes she looked down. Well, hell! She had on her open-toed shoes, and it looked like the knife had cut her when she kicked it out of the bastard's hand. The sound of the sirens brought her back to herself, and she looked up from her dripping toe. The garage seemed even dimmer than before. It wasn't until the police car pulled up to her that she fully realized what had actually happened. The sudden spots in front of her eyes announced that she was about to faint. As the cops got out of their car, she sat right down on the concrete, crossed her legs and dropped her head into her lap.

It didn't take long to cuff the perpetrator, who was slowly starting to come to, and to stuff him into the backseat of the squad car. Hope's slow and deep breathing helped chase away the spots in front of her eyes and soon she was pretty sure she wasn't going to pass out or throw up. "Whew," she said as she wiped a hand over her sweaty brow, "that was close."

"We have to stop meeting like this." Hope looked over at the officer who squatted down beside her and recognized him as the cop she had spoken to on Sarah's porch not so very long ago. His partner, with the sexy blue eyes, was standing nearby looking down at her. The first cop asked, "Can I help you up?"

"Better not. Not yet." Hope smiled a wan smile. "I think I'd better get my equilibrium back first."

The other cop approached and sat next to her on the concrete floor crossing his legs in what they used to politically incorrectly call *Indian style*. "Why don't you tell us what happened?"

She took her time filling them both in on the assault.

Sexy blue eyes said, "I'm surprised you didn't pull a hamstring."

She laughed. "Probably thanks to the yoga stretches I've been doing."

When the guy in the back of the squad car started yelling at the trio, the first cop excused himself and went over to talk to the suspect.

Sexy blue eyes said, "Better now?"

Under normal circumstances, Hope hated looking foolish but right now she didn't care. Sitting there on the cold concrete, she tried to act blasé — as though fighting off an assailant was an everyday occurrence. "Yes, things are no longer...blurry or woozy."

"Why don't you let us help you back upstairs? They'll be able to take care of that cut on your toe."

"No, thanks. I'm not going in there; it's not a big deal."

"I think you should."

She simply shook her head.

"Why?"

"Because I don't have any insurance that's why. They'll charge me two thousand dollars in the emergency room just to slap a bandage on the cut, and I can do that at home for free."

The cop cupped her shoed foot in his hand and inspected the wound through the open-toed peek hole. "Pretty pink polish."

She smiled and said, "Say that three times real fast." At his little frown she continued, "You know, all those P's. The alliteration. Never mind."

"Yeah, I got it." He then said, "You might need a couple of stitches." When her answer was an exasperated sigh he added, "Not to mention a tetanus shot."

"Perfect." Hope, whose phone was still in her hand, punched in Dr. Lee's office.

The doctor answered on the second ring. "I'm with a patient now, Hope. Can I call you back in a few minutes?"

"Sure, Dr. Lee, thanks." Hope clicked off and looked at the cop. "When she calls back, I'll set up a tetanus shot. Satisfied?"

"You got right through to your doctor? Just like that?" The amazement in his voice made Hope smile.

"Not all doctors are on the payroll of the machine."

"Well, time to get that guy booked." Sexy blue eyes stood, stretched and held both hands down to Hope to help her up.

Taking his hands she noticed he didn't have a ring. Feigning nonchalance, she brushed the grit from the concrete floor off the backside of her skirt and asked, "Are you married?" He looked at her with a raised eyebrow. "I mean I noticed you weren't wearing a ring."

At that he looked pointedly at her ring. "No, I'm not married. What about you? I noticed you were wearing a ring."

Hope wiggled the ring finger of her left hand. "No, it's just for show."

"Ah."

It looked like he was waiting for her to finish what she'd started. "So what do you say to having dinner with me some evening soon?" She handed him one of her business cards.

Without glancing at it, he said, "How about I give you a call?"

"You do that. But first, tell me your name, so I'll know who it is when you call."

"Cliff."

"Short for...?

"We don't go there."

She grinned. "As in the big red dog?

Laughing he repeated, "As I said, we don't go there."

"Okay, Cliff. I'll await your call." They smiled at each other then got into their respective vehicles.

●●●

"Aren't you going to say, ouch?" Dr Lee pulled the needle out of Hope's flesh and once again swabbed the area with an alcohol-soaked cotton boll.

"Ouch."

"That's better."

"I'm just glad the toe didn't need stitches." She looked down at her nicely bandaged foot.

"You lead an exciting life, girlfriend. I didn't realize taking care of the elderly could be so dangerous."

"You have no idea."

"So tell me. What don't I have any idea about?"

"Morgan just makes wrong choice after wrong choice. It just is so... wrong."

Dr. Lee asked, "What is it that makes Morgan's actions right or wrong?"

"It's hard to explain."

"Haven't you ever wondered how and why so many people have lost sight of the fact that our choices define who and what we are?"

"Morgan doesn't care about that. Our clients die and...God, death, it's so final. I've really had death rubbed in my nose these past few weeks, four clients and counting."

"Pretty soon you won't have any more clients. What then?"

"There's always more where they came from. But, breaking news, I did tell Morgan I don't want to take on any new clients...but he gave me a new one last week anyway."

"Who?"

"A guy named Gene. Would you believe he's younger than Ross! God! A client younger than my ex."

"And? Is this new one demented?"

"Hardly. He's the sanest man I've basically ever met. Life just tossed him a grenade and he unfortunately caught it with both hands. Luckily he won't be dying soon. It's Ann and Hector that I'm all messed up about."

"Is it the finality that disturbs you?" Dr. Lee wanted to know. "Maybe you need to determine where eternity fits into your schematic. Some of the finest minds throughout time have speculated that death, the seeming final event, is in fact not the final event in the soul's journey."

"Yes. Those age-old questions..." Hope mused.

●●●

That night, bundled up in her bathrobe, Hope stood on her balcony breathing in the chilly night air. She felt different. Somehow lighter. She'd had her rant and managed to purge something out of her system in the process. Instead of feeling stuck, she felt as if something was starting to move, just a little, but movement nevertheless.

Her conversation with Dr. Lee that afternoon had started her thinking, once again, about moral obligations. Yes, she was firmly of the opinion that those who cared for the elderly had a moral obligation. Easier said than realized. The landscape revealed a moral diversity. There was right and there was wrong, and the shades of gray between those two poles rendered the treatment of one client *not completely wrong*, and the treatment of another client *okay*, and the treatment of yet a third client *the best it could be under the circumstances*.

It was the fact that her clients had their choices taken from them that she saw as the most grievous wrong. Oh, not all her clients, not the ones who had dementia or Alzheimer's. But the ones like Ann or Hector who were of sound mind. Why couldn't they make up their own minds? No, it wasn't that they couldn't make up their own minds. It was that the choice to make up their minds had been taken from them. Philosophers and theologians all taught that life was a gift and living it to the fullest was a person's responsibility. But how did aging and dying factor in to living the well-lived life? And especially, what happens when the system refuses to let you die in your own way? Refuses you let you die like a warrior symbolically falling on your own sword or knocking back your own potion of hemlock. Should Ann have been enforced to live a decade of life against her will? Should Hector be denied his choice to stop eating so he could join his beloved departed sooner rather than later? Why weren't they allowed to make their own choices?

17

Hector

> "It is, I believe, the greatest generation any society has ever produced."
>
> — Tom Brokaw

Hope sat by Hector's bed while he slept. Every now and then she would reach out and pat his hand. What a sad twist of fate it was that had landed Hector in Morgan's clutches. A year ago he was as spry and vibrant a ninety year old as anyone could imagine. But watching his beloved Wren fail and slowly die over the course of months had taken its toll. After the death of his wife of sixty-six years he had fallen into a depression and lost his appetite. It wasn't long before Morgan had taken Hector from his home, institutionalized him, and gotten the inevitable PET tube inserted. Hector, a shell of his normal self, refused to get up to exercise and slept most of his days away. Hope was fairly certain it wouldn't be long before the predictable pneumonia would settle in to his lungs and drown him. At least Morgan hadn't fired his caregiver, Mary Lou. She and Hope spoke in undertones so as not to disturb Hector.

"Does he have any visitors?" Hope wanted to know. "I mean, besides me?"

"Only his brother calls him once a week. Nobody else."

As with so many of her clients, Hector had outlived the majority of his friends and family. And what family he did have lived so far away: one brother in San Diego and a niece in Minneapolis.

Mary Lou pulled the curtain back from the sliding door that led out to a patio. It was a pleasant little spot with tables under colorful spreading umbrellas. Large pots full of plants and flowers were scattered here and there and a few little birds hopped about looking for sustenance. Spring had sprung, but as most of Hope's clients were living the winter of their lives, it was bittersweet to see all the newness and freshness.

Hope looked down at the sleeping man whose hand she held and vignettes of their past few months scrolled through her mind.

A couple of weeks before when she had come to visit, he had been sitting up in his wheelchair and was happy to see her. He asked her if she would take him for a little ride past his house. He just wanted to see it, he told her. Wren's camellias should be in bloom and he yearned to see them for the last time. Hope didn't chide him telling him it wouldn't be the last time. She knew better, as did Hector. But what the heck a pilgrimage back to the house he had lived in with his wife for more than half a century seemed like a good idea! Morgan wouldn't be any the wiser, unless one of the people in the facility snitched on them. She got help getting Hector into her car and off they went on their little trek.

The drive was pleasant. Hector related a story of the time he and Wren had gone hiking in a park in San Diego. They had stumbled across this neglected garden near a ruin of a building. The camellias were climbing up the crumbling walls of the edifice all white and pink and red. It was a sight to behold, Hector told her. "When we got home," Hector said, "from our weekend in San Diego, Wren planted the shrubs that surround our house. She tended them and babied them, those camellias."

The story was so lovely that Hope didn't have the heart to break the spell that it had woven with conversation. They drove the rest of the way in silence.

When she pulled up in front of his house, both of them were stunned. And it wasn't just the For Sale sign in the lawn. The beautiful sky-blue front door that was always so welcoming had been painted white. It was wrong. And most of the camellia bushes had been cut back or pulled out as well. Only a couple remained. Hope felt tears glisten in her own eyes as she reached out and took Hector's hand. The question *why* hung in the air between them. "I'm so sorry, Hector. Morgan shouldn't have done that." Even the few remaining blooming flowers couldn't take away the blow. Hector sputtered once then sat back beaten and glum. Neither of them spoke on the way back to the facility. When they got there, Mary Lou helped Hector back into bed. Hope never saw him out of bed from that time on.

When Hope had gotten home that evening, after making an emergency detour to see Ann who had nearly flat-lined, Hope, beyond exhausted, collapsed on the chase lounge on her balcony. It wasn't cold out but it wasn't warm either. She pulled the afghan over her and tried to relax.

She felt slightly ill and was too sad to even cry. Ann was dying, Hector was devastated. Why oh why had Morgan painted the blue door white? Why had Morgan had so many of the flowers uprooted and destroyed? What was that all about? What possible reason was there to take even that from Hector? The fact was, when her clients were hurt she was hurt too. It was a symbiotic thing she couldn't explain. It just was.

Bites were being taken out of her soul. Little bites at first, bit by bit then bigger bites, and finally huge chunks were being torn away. She felt a kinship with Prometheus whose liver was torn out by the raven. And what she did, taking care of her folks and living their pain with them, it was unbearable, but like Prometheus she had no choice but to bear it. And finally she wept.

●●●

Hope saw Hector more often than Morgan knew. It was only right, she thought, that she sit vigil for him the way he had done for his wife. In fact Hope had, more than once, sat side by side with him while Wren slept. She recalled during Wren's last days, a mere few months ago, Hector reaching over and patting his wife's hand the way she did now with him. One time he said to her while Wren slept, "I wasn't always the best husband, but I always loved her with all my heart."

"She knows you love her," Hope had told him. "But I have to disagree with you. You are the best of the best as husbands go. When Morgan first had Wren in that lock-down facility, you visited her every day. And you fought the good fight to get her back home."

"I wish I could bring her home now." His anguished expression as he looked down on his dying wife broke Hope's heart. Nor did Hope respond to his comment as they both knew his wife would never go home again. Wren had been failing at a very rapid rate. She had contracted pneumonia and landed in the hospital weeks before, and it was a down hill progression from that point on. Up until that time, Wren had made some remarkable progress. Her young and energetic neurologist had managed to wean her off most of the psychotropic medications the lock-down facility had her on, and the results were remarkable. While it didn't prevent the continued deterioration from the Alzheimer's, she was no longer in a perpetual stupor. She sat up straight, was alert, could carry on conversations, and laugh and smile at jokes. For example, when Hope would go over to the little cottage where they lived with the two caregivers, Wren would always say, "Oh it's Hope, how nice to see you, Hope. But don't buy anything from her Hekkie, we don't need what she's selling." Asking for help or stating an opinion, which would have been an impossibility when she first got home, had become an everyday occurrence. Then winter rolled around and with it flu season landing Wren in the hospital. She'd gotten over the flu within a matter of days, but had become dehydrated and weakened. Weak to begin with, she was almost completely bedridden at this point. And yet the hospital said time was up, she had to be released. It was probably an insurance thing.

Hope was meeting Hector and the two caregivers at the hospital the day Wren was to be discharged. As she got off the elevator her phone rang. It was Morgan. "We're going to be moving Wren to a rehab facility," Morgan jumped right in. "She's too weak to go home."

"She has two caregivers, Morgan. I think it's safe enough to send her home."

"No, not for a few more days."

"Have you told Hector?"

"I'll leave that to you."

Of course you will, she thought to herself. Then aloud she asked, "How long before she can go home?"

"It depends. You know how it is."

"Will the caregivers stay with her at rehab as they did here at the hospital?"

"No reason for that. The facility has enough people there to take care of their patients."

When Hope got to Wren's room the caregivers already had her dressed and in the wheelchair. Wren looked up at her and said, "Oh, Hope. What a cute little jacket, Hope."

"Why thank you, Wren." She patted the woman's shoulder while breaking the news to Hector. He wouldn't be taking his wife home. An ambulance would be transporting her to a rehab facility nearby.

The next day when Hope popped into the facility to see how things were going, all hell had broken loose. Used to twenty-four seven attention from the two live-in caregivers, being put to bed in the rehab facility and essentially ignored had pushed Wren's fragile mind over the brink. Hope could hear Wren crying out from down the hall. She broke into a jog and rounded the corner into the room. Wren was weeping and mumbling. The only words Hope could understand were "Help me. Help me." If that wasn't bad enough, her nightgown and bed sheets were sopping wet. She summoned the attendant not daring to say a thing other than that Wren needed cleaning up. She knew if she let go of that grasp she had on her temper, it would come to no good. All she could think was: "Damn Morgan! Damn Morgan!" Morgan had ruined everything by sending Wren to rehab instead of letting her go home with her husband and caregivers. Two caregivers giving her full-time attention compared to the abandonment that happened here. Talk about criminal negligence! All those months of drug adjustments and moving forward a slow pace at a time, all for naught! It was essentially over for Wren; it was just a matter of time. And Hope was enraged at the injustice of it all.

Hope never heard Wren speak another coherent sentence again. Over the next month she spiraled downward into a bottomless chasm.

But that was weeks ago. Wren's death had made Hope angry because it was so unnecessary. And now Hector wasn't long for this world. One by one her clients were leaving her. And as hard as that was, Hope knew that soon she would be free. The word *soon* became her mantra. Soon she would no longer be working for Morgan. Soon a new chapter in her life would begin. Soon. But for the time being, the constant needs of her clients kept her going. There was comfort in routine; the sameness wasn't a rut, it was a choice. If nothing else, working with her failing clients taught her to savor the moments. It also taught her that there were fates far worse than death. When she was thirty, forty seemed old. When she was forty, it was fifty that was over the hill. Now that she was just a blink away from sixty, well, eighty didn't seem so far away. And after dealing with the elderly everyday, even on weekends and holidays, she knew the nineties, for the most part, were no place to be. And yet, not all of her clients were old. There was Sarah, just shy of sixty. And when she thought of Gene, who had just turned seventy-four, she couldn't believe he was still stuck in the system. It was time to visit him again. She'd try to get over to The Crescenta Arms tomorrow.

She stood and looked down on the sleeping Hector. Well, my God, but she needed some cheering up. Maybe Darling was around. She'd give her a jingle and tell her that it was margarita time.

●●●

Darling was quick to respond and showed up at Joselito's not long after Hope had started on her first drink. Plunking herself down in the booth, she said, "Well, we came to the right place to drown our sorrows." She pointed to Hope's dwindling drink. "Hey, garçon, I need one of those, and make sure it has mucho tequila." Hope chuckled. "What's so funny?"

"Garçon is French."

"Oh, yeah, I knew that."

"You know Darling, every day gets worse. And I carry around all these unwept tears."

"Why keep them bottled up? Shed them now."

As if on cue, Hope started to cry. Not big sobs, just a slow leak with the tears trickling out of her eyes. "I feel so helpless. There's nothing I can do to stop this." She took another pull on her margarita. "I don't know how much longer I can keep up with this job."

"You just get so wrapped up with the clients. That's all. You need to try and keep more of an emotional distance."

Hope made a pffftting sound and took another sip of her drink.

Darling knew she needed to distract Hope. But sometimes the best thing was to talk about what was causing the pain. "Tell me, 'bout poor Hector."

"He just wanted to be with Wren. That's what it's all about. When Wren died, Hector just started losing ground. Didn't want to eat. It was all very natural. Nature knows what its doing. But Morgan wasn't about to let Hector pass away and join his wife, not while some of the estate still exists to exploit. Their house was supposed to go to a niece in Minneapolis. Morgan is selling it and will have all the money spent before Hector dies. The niece won't inherit a thing."

"That doesn't seem right."

"No, it doesn't. If I were in charge, I'd get hospice involved more often... well, I was going to say more often than Morgan does. But Morgan never gets hospice involved at the end." Hope took another sip of her margarita.

"You know, so many of my male clients are World War II veterans." The non-sequitur didn't bother Darling. She knew Hope just needed a sounding board. "Mr. G was. So is Dennis and also Hector."

"What did Hekkie do in the war?"

"He was a fighter pilot. These guys, they're all the best of the best, you know. And look how they are treated by the world that they saved for democracy. Democracy, hah!"

"That's better, girlfriend. I like it better when you look like you're ready to skin someone."

Hope's response was to snort. Then she sighed. Then she said, "Enough of this. I can't talk about it anymore."

"Okay, change of subject." Darling sipped her drink and thought for a moment, "So, let's talk about men."

"Okay. What's going on with Mr. Derek?"

"Oh, man, girlfriend. I need to get me a *new* boyfriend." And Darling went on and on about her affair with Mr. Derek. She finally wound down saying, "He says he can get me a job in his law office. But he won't pay me what that other law clerk is getting. When are we women going to start getting treated on an equal basis with the men?"

"You know what Marilyn Monroe said don't you? *Women who seek to be equal with men lack ambition.*"

"Good one. Maybe I'll tell that to Mr. Derek. Oh, to hell with him! I got to get me a *new* boyfriend!"

Hope smiled and ran her fingertip around the salty rim of her margarita glass then licked the salt off her finger. "You know, Darling, I do love you. I love you for many reasons, but mostly because you make me laugh at the human comedy."

"Uh huh. So back on topic. Men."

"Well, it just so happens I have met a new man."

"Do tell!"

"Only he hasn't called me yet, so maybe it's not anything."

"So why don't you call him?"

"A, no, we kind of left it that he'd call me."

Darling was shaking her head. "Don't you know anything, girl. Call him."

And on that note, Hope's phone rang.

Looking at the readout, she shook her head, and shrugged her shoulders. "Don't know who this is." When she answered her jaw slightly dropped and she looked at Darling and pointed to her phone mouthing, "It's him!" She listened for a moment then said, "Yes, I know where that is; why don't I meet you there, say, around seven?" When she hung up Darling guff hawed. "Don't say a thing," Hope warned her, "not a thing."

Darling, who had been wolfing down chips and salsa with an unladylike gusto, wiped her fingers on a napkin. "I was going to suggest we order another drink and something to eat, but looks like you'll be eating elsewhere."

18

Cliff

"The healthy and strong individual is the one who asks for help when he needs it. Whether he's got an abscess on his knee or in his soul."

— Rona Barrett

Cliff had reached the point in his career where he could retire at any time, but then what? The future was a long, dark place to him with the boring sameness of everyday a potential hell on earth. So he stuck with the job, the only interesting thing in his life — until lately.

Shortly after getting out of the police academy Cliff had married his high school sweetheart. That marriage lasted about seven years. One day he and his wife looked at one another and both said, "What the hell were we thinking?" The divorce was amicable, well — as amicable as could be considering that it was a divorce. For the next couple of decades Cliff had thrown his all into his work and moved up the ladder in the department until he was riding a desk and calling the shots. He had dated occasionally, just met women in bars more often, and was a content singleton. When he was in his early fifties, he met the woman who was to become his second wife. To find love at that stage of his life, real love, had stunned, surprised, and thrilled him. Cliff was certain that he and Eileen were the two happiest people in the world.

About five years into the marriage he had to spend a couple of days in San Diego at a seminar. On day two before the morning meeting he called home. No answer. He had planned the call between the time Eileen usually took her morning shower, when she wouldn't hear the phone, and before she actually would head out the door to work. So it surprised him when there was no answer. Between meetings he dialed her work number. There was no reason for his calls, just that he was missing his wife and wanted to touch base. After several rings the phone was finally answered. He spoke with Eileen's co-worker then hung up scratching his head. Eileen hadn't showed up to work that day. He called home again. Still no answer. He started to feel apprehensive. What was going on that Eileen was incommunicado? Calling a buddy to do a drive by and check up on her, Cliff admitted to his friend that he was really worried. He put his phone in his pocket and headed in to the next meeting.

About twenty minutes later, when his phone vibrated against his thigh, Cliff felt a chill slither through his entire being. He excused himself from the meeting and went into the hallway to answer the phone. It was his buddy. There had been no answer when he knocked on the door, so he found the key that Cliff had told him was hidden among some potted plants. Letting himself in, he had found Eileen. She had apparently had a heart attack and died before she could summon help.

A stunned Cliff went through all the necessary motions getting his beloved wife laid to rest. Then the empty sameness of each day that followed nearly killed him in turn. Time had morphed into a circle and he was just going around and around and around making the rut deeper with each revolution. He'd go to work, sit behind his desk and issue orders and do what he had to do, but his heart wasn't in it. He'd come home turn on the television, not really watching it, and eat a tasteless something he'd torn open and tossed in the microwave. It wasn't that he had to work anymore. He and Eileen had taken out sizeable life insurance policies to hedge bets against some future health issue that might end up putting the financial bite on a remaining spouse. But both had been healthy, or so it seemed, and they were one of the rare couples who were completely debt free. So after paying for the funeral expenses, Cliff put the remaining money from the life insurance in an investment package that included a mix of this and that. No, he didn't need to work, but he did need to keep his mind occupied. However, no matter what he did or didn't do he did know he wasn't happy. He wasn't happy at home. He wasn't happy at work. He realized he had no hope. He also realized he needed some help.

He started seeing a grief counselor and between the two of them Cliff came to realize that riding a desk no longer suited him. He went back on patrol, taking a pay cut in the process, and slowly started to appreciate life again. He was out and about making a discernable difference and before he knew it another five years had passed. And while he wasn't what he would call happy, he wasn't miserable anymore. Life outside the job held a boring sameness; it was the job that kept him going. Then he met Hope.

The first few times they went out to dinner or took in a movie, he wasn't interested in anything more than companionship. But with each date, and even against his will, he was becoming more and more attracted to her as a woman. Last night she'd invited him over for dinner at her condo. She set up a cute little table out on her balcony and they ate under the stars. It was an unseasonably hot spring evening, but the breeze kept the heat from being unbearable and their conversation as usual was interesting even stimulating. He barely caught himself leaning in to give her a goodnight kiss before he realized it. He turned the potential kiss into a mere peck on the lips, said good night, and that was that. But he found himself whistling on the way home. When was the last time he had whistled? He couldn't remember.

Their conversation over dinner had taken interesting twists and turns. When he'd asked her about her job, she made a statement that made him sit up straight and stare at her. She'd said, "You'd actually be a perfect candidate for being under conservatorship." At his bug-eyed look, she just laughed at him. "I mean your circumstances. You have no spouse, you have no children, and, I'm speculating here, as you had no kids, that translates to no college tuition, no braces, no etc. So I'm guessing you have a pretty decent portfolio too. That would make you very attractive to conservators like Morgan. That's what they want, someone with a substantial estate. Being forewarned is forearmed, so they say. Just watch out." She softened all that with a smile.

"I'm only sixty-five. Isn't that a little young to be worried about a predator like Morgan snatching me up?"

"My client Gene is only in his early seventies and he got sucked into the system."

"Does he have Alzheimer's?"

"He's sharper than most people. The thing is I think he'll be able to shake the conservatorship eventually, but that he ended up under conservatorship in the first place is the concern. Or it should be a concern to people who are aging and likely to be the next victim. But Gene is the exception to the rule. Most of my clients are much older than Gene. And one by one they are dying. Each life is in the process of being extinguished, but... though they are no longer here, they were here. They lived. They mattered. They made their marks, laughed, cried, made love, and then one by one grew too old to care for themselves and fell into the maw of the great beast."

"Tell me about the beast. Is it simply old age?"

"No. Old age isn't bad or wrong. In past centuries the elders were admired for their wisdom. There is a saying that goes something like: elders see more from a sitting position than the youth do standing up. I don't know who said it. So no, old age isn't the beast. The beast is like the Minotaur. In ancient Greece Athens' youth were deliberately fed to the Minotaur. In our society it isn't the youth who are fed to the beast; it's our elderly. The inhumanity, the way we treat them, it overwhelms me at times and I just feel so impotent. And conservators like Morgan are the right-hand of the modern-day Minotaur helping the beast to devour these, these castoffs of society, these elderly citizens of the Greatest Generation! It's just one example of...okay...sorry. I'm starting to rant."

"That was fascinating...as well as intimidating."

"Sorry, I got carried away."

"You really do get passionate about things. Maybe you need to run for office."

"Not interested in that thankless job."

"Well, what about doing what Morgan does? If you were calling the shots...let me rephrase that. If you were making the shots, their trajectory might be in a better direction."

"Oh, Lord. I don't know if I could handle the responsibility. I know I'm a good case manager, but I don't know if I could or would be a good conservator." And on that note she stood and started to pile up their dirty dishes.

He helped her clear off the table then standing at the kitchen sink, she washed the dishes and he dried. "Something wrong with your dishwasher?" He nodded his head at the appliance.

"Not a thing." She smiled at him. "I find I like doing the dishes by hand. It's a fine time to let the mind wander and go to that Zen-like place. It's a time to think."

"And what do you think about?"

"My life, I guess. You know what they say about an unexamined life is not worth living and all that."

"Did you ever think you think too much?'

"Why do you say that?"

"Because I know that at times I think too much. I'd like to imagine I'm not the only one." They shared a smile that lit up both pair of eyes.

Back on the balcony, over coffee they discovered they were both Lee Child fans. "Have you ever wanted to do the Jack Reacher thing?" she asked him.

"Oh sure. After Eileen died I almost chucked everything...but, well, at the time my heart wasn't even in that. What about you?"

"I've always thought I'd like to be a Reacher-like vagabond—for about a year. Oh, I wouldn't hitch-hike or even take a bus. I'd stick with my Honda. But wouldn't it be fun just to get into the car and drive without any definite destination, just follow one's nose and end up where you end up?"

In a jocular way he said, "We should do that, but instead of a Honda, get a motor home and just chuck everything and go."

Using his same playful tone she asked, "You wouldn't get board being a vagabond?"

"Would you?"

Hope looked thoughtful. It had been years since she'd played the "what if" game with someone. So she speculated. "I think I'd take the time to mentally pull all I've learned on this job into perspective. I can see myself sitting at a little motor-home kitchen table with my computer writing about my folks."

"You want to write about them?"

They heard a coyote howl in the hills, and then an answering yip.

"I guess if I did write something, it wouldn't be anything more than that," she gestured toward the sound of the coyotes, "a yip in the night. But it would just make me feel better to tell their stories. They were people who lived and...they mattered."

He looked at her over the rim of his wine glass. "Admirable. I think you should do that."

"Some day down the road, maybe. But there's this." She spread her arms and encompassed not only her balcony, but the hills, the night sky, the whole environment. "I'd miss all this if I took off in a motor home."

"I kind of sensed this balcony is your spot, a favorite place."

"It is. I can sit up here and look out at my hills. For some reason they sustain me. This balcony is like my perch. If I didn't have this place to retreat to at times, I'd just feel so lost."

Well, Cliff knew all about feeling lost. The place that sustained him was work. But lately he was discovering that Hope sustained him too. He just wasn't sure how he felt about that.

●●●

A few days later she invited him over for another dinner on her balcony and he found he was looking forward to that very much. When he arrived with flowers, he was stunned to see that she was stunned.

"What?" he asked her.

"I...I just don't remember the last time I received flowers." She actually blushed and that made him smile.

"Maybe when your kids were born your husband gave you flowers?"

She tried not to frown. "No, that never happened. But...don't want to go there. Okay?"

He agreed. "Okay."

"Come on back. I have guacamole and chips ready. I thought we'd just talk and get to know each other better before we eat."

Dinner was fun. She lit up the BBQ and cooked buffalo burgers—actual buffalo as in bison—that and her potato salad and green beans for a vegetable. The dinner was simple but yummy at the same time. And before they knew it, the sun had dipped behind the hills, the night grayed, and soon it was fully dark. The whoosh of an owl's wings floated on the air causing Hope to shiver. She looked quickly to see if she could spy the predator, but it was gone.

"Look." She pointed over to the hills. "There it is again, see that house all lit up from one end to the other? Most nights you don't even know a house is there. But every few weeks or so, there it is, all lit up like a beacon saying, 'Come and find me.'"

"Hummm." Cliff focused on the house.

"I always wondered if it was maybe a meth house sending out its signal to buyers." When he gave her the raised eyebrow look, she blushed. "I mean, what the heck else could it be?"

"It could be any number of other things. Maybe the owners just travel a lot and are only home occasionally. I doubt it's a meth house."

"You're right. It's just my overactive imagination. But things have changed so much around here. In the old days nothing like a meth house would ever happen around this neighborhood, but in the old days they didn't have homeless people sleeping on the sidewalks either. And the fact is I have to step around one guy sleeping on the sidewalk up on Montrose Avenue just about every morning when I take my walk."

"We are seeing a lot more homeless."

"And just the other day I saw a new pan handler standing at the freeway off ramp: begging. This guy wasn't like others I've seen over the years. The others were mostly professionals. You know the guys who make livings at what they do, and, truth be told, probably better livings than me. But this man had a haunted and stunned look on his face—humiliation in fact. One of the new homeless. His expression said, 'Why me?' It said, 'I never expected this to be me in a million years!' It said, 'I'm helpless, in despair, I feel shame.' It said, 'I'm embarrassed, and I am in great need!' It was heart breaking. For the first time ever, I pulled over, rolled down my window, and handed the man a twenty dollar bill."

"It is horrible. The discrepancy between the haves and the have nots is widening every year and the middle class is shrinking as a result. It took the Roman Empire centuries to complete its decline and fall; sadly, the United States of America is going in the same direction, but in record time. It's going to be over within a matter of decades if things don't turn around soon."

"And on that happy note," Hope emptied the bottle of wine in to their glasses.

Cliff kept staring at the house that had started the whole conversation. "I think we should take a walk and go see what's going on there. Not that I buy into your meth house theory, but I think some investigation is in order. Let's go"

"I don't think so."

"Why not?"

"Call me chicken, but if it's something fishy going on, I don't want to be part of it."

"This from a woman who disarms assailants with her big toe?"

That made her laugh. "That was a fluke and you know it."

"Come on." He took her by the hand and pulled her up. "Instead of walking, we'll drive over there. Distances are deceptive and it's probably a lot further than it looks from here.

They parked a little way down the road and watched the house. A few people came and went. "It's just a party, nothing suspicious."

"Is that your professional assessment?" Hope was snuggled back against his arm that was around her shoulders.

"Yes, it is."

"So, then we can go home?"

"What's your hurry?" he wanted to know. Then he cupped the side of her head, turned her toward him and laid his lips on hers.

●●●

Watching Hope as she slept, Cliff brushed the back of his fingers over her soft cheek. Her eyelashes fluttered open and there Cliff was, propped up on one elbow, gazing down on her.

"Good morning, sleepyhead."

"Is it? Morning?"

"Barely. I have an early meeting so I've got to get moving."

"What time is it?

"Nearly five."

Hope started to push the covers back. "I can put some coffee on."

He smiled. "You don't drink coffee."

"No, but you do." She was only halfway sitting up.

"Don't bother." He gently pushed her back down and pulled the covers up to her chin. "You go back to sleep. I just didn't want you waking up alone and thinking I'd snuck out on you."

"Thanks."

When she heard her front door click shut behind him, she smiled as she drifted back to sleep.

An incessant ringing in her ear awoke her. She fumbled for her phone and answered; her voice husky with sleep, "What time is it?"

"Time for you to be up and at it. Just after six."

"Oh, hi, Morgan, you're up early."

"I just checked my calendar and today's the day they have the monthly evaluative meeting for Miguel, so you've got to get down to LA this morning."

"I thought that was next week?"

"Nope, they switched it and I forgot to let you know. Is the meeting going to mess up anything else you had planned?"

"Not really."

"Remember we talked about getting a Spanish speaking caregiver to come in and read to Miguel during the day?"

Of course she remembered. It had been her idea, but she knew better than to remind her boss of that. She simply demurred with a, "Yes."

"Let them know that's on our agenda."

"Ah...okay. Anything else I need to bring up at this meeting?"

"That's it on our end. Just take notes regarding his progress or lack thereof. The usual."

"Okay, got it."

"Good. Good. Talk to you later."

Hope clicked off and mentally took her morning walk off her to-do list. She'd have to get dressed and try to beat the LA traffic downtown. The meeting at the hospital never lasted more than an hour, but it was always scheduled for the most inconvenient time of the day, right smack in the middle of the morning rush hour. So Hope always got there early, avoiding the worst of the rush hour traffic then sat in the lobby reading a book until time for the meeting.

Poor Miguel. He had been injured at work, an industrial accident that could have been avoided, and was now little more than a vegetable, hence the big payout from the insurance company. Not that the insurance company had just handed over the money. There had been a lawsuit and naturally the lawyers got the lion's share of the compensation. What was left should have been put in the hands of Miguel's wife, but the court had different ideas. They were afraid that if the money for Miguel went to the wife she wouldn't use it to care for her husband but spend it on unnecessary luxuries for herself and her kids. So the court put Morgan in charge of the millions, and that suited Morgan just fine. Morgan did need to be able to justify the expenditures to the court; and the fact was Morgan could be tight-fisted, particularly with Miguel's family. Hope was always stepping in and reminding Morgan that Miguel had been the breadwinner and his wife had been a stay-at-home mom raising the four kids. Getting Morgan to buy the kids computers for school had been a battle of almost epic proportions. Why, Hope didn't know.

When Hope would pop into the hospital room to see Miguel – she couldn't call it a visit because he was essentially the next thing to brain dead – she began to notice that while he was certainly a victim of terrible circumstances, he also did respond to stimuli. If the room was dark and gloomy when she got there, Hope would pull up the blinds to let some sunlight in and she'd see that he'd blink and turn his face toward the sun. When she spoke to him, he'd turn his head in the direction of the sound of her voice. Hope didn't know if that was just basic stimulus-response, or if there was something still clicking inside Miguel. Yes, the brain was damaged, but what about the mind? Weren't they two different things? She recalled reading something about a person who had had a stroke and who had slowly gotten better. That person explained what it was like being trapped in a body. He was still able to think, but couldn't get his thoughts out to the world. She wondered what Miguel's thoughts were? And if he had thoughts, was he feeling abandoned? Maybe he was like a Stephen Hawking trapped in a body that wasn't cooperative. That was when she got the idea to have someone come in and read to him: a newspaper in the morning, maybe some magazine articles, or perhaps a chapter of a novel each day. Maybe stimulating Miguel's mental faculties would be beneficial in some way. If she were lying in a hospital bed like Miguel she would love to be read to. It would be a very justifiable expense in Hope's mind and she had broached the subject with Morgan a couple months back. Yes, paying a caregiver to come and read to him would be a fine way to spend some of those millions. Of course, she'd have to be a Spanish-speaking caregiver as Miguel only spoke Spanish, but that wasn't a deal breaker.

Last fall they had spent some of the millions another way. At the October meeting the nurses had asked Hope to get Miguel a costume so they could dress him up for Halloween. Morgan approved the expenditure so she went shopping at some party store and got him a Phantom of the Opera cape and mask. Hope knew if she were lying in a hospital bed nearly brain-deal, she would not want to be dressed up and put on display at some hospital party. But that was just her. Maybe others wouldn't mind. At the time Hope remembered that Zen koan that went: If a tree falls in the forest and no one is there to hear it, does it make a sound? And she thought: If someone strips a person of his dignity, but the person's brain is so damaged that he doesn't know it, is it okay? Hope expected she'd be asked to get another Halloween costume for Miguel next fall; unless they'd had the foresight to keep the one she already bought. Shaking her head, Hope headed for the shower so she could get on the road.

●●●

Cliff and Hope's next date was a trip to the museum. It seemed that Cliff was a bit of an art lover. "So what do you think of this painting?" he asked Hope. It was the picture of a man standing on the end of a dock, hands in pockets, staring down into the rippling water of the lake. He was all alone and the trees along the distant shore were mostly barren.

She smiled up at him. "I think...I don't know much about art, but I know what I like."

"Come on. I'm not going to let you get away with that. Look at it," he coaxed. "Look closely. Art lays bare life, sometimes subtly, sometimes boldly. So...tell me, what do you see?"

So, she looked closely. "I see," she started to tear up. "I see something that makes me feel very sad. It's kind of lonely. There is pain there." She shook her head. "I don't know why I say that."

"I do. You're right. I used to come here often and look at this painting after my wife died. I sensed the loneliness too. It's funny, but for some reason looking at it made me feel less alone. Then the museum lent it out to another museum somewhere, and it was gone for a long time. I missed it. It was like my buddy was getting on with his life and I was still stuck in a rut."

Hope slipped her hand in Cliff's. "Well, now I think you are out of your rut."

He gave her hand a gentle squeeze. "So do I."

The plan was to have another BBQ, but this time at his house. Cliff lived in a nice one-story ranch with a cute little bay window. It was on the edge of a little valley, but nestled against some foothills. The area was zoned for horses, but while Cliff didn't have horses, he had neighbors who did.

Luckily all the properties were on large lots; the neighbors on both sides were a nice distance away. It felt isolated, almost rural, but also cozy. In the back of Cliff's house was a patio made of pavers and it was furnished with a nice, manly Weber BBQ.

Hope sat at the little table drinking a glass of wine and watching her... well, yes, she guessed she could call him her boyfriend, cooking marinated chicken breasts and sipping beer out of a long-neck bottle. There was the faint whine of a power drill reinforcing the realization that the nearest neighbor was way over that-a-way. She barely heard it while she admired Cliff's butt. Nice! She was still observing him when he turned. At first he looked at her, long and deeply, then his eyes swept the back of his house and his gaze moved upward. She could tell a lot was going on in his head. "You're practically thinking out loud," Hope said. She looked up at the roofline where he had been concentrating. "What do you see?"

"I just had an idea."

"Tell me."

So he did, painting a picture with words of building a second story on the house, master bedroom with a bath and sitting area. "Walk-in-closet goes without saying. Then I could build a balcony right there." He pointed and turned. "See it would face those hills and kind of overlook that distant golf course on that side over there."

When he turned back to look at her, Hope felt her breath back up in her throat. She felt a pressure building, pushing then something broke through and whooshed through her system. He was suggesting building a balcony, for her? Hope didn't have words.

He cleared his throat. "You look like you've just been pole axed. So let's table a discussion of that idea and eat." He placed the platter of chicken breasts on the table.

19

Morgan

> "Our prime purpose in life is to help others. And if you can't help them, at least don't hurt them."
>
> —Dalai Lama

Cliff had asked Hope to move in with him. But she found she was waffling. The temperature had dropped and it was cool again. She wrapped up in an afghan on her chase lounge out on her balcony and just sighed in contentment. It was here she came to contemplate, to think, to dream. If she moved in with Cliff, where would she go to replenish her sense of self? Of course, he had said he'd build her a balcony. That he knew, that he understood how much she loved her balcony made her feel so loved and cared for — but that balcony wouldn't be *her* balcony, it wouldn't be *this* balcony. Nor would his hills be *her* hills. The hills she was looking at now. Things were happening quickly, moving quickly, and she felt the need to slow down and think it all through. So here she was on her balcony doing just that. She knew life was all about change. Nothing stayed the same. But was she ready for change? The answer, yes, was on her lips. But still she felt the need to slow down, to pull back, and to think. She caught herself drifting off, just floating on the wings of some peaceful cloud. What? What had snagged her attention? Then her phone rang again.

"Hi, Morgan, what's up?"

"Ann just died."

"Oh," was all she could respond. Hope felt her heart clutch, then release. She eventually said, "Ann finally got her wish."

"Yeah, I know." Morgan was silent for a moment. Then, after a good throat-clearing said, "I know you usually go see her on Tuesdays, so, well, no need to go tomorrow."

Hope was curious at the note of sorrow she was detecting in Morgan's voice. "You okay, Morgan?"

"Did you know Ann was my very first client?"

"I guess I did. I mean I know she'd been under conservatorship for over a decade."

"Yep. My very first. I don't...know...this one's hard."

"What was it? That viral pneumonia?"

"Yes. Anyway, just wanted to let you know. The funeral is bound to be a big deal. Franklin and all that crew and...well, you know."

"Sure, Morgan. Thanks for calling." When she hung up, Hope just stared at her phone for a moment. That was odd, seeing Morgan kind of shaken like that. Very unusual.

●●●

The funeral was so well-attended that the mourners spilled out of the chapel and onto the steps. Morgan and Hope sat near the back. While Morgan perused the program Hope looked around. Lucy, Ann's long-suffering caregiver, was sitting up front with Franklin and his family. That was as it should be. When Morgan made a surprised little sound, Hope whispered, "What?"

Morgan tipped the program toward Hope. "Ann didn't believe in the afterlife."

"Didn't she?"

"No, I mean, she was always saying she'd see me in hell, but those were just words. When I talked to her seriously, way back when, about what happens after a person dies, she said, it was just nothingness and that's why she wanted to go there, which makes it kind of weird that they'd choose this poem to have in the program."

"What poem is that?" Hope opened her own brochure and saw the first stanza of the poem *Death* by Emily Dickinson printed there: *Because I could not stop for Death / He kindly stopped for me. / The Carriage held but just ourselves / And Immortality.* "Yes, it certainly is an interesting choice," she told Morgan.

There were hymns and prayers and eventually a sermon. The priest's voice was sonorous and it was putting Hope to sleep when something he was saying pulled her back to attention. "What is letting go to you? A risk? An inevitability? A lot of life is learning how to let go. It's a lesson that needs repeating over the decades. Those experiences are all trial runs, so to speak. So when one is faced with the ultimate letting go, that person jumps with abandon into the vast unknown trusting that Loving Arms will be there to catch one, or at least help to break the fall." The attempt at humor resulted in some tittering amongst the congregation.

"Hummm," was Hope's thought.

When Franklin got up to eulogize Ann, he had everyone's attention. At first it was the usual spiel—she was a wonderful person etc. etc. But suddenly he switched gears and in deference to the woman he had worked for and loved as a friend and mentor for most of his life, he changed his tactic and stopped sugarcoating her. In his usual folksy tone, he painted a truer and more realistic picture of Ann right down to her mustache and everybody murmured in agreement when Franklin said, "And that woman could swear, but as we are in church here, I won't share her favorite vulgarities." Franklin told the story of an Ann that Hope had never met. She had known the shadow, the ghost of the woman who had lived and worked shoulder-to-shoulder with Franklin and been loved for who she was: a savvy business woman and a beer-drinking buddy. Franklin was bringing to life that woman and Hope was so glad to finally meet her. At one point he strode across the front of the group imitating her swagger when on the job; the audience literally laughed out loud and some even applauded. And then he thanked Hope for all her good work and attention to Ann the last couple of years, but didn't even mention Morgan. That might have been what they called *chickens coming home to roost*, but Hope knew the omission was a blow to her boss. Moments after that Morgan whispered, "Excuse me," and left the chapel. Franklin was winding up his eulogy when all of a sudden the church bells started clanging and clanging drowning out everything except their own cacophonous noise. Hope glanced at her watch. It was twenty to the hour, a very strange time for bells to start ringing. They soon stopped and Franklin finished speaking and the funeral ended.

Looking around at the departing mourners, Hope caught up with Charlene. "I didn't see Edna."

Charlene made a sour expression, as if she'd just bit into a lemon. "That...bitch...she got a hold of Ann's safe deposit key, cleaned out the box the day Ann died, and vamoosed out of here."

"Oh, oh, what'd she get?"

"A shit load of cash."

It was some time later that Hope spoke with Morgan again. "You missed the weirdest thing. All the church bells started ringing shortly after you left; it was very strange."

"That's not the weirdest thing," Morgan added. "Just as I left the church, I flipped open my phone to check messages and there I was out on the sidewalk and the phone flies out of my hand and smashes facedown on the sidewalk. Cracking the glass, what a pain! It was then that the bells started ringing."

Hope started laughing. "Well, well, looks like maybe there is an afterlife after all and ole' Ann had a few things to share with you, doesn't it?"

"Well, it did give me the creeps. I'll say that."

●●●

Conservators, with the California court system behind them, enjoyed an invulnerability. They could decree this and order that, and the caregivers and the medical community essentially kicked their heels, held an arm out and said, "Heil!" Not all conservators were morally corrupt. Not all of them had God-complexes. Not all of them made Hope want to pull her hair out by the roots. But more often than not, Morgan did.

One thing that bugged Hope was that Morgan liked to label the conservatees: one was the Kook, one was the Numbskull, one was the Crackpot. Perhaps labeling them was Morgan's way of dehumanizing them so that making life-altering decisions would be easier. Hope felt that dehumanizing them was just one more step down the slippery slope of dehumanizing one's self. She had to grant that Morgan had a tough job, one she wouldn't want. She had said more than once that she liked to be good cop to Morgan's bad cop. But one good thing about her boss was she was never told to cease and desist with her challenges regarding decisions. She recalled one time asking Morgan, "How do you know that's the right decision?"

Morgan had come right back at her and replied, "Can you be absolutely certain of what is right and what is wrong in any particular situation?"

Hope thought about it. "Of course not, but I know what I know."

"And what do you know?"

I know our clients are human beings and they deserve respect."

"And you think I don't respect them?"

"I know you rarely respect their wishes or choices."

"Hope, most of our clients suffer from one form of dementia or another. They need someone else to make the choices and the court has appointed me. And if not for my job, you wouldn't have your job."

All that was true and while she often challenged Morgan, she had never before outright tried to undermine any of Morgan's decisions. Until now.

Hope wasn't sure how it had happened, but she and Gene were in cahoots. They had hatched a plan and now they were in the process of executing it. Looking back, Hope realized that Gene had gained some new respect for her after her encounter with the assailant in the parking garage at the hospital. Shortly after that incident, the two of them had been visiting on the roof-top patio of the facility where he lived. Hope had showed up for a visit and Gene, looking up from the newspaper he was reading, gave her the casual up and down look that was his habit. Seeing her bandaged toe peeking out of the sandal he asked, "What happened to you?

"Knife fight." He gave her a bland look as he blew smoke out of his mouth and tapped out the cigarette in the nearby ashtray. His look clearly suggested that he thought she was pulling his leg. "You think I'm kidding? I'm not. I was mugged and I fought back."

"With your big toe?"

"Yes, with my big toe. I kicked the knife out of the bastard's hand and ended up a little sliced for my effort."

He was grinning at her now. "My, my maybe you are the one to help me fight my battles with the big, bad conservator."

"You have a plan?" she had asked.

"I've got a...notion."

"Want to share?"

"No." Gene shook his head and grinned at her. "It's still under construction. When it becomes a plan, maybe you'll be the one to help me execute it."

She grinned back at him. "Maybe I will and maybe I won't."

"Didn't you ever want to be Nancy Drew?" he asked her.

"No, sleuthing was never really my thing."

"What was you thing?"

Hope considered the question for a moment. "Observing others, making up stories about them."

"I think we've had this conversation before."

She had just laughed. But she wasn't laughing now. Here they were, a few weeks later, going over the plan. Gene, realizing what he was asking of Hope, said, "Are you sure?"

"I'm sure. I'm so close to quitting this job, but I'm going out with a bang, not a whimper. I can't save most of my clients, but I'll at least give you a fighting chance."

At the same time, Hope hadn't wanted to commit any crime. She was, after all, dating a cop. But she had decided that she was willing to help Gene help himself. She wasn't going to do much; she was only going to create a diversion if that became necessary. Gene was the one who was going to be breaking the rules. He had decided he needed to see the paperwork about himself, and that would be located in the administrator's office. Hope pointed out to him that *paperwork* was a misnomer anymore as there were not likely to be file cabinets. Everything was probably on the computer and computers had passwords.

Gene simply gestured toward his laptop and said, "I'm a bit of a geek, plus I've been reconnoitering. That ditsy administrator pops in and out of her office all the time and my educated guess is that she doesn't shut down the computer and then boot it back up each time she's called out of the office to deal with this or that. Plus, Thursday afternoons she's usually gone for about a half hour sometimes longer."

"Because...?"

"I think she's having a bit of a flirt with that dentist who comes in once a week to see the bed-ridden patients."

"Ewwwee, that oily guy?"

Gene laughed. "To each his own. At any rate, I'll get to the computer, download my files, print them so I can go over them at my leisure, and see if there's anything I can use to get out of this mess next time I'm in court. All you have to do if you see her coming back toward the office is stop her in her tracks and start talking to her loudly so I'll hear. Then I'll back off from the computer and sit in the chair like I was waiting for her to get back to her office to ask her a question. Got it?"

Hope was nodding then she looked him squarely in the eye. "Are we really going to do this thing?"

"With malice and aforethought."

"What if Sasha ignores my diversion and walks in on you?"

"I'll improvise. So I ask once again, you ready to roll?"

Hope was ready. "I just have one question?"

"Yeah?"

"Why can't we go incognito?"

"Come on," he laughed. "Let's get this show on the road."

So there Hope was loitering in the hallway and after what seemed like an eternity she heard the printer whirring. Almost home! Her fingers were crossed that she didn't have to create a diversion, but as her father used to say, "If wishes were horses beggars would ride" because sure enough there was Sasha sauntering down the hallway. Her tête-à-tête with Dr. Oily must have been what put that little grin on her face. Hope made it look like she had just briskly come out of the dining room and was heading for Sasha's office. "Oh, hi," Hope sang out. She was pretty sure there were no more printing noises coming from the office. Standing in front of Sasha right in the middle of the hallway so it would be difficult to skirt around her on either side, Hope smiled and gestured toward the office as if that's where she'd been going. "I was just coming to find you."

"What's up?" Sasha wanted to know.

"I'm looking for Gene. He wasn't in his room or in the dining room. Any idea where he might be?

"He might be on the roof smoking one of those stinky cigarettes of his."

"Oh, thanks, I'll head on up there and see if I can find him." They maneuvered around one another and just as Hope reached the corner of the hallway, Sasha gave her a holler. Hope turned around to see Sasha standing in her office doorway. "He's in here, Hope."

"Oh, great." Hope retraced her steps and headed back to Sasha's office.

Gene was sitting in a comfortable chair with his legs outstretched and a manila folder on his lap. When Hope arrived he was just extracting a piece of paper from the folder. "Here's the proposal I ran by you the last time we chatted. It's a list of the different movies and the times they are playing afternoon shows. I think the bus driver is on board too. It will be a great optional outing for the seniors to see a real movie instead of always watching them in the TV room."

Sasha took the proffered paper from Gene. "Thanks, Gene, I'll give it a look-see when I have a few minutes. Good idea."

With that he appeared to be dismissed and Hope said, "I've been looking for you Gene. Do you have time for a short visit?" And they escaped down the hallway.

They headed up to the rooftop to debrief. Hope fanned her hand in front of her face. "Whew! See what you've done, Gene. You've turned me into an accomplice."

He grinned at her. "You did fine."

Hope pointed to the folder. "Do you think there's anything in there that will help you make your case to the judge?"

"Let's hope so."

Reaching out, Hope touched Gene's arm and said, "You didn't deserve what happened to you. Maybe when this is over and you have your life back, you'll be able to sue the state — get some reparation for your financial losses."

"Maybe. I don't know. You know as well as I do that you can't unring a bell. Or, to use another analogy, you throw mud at someone, some of it is going to stick, even if the person isn't guilty of the accusation. Like me. But the good news is that I've been assigned a new judge. A woman this time. Maybe she'll be more reasonable."

"Here's hoping...what was that?" Both Gene and Hope were looking in the direction of a muffled explosive sound that came from a distance away.

"It wasn't a sonic boom."

"God, you just dated us. I haven't heard a sonic boom since I was a kid. And you're right, it wasn't that." Then the blaring of sirens rent the air. The fire department was just down the street from The Crescenta Arms and, from the sound of it, they had been summoned adding to the mystery of what had just happened. And then another siren shrilled as a vehicle raced in the direction of what could only have been an explosion. Because the rooftop patio was surrounded on all four sides by upper-story apartments that opened out onto the patio, there was no way to go to the edge and look out to see what was going on, but over the top of the west-facing apartments a curl of smoke could be seen in the sky.

"Looks like whatever is going on is happening over in the direction where you live."

Hope picked up her purse and her briefcase. "And on that note, I'm going to head home and see what's what."

•••

What it turned out to be was a disaster. The condo directly next to Hope's had experienced some kind of a gas leak in the fireplace and the explosion took out not only that condo, but a large portion of Hope's as well. The engulfing fire was in the process of finishing off what the explosion had started.

Hope stood on the sidewalk with other neighbors and onlookers; her shock evident in her pale face and shaking hands. She felt an arm come around her shoulders and realized Cliff was standing beside her.

"I heard on the scanner and came as soon as I could." Even from the distance she could feel the heat on her face as flames engulfed the entire building. It was evident that nothing would be saved. Everything she owned with the exception of what was in her car or on her back was going, going, gone. "Come on, Hope, let's get out of here. There's no point in watching any more."

"I can't...I don't...I don't know..."

"Shush, now, come on, let's go." He bundled her into his car.

"Where are we going?"

"Where do you want to go?"

"Umm?" Lordy, had she actually said, 'umm?' "I think I need to go talk to Morgan. The office isn't far. Do you mind driving me there?"

"I think you can talk to Morgan over the phone." He then drove to her favorite watering hole.

"Are you okay, Hope?" The waiter hurried over. "You don't look too sturdy."

Cliff had his arm about her. "She's had a bit of a shock. Let's have a couple of your best margaritas," he told the waiter.

Hope played with the straw more than she drank the drink. Her mind kept jumping from thing to thing, not staying still, so there was nothing for her to focus on.

Cliff kept contact with her, rubbing the back of her hand, or murmuring that everything was going to be fine.

Hope called Morgan and said that she'd most likely not be seeing clients for the next couple of days.

"What's going on, Hope? You sound...spacey."

When she just started shaking her head, Cliff took the phone from her and filled Morgan in.

Hope suddenly pushed the remainder of the drink away. "I need to get back. I need to see what's happening."

"Soon. Right now you're going to get something warm in your stomach to go along with that alcohol."

"I couldn't. I'm too queasy."

"Just something light."

She let Cliff take care of her. He ordered her some food and watched as she nibbled at it. But when he suggested she come and stay with him at his house, she pulled herself together enough to say, "No thanks, Cliff. I really need to be with Faith now. I need my sister."

Without missing a beat, he said, "Why don't you give her a call and make sure she knows you're coming. Then we'll go see what's happening back at the scene before I take you over there."

By the time night fell all three condos in the complex had been gutted with fire, doused with water, and were completely uninhabitable. What remained standing was a merely the shell of the original house. Hope and Cliff stood on the street looking at the smoldering building which was only a ghost of its former self. Hope could taste a smoky flavor on the back of her tongue. She thought it might never go away. God! What if she'd been home? What if she and Gene hadn't set up their sting? If she'd been home lounging on her balcony...it was too horrible to consider.

"Come on, I'll drive you to Faith's."

"My car's right here. I'll be fine."

She didn't look fine. "Tell you what. I'll follow you just to be sure you arrive safely."

She thought about that for a moment. "Okay."

Cliff pulled up in front of Faith's house just as she was getting out of her car. Buzzing down his window, he asked, "Do you want me to come in with you?"

"I'm okay, really. Thanks." She leaned in to give him a hug.

"I'll call," he said into her hair as he kissed her on the side of her head.

"Okay." She tried not to stumble as she walked up Faith's driveway, barely aware that Lola was barking her head off behind the front door.

Faith flung open the door before Hope reached the doorstep. "Lola, stop!" She waved at Cliff, pulled her sister into the house, pointed a finger sending the dog into the other room, got the Kettle One out of the freezer, mixed a couple of vodka and tonics, and squeezed in the lime. "Here." She handed one to her shell-shocked sister. "What now? Never mind." She brushed her hand through the air. "Stupid question. Let's go sit in the family room and just knock these back."

They drank in silence then talked in fits and starts. "So, Cliff was with you. That's good."

"Actually he happened by while I stood watching my place go up in flames. He wanted me to go home with him, but I just felt better coming here."

"Of course you did." Faith reached over and rubbed Hope's arm.

"I'm numb right now, but I'm going to fall apart. I'll cry and my nose will get red, and my face will get blotchy. I don't want him to see me at my worst."

Faith laughed. "That's great, honey, even in the midst of a disaster you don't want Cliff to see you at your worst. Oh, the luxuries of the early stages of a relationship."

"Don't make fun of me."

"I'm not. Not really."

"I just needed to be with you."

"Yes, in times of crisis family matters."

"Well, *some* family."

"Now, don't go there tonight." Faith mixed them another drink.

"Everything's gone." Hope repeated for the umpteenth time. "Everything."

"Time for a fresh start then. Maybe this is just the universe stepping in and cleaning your slate for you so you can move on...stop looking at me like that."

"Like what?" Hope wanted to know.

"Like I'm crazy. Look, it's the symbolism of the fire. Fire purifies, you know."

"It was real, Faith, not a symbol of something."

"I know, honey, I'm just blabbing."

Hope covered her face with her hands. "I don't know what to think."

Faith pushed her drink away and asked, "Say, you were insured?"

"Oh, sure."

"Well, thank God for that."

"Everything's gone," Hope repeated. "All I have is this business suit." As she gestured her hand shook and the tears started to fall.

"No baby, clothes are the least of your worries. Trust me on that one."

Hope perused her sister's statuesque form. "We don't wear the same size, so, yeah, clothes are something to worry about."

"You're forgetting; I own a clothing store. So...come on." She grabbed her keys off the table as inspiration hit her.

"What?" Hope sniffled.

"We're going shopping," Faith told her.

"Now? It's late, plus we're plowed. We can't drive over there."

"You're right. Well, it's only a few blocks away, we'll walk."

"Hope glanced at her wristwatch. "It's midnight."

"Yes! A midnight shopping spree! Get ready to turn into a fashioneista!" And taking her sister's arm she led her out the door and into the night.

●●●

Hope sat in Morgan's office going over the logistics of her situation.

"You will probably start having to managing without me. I'm thinking of opting out of this job...soon. The timing seems right. With no condo, and most of my clients dying off, I need to regroup and do something different with my life."

"Don't make any hasty decision, here, Hope. No need for you to bolt."

"It's not just the fire, Morgan. We've talked about this before." Hope tried to find a diplomatic way to say what she wanted to say, and then gave up, "It's just time for me to quit. And to be honest, I haven't always liked or approved of your high-handed or tight-fisted manner of treating our clients."

Morgan sat behind the huge desk just staring at Hope. "You could try being a little more subtle."

Hope gave a self-deprecating little nod. "Silly me. What was I thinking?" When Morgan didn't answer, Hope added, "Why didn't you ever fire me? Didn't it piss you off when I challenged your decisions?

"Not really. You keep me on my toes, Hope. You might even be my moral rudder. I don't know how I'll ever manage without you. I know that sometimes you found my approach to things...unsavory. But I do take my job seriously. I don't just bop along making willy-nilly decisions. I follow a strict protocol. First this, then this, then the next thing. A basic standard operating procedure. I won't say that every decision I've made over the years is the right one, but I can say, unequivocally, that I regret nothing."

Hope didn't begrudge Morgan the soapbox. Lord knows, she climbed up on her own soapbox a time or two. But the thought about *protesting too much* did flash through her mind.

"No hard feelings?" Morgan asked.

"No hard feelings," Hope affirmed.

"I want you to know, if you ever want to come back, I'll always have a job for you."

"Thanks."

"So, you'll finish out the month?"

"That's the plan."

"Good. Well, then, what are your plans, for next...month?"

"Don't know yet."

"Something will come along."

"It usually does." Hope stood up and looked at Morgan. "Thanks for taking me on two years ago when I didn't know a thing about this kind of work. I learned a lot."

When Morgan's phone rang, Hope took her leave. Stepping outside she attempted to assess her feelings, but couldn't determine if she was happy or sad. She got in the car and started the engine. Glancing at the clock on the dash she realized she was barely going to be on time for her appointment.

•••

Faith and Hope met in their attorney's office. Today was the day they were to sign the documents they'd had drawn up that would prevent Charity from overriding their DNR's. The attorney had explained to them that they no longer used Do Not Resituate forms. It was now called Advanced Directives, but it amounted to the same thing. An Advanced Directive was a legal document spelling out a person's end-of-life wishes. It still didn't mean a doctor would honor it, but there was a better chance of having one's desires honored than not if the Advanced Directive was in place.

Unfortunately while Faith and Hope had arrived on time for their appointment, the attorney was stuck in court and would be about an hour late. As it was lunch time and there was a nice little Italian place down the street, the two sisters opted for lunch while they waited.

"It's just too bad Frank died so very young," Faith was saying after their wine was served. "Marrying him was the only good thing Charity ever did."

"He certainly made her human...or, at least, she pretended to be human while he was alive."

"Look enough about sister dearest. Tell me about what's going on with you and Cliff."

Hope smiled a soft smile. "He's been a rock though all this. He keeps saying he wants me to move in with him. The first time he asked me was before the fire, so it's not like he's just offering because I'm homeless."

"Were you considering moving in with him, before the fire?"

"I was thinking about it."

"Yeah, and sometimes you think too much. There are times in life when one needs to stop thinking and start doing."

"I know."

"Let me guess, you were setting up a plus and minus balance sheet, weren't you?"

"Not exactly."

"Yes, exactly. So what was on the plus side?"

"A few things."

"I'm waiting..."

"You mean other than his good looks, his blue eyes, his great bod, and his adorable butt?"

"I'm still waiting..."

Hope considered then said, "One day when he was over, before the fire, he needed to use the bathroom. And I told him that he'd have to remember to jiggle the handle after flushing or the toilet would run and run and run. And you know something? He ended up fixing my toilet."

Faith nodded sagely. "Nice to have a man around the house, I call that a plus."

"Yeah, I thought so."

"So tell me, is the bathroom plumbing the only plumbing he's fixing?" Faith raised her eyebrows a la Groucho Marx. Never mind. Your smug look says it all." She flagged down the waiter. "We'd better order or we'll never get back to the attorney's office in time."

20

Hope

"Not everything that is faced can be changed, but nothing can be changed until it is faced."

—James Baldwin

Hope pulled into Faith's driveway, killed the engine, and just sat there for a moment. She had bought Sarah's groceries for the last time and was, one by one, clicking her final obligations to her clients off her list. She had to admit to herself, she wasn't going to miss those frustrating visits to Sarah. Nor was she going to miss the stress of seeing her people fading away bit by bit. She was, however, going to miss some things. These past two years had been two of the longest and hardest years of Hope's life. She loved her clients, but she just couldn't do it anymore. Talk about a burn out job, and yet, these past few days as she was winding everything up, she felt more vitalized than she had in a long, long time. Her future was wide open and while she didn't yet know what direction she was going to take, she wasn't afraid. It was going to be an adventure. She'd get through tomorrow then she'd start on planning the next day and then the next. She got out of the car and stretched before heading toward the door.

She could hear Lola barking her head off. After nearly two weeks of staying with her sister and that dog still set up a racket whenever she got anywhere near the front door. She really wasn't going to miss that animal when she got back on her feet. Lola eventually shut up by the time Hope got herself settled at the dining room table to write up her client notes. Tomorrow she would see her last two clients, then that would be that. The dog curled up at her feet, actually literally on her feet, while Hope clicked away on her newly purchased laptop.

Faith stumbled in with grocery bags in her arms. When Lola jumped up and ran over to her mistress, Hope said, "Sure, you don't bark when it's her. Why doesn't she ever set up a ruckus when it's you?"

"Cause she knows better. Don't you du mas?"

Hope knew that was Faith's variation on the endearment "dumb ass" as did the dog. "You need help bringing more groceries in?"

"No, this is it. Now that the kids have all moved out, there's a lot less shopping."

Faith put the groceries away and was unloading the dishwasher when Lola leaped to attention and started, once again, barking at the front door. "Somebody's coming." Clearly Hope didn't need to state the obvious, but she did anyway.

"Yeah, I'll get it." Faith put the glass down she'd just retrieved and headed for the door. Glancing through the window, she added, "Oh, it's Cliff."

Faith swung open the door and smiled at the man she expected some day would become her brother-in-law. "Greetings." As he stepped into the living room, Faith started to shut the door then, looking over his shoulder to the curb out front, she swung the door back open. "Well, well, well, what do we have here?"

"A surprise." By that time Hope had saved her work, and powered down the computer. When she smiled over at Cliff, he beckoned her forward with his fingers. "Come here."

"I think I'll just give you two a little time..." Faith headed on back to the kitchen to finish her chore.

Hope looked first at Faith's retreating back and then over at Cliff. "Come over here," he repeated. As she approached him he took her hand and pulled her outside. Parked at the curb smack dab in front of her sister's house was a shiny motor home. "You like?" he asked her.

"You bought a motor home?" He was leading her to it and opening the door so she could step inside.

"Come on. Get in here." Hope stepped up and into the motor home. "It belongs to a buddy of mine. He bought it a few years ago and then after a couple of trips, it's just been parked on his property taking up space. I asked him if he wanted to sell it and well, what he's asking for it is less than it would cost to rent one for a year."

"A year?" Hope was trying to keep up.

"Yeah, remember what you said one time, that you'd like to just take off and live like Reacher for a year?"

"Yeah, I do remember that conversation."

"So I thought I'd bring it by and we could look at it together, decide if I should take it off his hands."

"So we could live like Reacher for a year?"

"Doesn't have to be a year. It could be a month here a month there."

"What about your job?"

"I'm in the process of filling out all my paperwork for retirement. I've been on the job long enough for full pension. It's time for me to move on to the next stage of my life."

"Okay." She was still processing what he had said when he reached down and picked up something from the booth that surrounded the little kitchen table. She watched him spread the rolled-out paper on the table. "Blueprints?"

"Yep, I thought we could do some traveling while my house is being remodeled. I have another buddy who's a contractor. He's looking in to getting the permits. But construction takes time and rather than living in a construction zone...well?" He gave her a quizzical look.

Hope sat down at the table and placed her hands on her cheeks not knowing what to say. This man who had become so important to her so quickly was quite literally sweeping her off her feet with his generosity. When she looked up at him her eyes were glistening with tears.

He sat down next to her, slipped his arm about her shoulders, and pulled her toward him. "I want us to be together, Hope, and I want to take care of you and live each day with you. We'll just take it one day at a time, you and me together. What do you say?"

"I say, I'm probably the luckiest woman alive."

"So tomorrow, before you leave to see your clients, how about packing all your new clothes and putting them in your car. Then when you've finished up for the day, you come home, to my home...to our home. And we can start planning the rest of our lives from there?"

"Yes," she told him. "Yes, yes, yes!"

●●●

Hector was so close to joining Wren. He slept most of the time now, rarely rousing when she popped in to visit him. Morgan had allowed his caregiver, Mary Lou, to stay on, so at least he had someone nearby. Hope would miss Hector most of all. But just because after today she'd no longer be working for Morgan didn't mean she couldn't still visit him. Hope sat by his side holding his hand while he slept and thought back to the very last conversation they had shared not so very long ago.

Hector had told her, "No matter how old a person gets, no matter how many things are taken away, there's something inside you that they can't take away."

Hope heaved a sigh kind of knowing where this was going, "Don't tell me, it's *Hope*."

He gave the hand that was holding his a little squeeze, "I was going to say your memories. As we get older we turn inward. Those places are more real...but as far as hope, hope is a good thing too...

"Here we go." She rolled her eyes teasingly.

"Because..." he tried to give her a stern look, "...hope, like energy, never dies."

"Well then," was all she could think to say.

"E equals Mc squared." He nodded sagely at her.

Today, looking down on the sleeping man, she wondered about energy, the energy that kept a body going; and she wondered where it went when the body released it. Was that energy what people called the soul? Did the soul move out of one house and into another one? Ah, more questions for the ages. She sat with him for an hour. Then rising to go, she bent down and kissed his withered cheek.

Mary Lou told her, "You're going to miss us."

"I'm going to miss all of you. All my clients. All the caregivers. I have learned so much from all of you, received so much from all of you. You've all pulled from me an immense capacity for love that I never knew was inside me. You were like midwives attending the birth of my humanity, my evolution."

"You talk fancy." Mary Lou smiled at her. "But I understand what you are saying. And I understand it's time for you to rest...for a little while."

"Do you?"

"But you won't rest for long. You are young yet, and young people must assert themselves in some way. Old people, they just wait. But you have more to do and you will find your way."

"Right now, I haven't a clue which way to go."

Mary Lou gave a slight nod. "Someday you will be doing something like this again. Only I think you will be the boss not the employee."

Hope just shook her head. "You know, you are the third person in the past few months who has suggested that."

"Maybe third time is a charm?"

"Maybe I need to step back and take care of me for a while."

"Yes, taking care of yourself is good. But..."

Hope chuckled, "Okay, no more advice." Hugging Mary Lou she promised to visit again some day soon. "I just won't be on the clock next time I show up."

"If he wakes up, I'll tell him you were by. But he sleeps so much now."

"I know." Hope took her leave, looking back once. The little old man curled up like a baby broke her heart. He'd never wanted to end up like this, but who did? She shook her head, brushed a tear off her cheek, and headed down the hallway. One more to go.

●●●

Hope pulled up outside of Lila's facility. She sat in the car looking at the building and thought to herself about all the people it house, had housed, and would house in the future; so many people, so much history. And so much of that history would die along with the patients and never be recorded. That in and of itself wasn't a bad thing, but it was a sad thing. Their lives are in the *falling star* stage, she thought. But instead of being allowed to go out in blaze of light they were slowly being suffocated; extinguished in slow increments until they were going, going, gone—but not Lila. Hope believed that woman would outlast them all. She climbed out of her car and went inside.

"Are you going to talk to me today, Lila?"

"No!" Lila's voice boomed.

"You doing okay?" Hope knew the answer she was going to get before she got it.

"No!" Lila turned her head away from the annoying questions and closed her eyes.

"Aren't you happy to have a visitor, Lila?" There was no response to that. Hope glanced around the sterile room. Not surprisingly, the second bed was still empty. Nothing new there. Hope took the shampoo and lotion out of her tote and put them in the drawer next to Lila's bed. "There, that ought to hold you until the new case manager gets used to the routine."

Once again Hope looked around the room. Lila was the first client she had visited when she started working for Morgan, so it was fitting that she be the last one too. She didn't reach out to hold this client's hand as she did Hector's. Lila was still a hitter and Hope didn't have any intention of ending her job by being smacked upside the head the way she had begun it two years before. What a long way she had come since then. When she first started working for Morgan she had taken the time to read Elisabeth Kubler-Ross's landmark book *On Death and Dying*. She felt it would give her some insight into what her clients were dealing with during the last stages of their lives. She recalled that Ross recognized that there were five stages that a person went through: denial, anger, bargaining, depression, and acceptance. She smiled down at Lila who was wearing a thunderous expression on her scrunched up face with her eyes tightly closed against what she considered a rude intrusion. Looks like Lila was still in the anger stage. She'd been there a long time. What a strength of will this woman must have, Hope thought. Too bad the Alzheimer's had robbed her of what might have been a rip-roaring final decade.

Hope gathered up her brief case and purse and was ready to head on out when she smelled, well, something you often smell in facilities like this. Lila had defecated. Hope once again looked down on Lila lying in her bed with no expectation for anything more than being fed via a PET tube and having her diapers changed. "You poor woman," Hope whispered as she turned to leave. She approached the nurses' station to find an aide. "Lila needs to be cleaned up," she told the person behind the desk.

As Hope headed down the hallway, she heard soft crying coming from a nearby room and the words, "Please, let me die." It was the plea of so many in nursing homes. These elderly people housed here and in facilities like this one were all engaged in the challenging work of dying, and they needed to be cared for while they did that work. And those who cared for them? Some were tender and loving; to some it was just a job. But what about doctors or conservators who decided to keep them alive past their expatriation dates? When conservators like Morgan could willy-nilly impose an alien will upon people who just wanted to be left to their own devises, well, that simply was not just. Hope knew in her heart that it was wrong to keep people tethered to life when all they wanted was release. That the system was corrupt was a given. Warehousing the elderly has become an industry. And often an industry becomes an entity. And entities, like all living things, fight back when they are threatened, even if they are in the wrong, or most especially when they are in the wrong. And yet, if the system could just be changed...

With a sigh in her heart, Hope Nightingale headed down the hallway leading toward the exit. She thought perhaps the sound of her heels clicking on this oft scrubbed tile would continue to echo for some time to come.

Suggested Readings

Angelou, Maya. *Wouldn't Take Nothing for my Journey Now*. New York: Random House, 1993.

Brokaw, Tom. *The Greatest Generation*. New York: Random House, 1998.

Genova, Lisa. *Still Alice*. New York: Pocket Books, 2009.

Johnson, Thomas H., Editor. *The Complete Poems of Emily Dickinson*. New York: Little, Brown and Company, 1961.

Keen, Sam. *Learning to Fly*. New York: Broadway Books, 1999.

Kubler-Ross, Elisabeth. *On Death and Dying*. New York: Scribner, 1969.

Milne, A. A. *Winnie the Pooh*. New York: Puffin Books, 2005.

Shakespeare, William. *The Complete Works*. Stanley Wells and Gary Taylor, Editors. Compact Edition. Oxford: Claredon Press, 1998.

Spark, Muriel. *Memento Mori*. New York: New Directions Publishing, 2000.

Tolle, Eckhart. *The Power of Now*. Novato, California: New World Library, 2004.

Readers Guide

1. The protagonist's name is Hope. What is the symbolism of such a name in the context of this novel?

2. Darling, Hope's well-liquored friend, is the story's comic relief. Does her character serve any other purpose?

3. The pronouns he or she are never used when the antagonist, Morgan, is in play. Why did the author choose to make Morgan gender-neutral?

4. In your opinion, is Morgan a man or a woman and why do you think so?

5. Does Morgan have any redeeming qualities?

6. What is revealed about Hope's character when juxtaposed with her sisters Faith and Charity?

7. In each chapter a curtain of time is lifted rounding out each elderly character's past. How successful was this device in terms of humanizing the aged who are often seen not as people but as burdens?

8. The PET tube (percutaneous endoscopic gastrostomy tube), more commonly referred to as a stomach tube was described thusly in the book: "That tube was nothing more than a man-made umbilical cord without which this woman and countless others like her would not be alive." Hope and Morgan have diametrically opposed perceptions of the value of stomach tubes. What is the debate and on which side do you fall?

9. Which elderly character did you relate to the most? Why?

10. There are many references to "time" in *Court Appointed*. Is "time" an appropriate motif for this story?

11. Throughout literature, Death wears many guises from grim-reaper to bridegroom. In what way does *Court Appointed* lift the mask of Death and teach the reader not to be afraid of the inevitable?

12. The recurring balcony scenes in the book emphasize the importance of the balcony to Hope. Why is it important to her? What does it symbolize?

13. Thinking past the end of the novel, what would you guess happens to Gene?

14. What is the likelihood that a court appointed conservator is in your future?

15. *Court Appointed* begins and ends with the bed-ridden client Lila. What is the significance of bookending the novel with Hope's visits to Lila?